LOVINGATE

A MONTREAL MURDER MYSTERY

JOHN CHARLES GIFFORD

 iUniverse®

iUniverse books may be ordered through booksellers or by contacting:

iUniverse
1663 Liberty Drive
Bloomington, IN 47403
www.iuniverse.com
844-349-9409

Because of the dynamic nature of the Internet, any web addresses or links contained in this book may have changed since publication and may no longer be valid. The views expressed in this work are solely those of the author and do not necessarily reflect the views of the publisher, and the publisher hereby disclaims any responsibility for them.

Any people depicted in stock imagery provided by Getty Images are models, and such images are being used for illustrative purposes only. Certain stock imagery © Getty Images.

ISBN: 978-1-6632-3032-4 (sc)
ISBN: 978-1-6632-3033-1 (e)

Library of Congress Control Number: 2022904304

Print information available on the last page.

iUniverse rev. date: 04/04/2022

Man is not what he thinks he is; he is what he hides.
—André Malraux

PROLOGUE

POINT OF DEPARTURE

Sunday, January 1, 1956
Sandy Hill, Ottawa

Colonel Alexey Ivanovich Trifonov was dead, but somehow, he still managed to stay on his feet. He was in his early forties, tall and handsome, an ambitious senior staff member at the Soviet embassy who made it his business to see that all the bolts were screwed on properly and that the i's were dotted and the t's crossed in a fashion most befitting a communist life raft in a sea of contaminated capitalist muck. If asked, he'd certainly tell you he was dead, but the truth of the matter was he was as alive as anyone else in the embassy. Exhausted? Without question. Testy? No doubt. But very much alive.

He had a magnetic appearance and a formidable bearing among his fellow officers that commanded respect, even from those who outranked him. Whenever he spoke to his ambassador about a problem—and there were many—he always felt that the man was deferring to him. That was how it should be; he had more responsibilities to ensure that the embassy ran efficiently than even the ambassador himself.

At least that was what Alexey thought, and because that was what he thought, then it must be so.

Despite the influence he wielded, the mustachioed Alexey believed that facial hair gave one power—not that he had had problems acquiring it clean-shaven in the early days. But Peter the Great had thought otherwise and issued an edict centuries before against wearing beards in the army, a ban that endured to this day, so Alexey had to be satisfied with his mustache. If a mustache had been good enough for Peter the Great, then it was certainly good enough for him. Furthermore, Alexey had the staying power of men half his age. Yet even with his closely trimmed mustache, he did have his limitations. He felt he was reaching those boundaries at the moment.

First, there had been the party here at the embassy last night. All the embassy personnel had partaken—it was mandatory. Of course, they had brought their wives and husbands and older children if they had any. They had been allowed to invite Canadian guests, but the guests had to be vetted a month prior to the big event. There had been nonstop music and dancing, and the vodka had flowed continuously. Being unmarried, Alexey had kept busy every minute of the night with women in their brightly colored evening gowns. The dancing itself turned out to be a physical feat comparable only to the infantry training he had undergone when he was a young lieutenant. The last guests hadn't left until nearly six in the morning, and Alexey had been so wound up that he was unable to sleep after that.

With only hours to spare and with a throbbing head, he then had been obligated to attend the annual Governor General's New Year Reception on Parliament Hill before going to the Railway Committee Room for a glass of punch and a light lunch. He had been one of many foreign dignitaries at the reception to shake Vincent Massey's hand and chat up

Ottawa's daunting mayor, Charlotte Whitton. He didn't much like her—he thought she was far too bossy for a woman—but he did remember to bring up her past skating abilities on the women's ice hockey team at Queen's University when she was a student. He had done his homework on the mayor and knew more about her than she ever could have guessed. Of course, he had worn his full regalia to the reception, but with his headache and lack of sleep, he had felt like anything but a dignified Soviet military leader.

After the reception, he had hurried back to the embassy for the embassy's own New Year's Day celebration, which was, by any calculable means, an accurate replication of the previous night, minus the midnight whoop-de-do. Now, with Ambassador Dimitri Chuvahin having gone off to make an appearance at the US embassy, and with the guests finally leaving, all he wanted to do was return to his apartment, take off his clothes, and go to bed. Yet he had other duties to perform before he could even think about leaving. With rank, he had obligations, and Alexey Ivanovich Trifonov was never one to shirk his responsibilities. He had a history and tradition to uphold.

His father had been a Bolshevik activist as well as one of the leaders of the Cossack revolutionary forces and, later, an important Soviet politician. His commitment to the ideology of the Communist Party, however, hadn't saved him from being arrested and executed during the Great Purge. Inevitably, the party had come to its senses, and he had been "rehabilitated" a decade later, dead as he was. He was now looked upon as a revolutionary hero, which had spurred on Alexey's career aspirations.

As Alexey stood in the lobby shaking hands and saying goodbye to the guests, his mind was elsewhere. He was thinking about Anastasia and how much he desired her and wished she could be here with him to enjoy the festivities.

They had known each other since childhood and had fallen in love when they were in their tender teens, but they'd been forced to part because of their respective government careers. The Kremlin forbade romantic entanglements among people in certain jobs. Their parting had happened a few decades ago, but he had never stopped loving her, never stopped desiring her. They had had no contact with each other since, and he'd often wondered whether she felt the same about him. And now, she had suddenly popped up on his radar again, but in a way that brought him the greatest heartache he could imagine.

As a young, emaciated-looking private closed the door behind the last guest, Alexey turned around and sniffed. What was that smell? Where was it coming from? Before he could answer those questions, he heard shouting from upstairs.

Then all hell broke loose.

———◉———

Across the street in an apartment building, Mrs. Diane Destonis, a widow, sat at her window watching the world go by, as she often did on Sunday afternoons, drinking a freshly made cup of green tea. The sky was clear and a nice shade of blue, but the snow was piled high on either side of the street, and there were large chunks of ice on them from the snowplows. In fact, there was so much snow that the street's width had been reduced by a third. She hadn't been outside for a couple of weeks, but she was certain that it was very cold out there.

Normally, the first day of the year was not a joyous time for her. Five years earlier, her husband Norman had had a sudden heart attack and died while reading the Sunday paper in the very chair she was now sitting in. There had been a lot of activity at the embassy in the last few days, and it had kept her mind off Norman. At the moment, she was particularly captivated by all of the rich Russians coming out of the embassy and getting into fancy cars. She didn't know much about Russians, except that they were supposed to be the enemy of all freedom-loving people. If they were the enemy of the Canadian people—certainly, Canadians were freedom-loving people—why were they across the street from her, having a party? She was baffled by that. She hated politics—Norman had thought politics divided people rather than united them—so she had never bothered to find out.

She watched the Russians through her binoculars, which she kept handy for just the occasion. She lived alone and was approaching eighty, and because the weather was subzero Fahrenheit, she had few options with which to entertain herself. She was a voracious reader, but one could spend only so much time reading. She had once read *War and Peace*, but that had been decades ago, and she didn't remember anything about it. Because of her convenient location across from the embassy, she had taken up the hobby of watching the periodic activities there. It was exciting! The lady across the hall had once accused her of spying on the Russians, but she knew better. It was only entertainment. She wasn't going to live forever; why not make the most of it?

When the last car pulled out and turned right onto Charlotte Street and disappeared, she refocused her binoculars to see if the show had ended and noticed smoke drifting from a window on the third floor of the embassy. *Oh my*, she thought. *Oh my.* Should she call the fire department? What if it wasn't an actual fire? What if it was just a fireplace backing up because they hadn't had the chimney cleaned? In that case she'd be really embarrassed, and maybe the Russians would resent her for making such a fuss. If they were enemies of Canadians, maybe they would do something to her. Maybe they would kidnap her, transport her to Russia, and then torture her. *Oh my*, she thought again. *Oh my.*

She decided to call the fire department anyhow and let the chips fall where they may.

———◦⦿◦———

Mr. William Dore, a retired city worker and the neighbor above Mrs. Destonis, was looking out his window at the same time. At first, he thought the smoke was coming from the kitchen. Then he realized the kitchen wouldn't be on the third floor. That would be the attic, of course. He wondered if those Russkies knew that their mansion was on fire. He limped across the living room to the hallway—he suffered from varicose veins, and each step was painful—and picked up the phone sitting by a vase of rainbow-colored artificial gerbera daisies. He dialed zero for the operator and asked to be connected to the Russian embassy. The operator let it ring ten times before she told Mr. Dore that there was no answer. Hell, he could hear that for himself. He didn't like those bloody communists, not even the slightest, but this was an emergency. He didn't want to see charred bodies being dragged out of there in an hour or two, communists or not.

"Their goddamn embassy is about to go up in flames!" he shouted into the receiver. "Call the fire department, call the police, call someone before it's too late!"

———◦⦿◦———

The Soviet embassy was located at 285 Charlotte Street, a stone's throw from the Rideau River in Sandy Hill. It had once been the mansion of lumber tycoon and railroad baron John Rudolphus Booth. But that had been decades before. It was a spectacular, imposing brick and wooden structure that had been built at the end of the last century and requisitioned by the federal government during the Second World War, but instead of using it as they'd planned, the government had turned it over to the Russians to house their growing Soviet legation. Now it was in danger of becoming a heap of ashes on the foundation of their Marxist ideology.

Alexey ran up the stairs to the second floor, where a dozen of his subordinates had gathered.

"Sir," one of them said, "the third floor is on fire. We need to call the fire department before it starts spreading."

The third floor! The communications room! Classified documents! Alexey was suddenly no longer tired, and his headache disappeared. The adrenaline kicked in.

"No! No one calls the fire department. You and you," he said, pointing. "Grab the extinguishers and start putting out the fire. You—get the fire hose. The rest of you, get your asses up there and start putting the documents in boxes. Take them out front. There will be cars outside shortly."

He ran down the stairs to the ground floor again, taking two steps at a time. Three privates were standing in the lobby, looking bewildered.

"Get the cars from the garage and bring them to the front. Go! Now!"

This was a nightmare. Of all places for a fire to start, the communications room was the worst. He was directly responsible for the cipher machines and all the documents in that room. There were top secret files in there with the names of every spy he had assigned throughout Canada, along with details of past and present covert operations. He wondered how the fire had started. If someone had been carelessly smoking up there, he'd have the person's head.

Suddenly, he heard something outside. He looked out a front window. *Goddamn it*, he thought. *Fire trucks.* Someone in the neighborhood must have called them. His men never would have disobeyed his orders. He opened the front door. *Damn it!* The whole Ottawa fire department must be out there—pumper trucks and ladder trucks and what looked like fifty, sixty, a hundred firemen. Three embassy cars drove around from the garages in the back and stopped in front of the building in the horseshoe driveway. Alexey watched a fireman—the chief?—get out of one of the trucks and jog to the front of the building and up the steps.

"Get your goddamn trucks away from here!" Alexey shouted at him in flawless English. "We didn't call for your help."

"If we don't get our hoses in action and our men in there, you're not going to have an embassy left. I need to go in to see what we're dealing with, and I need you to open the gate so the trucks can get in." He started to pass Alexey.

"Do *not* go in this embassy," Alexey said, stepping in front of him and blocking his way. "We have diplomatic immunity. This is the Soviet Union. I'm ordering you not to enter."

"I'm the chief here, and this is my fire in my city. Get the hell out of my way."

As the chief tried to brush past him, Alexey pushed him back and then punched him in the mouth with his fist. "This is Soviet territory, and I forbid you to enter."

"Are you crazy, you bastard?" the chief said, taking off his glove and holding his mouth. "Your embassy is about to be kindling wood. The fire could spread to these other buildings." He pointed to his left at the other embassies. If the wind changed direction, the fire department would have not only one disaster on their hands; they'd have several.

"Get off the property and stay off."

The chief turned around and shouted, "Get the hoses ready! Knock the gate down with the trucks if you have to."

Just then, Alexey's men stepped out of the embassy carrying boxes of classified documents and loaded them up in cars. They did so for the next fifteen minutes, until the cars were full.

Alexey leaned into the first car. "You know where to take them. Go! And don't stop for anyone." He turned around and yelled at the guard, "Open the gate!"

⸺ ❦ ⸺

Sawyer Nash stood near the driveway with his back to the building, freezing his ass off, watching the embassy vehicles drive away. He was wearing a heavy winter coat with the collar up, a woolen scarf wrapped around his neck, and a felt hat pulled down on his head. A white "Press" card stood up on the brim of his hat for all the world to see, if the world were interested. During the commotion, he'd managed to squeeze by the guards unnoticed. He watched the trucks move through the main gate and the firemen getting their equipment ready. He took off his gloves to light up a cigarette. The wind was stinging his face. He could barely keep the match lit. He lowered his head and cupped his hands, the flame dancing around the tip of his cigarette.

There had to be to be a better way for him to make a living than chasing fire trucks and prowl cars around the city. He had been doing just that for the last thirty years. He didn't know how to do anything else, but he nevertheless was getting tired of it. He should be home now with a beer, watching something on the TV set—warm and cozy in front of the fireplace. Instead, he was standing in subzero weather like some lunatic, covering a story. He could tell it in one sentence: "The Russki embassy went up in flames." Who the hell would care anyway? Most of the people he knew would cheer.

Thank goodness he had a lead for his story—the little scuffle out front would make good copy. *A Russian army officer punched the Ottawa fire chief in the face with his bare fist and ordered him off the embassy property while flames rose high behind them, endangering the lives of countless people.* That would give him a little in with the chief, but the Russkies wouldn't like it. But who gave a damn? Certainly not Sawyer Nash. He would have had a picture to go with the story had his photographer been here. Most likely, he was still at the Parliament Bar, drinking Rum and coke. Since it was Sunday, the bar was closed to the public, but it was always open through the back door for members of the press and a few select politicians of the right party.

It was so cold that for a moment Nash thought about leaving and then decided against it. Something else of interest might happen. Maybe the Russkies would engage in mortal combat with the firemen; after all, they had the firepower. That might be good for a follow-up story—spread the gossip around a little. They must have a lot of secrets in that building. Otherwise, why wouldn't they want the chief to go in? Why would they risk the building going up in flames? Maybe the Russkies were trying to put the fire out themselves—the idiots. In any event, Sawyer would have a story ready for the morning edition of the *Citizen* bright and early on Monday.

Just then, something caught his eye on the ground near the driveway. Something must have fallen out from one of the boxes as the Russians were loading the cars. He walked over, bent down, and picked up the folder. He opened it and looked inside—papers with some sort of Soviet seal on them. They were written in Russian, of course; he recognized the Cyrillic letters. Smoke from his cigarette was getting into his eyes. He shrugged his shoulders, folded the folder in half, and stuck it inside his coat pocket.

He heard someone yelling at him. "Get away from that building!"

He jogged across the driveway and then to the street in front. He was freezing now—a good time to warm up a bit in his car. In spite of the weather, a huge crowd was beginning to form. *More idiots.*

As he made his way to his car, he thought about the folder. Maybe there was something in it for another story. Maybe.

Whom did he know who could translate Russian?

Chapter 1
THE BIG BANG

Tuesday, January 3
10:45 a.m.
Montreal

GISELE LACROIX'S FEET HURT.

And it wasn't just her feet that were giving her problems. Her legs, too, were swollen and throbbing, especially her ankles. The pain was unremitting and intermittently radiated up the sides of her body and into her eyes, or at least that was what she thought was happening. She wasn't a doctor, you know, but she was the person experiencing it, after all, and that counted for something, didn't it?

She had no pain in her eyes until she felt a strange sensation creeping up her sides, slowly, like a cat climbing up a tree, getting ready to pounce on a nest of baby sparrows. As it intensified and reached her neck, her eyes began pulsating in much the same way her mother's had. Her mother had once described her migraines to Gisele when Gisele was a young girl. She hadn't had problems with her legs and feet, or at least Gisele didn't think so, but Gisele could certainly relate to the pain in her mother's eyes. Gisele had stopped going to doctors years before, having concluded that it was a frivolous expense to be told something that she already knew.

But what was she to do? She had to make a living, and doing so required the use of her legs and feet. There was no way getting around that. It was simply a fact of life that she had to face each day as she rose from her bed. When facts presented themselves in certain ways, there was no way she could deny them. Oh, she had tried for many years to ignore them, but she had finally reached a brick wall. She had to be honest with herself and face the consequences; she was in no position to face the dreadful penalties of being intractable.

There was rent to pay, and God knew she had to eat. She could cut down on expenses, buy used clothes instead of new ones, which she did mostly anyway, and cut down on meat from once a week to once a month, but that went only so far. She lived alone in a tiny one-bedroom apartment in a crummy section of town. If she cut down on that, she'd have to find some twenty-five-cent-a-night flophouse on skid row. She wasn't far from that as it was. Having never married, she had no one on whom she could lean. If she didn't work, she was quite aware that she'd be one paycheck away from living under some godforsaken bridge or on a bench in one of the public parks. And Jesus, Mary, and Joseph—it was the middle of winter!

With that on her mind, she took one last look at room 309 and sighed. Satisfied it was spick-and-span, she patted down her dark-mustard-colored uniform and backed out, closing the door behind her, which locked automatically. She slowly turned around and bent over at the waist to pull up her socks. She'd bought them several months before from a catalog that advertised specially designed "medical socks for tired legs." Her legs did feel better to a degree, but the socks didn't entirely solve the problem. However, at the moment they might be the only thing keeping her on the job and off the streets.

When she was finished adjusting them, she straightened up again and noticed that the pile of linens on her housekeeping cart was hanging off the edge. If she pushed the cart forward, the pile would tumble over, and she'd be picking up sheets and refolding them for the next fifteen minutes—time wasted. Like the linens, she knew that she too was hanging off an edge. She didn't need to pay anyone to tell her that either.

She slid one arm under the bottom of the pile and with the other one hefted it backward, away from her, centering the pile in the middle of the cart. She had been cleaning these same rooms for the better part of twenty-five years. Before that, she'd been a waitress in some two-bit greasy spoon, which had gone out of business long since, near where the ships offloaded their cargo at the port. She still knew a few of the longshoremen who had come in for coffee, stew, and a chat.

She stopped for a moment for a quick memory, something that always sustained her in her old age. She had been beautiful in those days, and the longshoremen had enjoyed talking to her—Lucien Chapelle in particular. He was young, handsome, and free. They had dated for a time, and he had taken her to restaurants and nightclubs, where they'd danced until the venues closed. When he'd worked up enough courage to ask her for her hand in marriage, she'd broken the relationship off. Did she regret it now? She didn't know. Before all that, she had had to quit school and wash clothes fifty hours a week to help her parents make ends meet. She was a woman who had always been on her feet. Just as fast as the memory came, it faded.

Now, at fifty-eight, she was beginning to tire of the same routine. Mind you, she liked the work, and she was quite prepared to continue until she dropped dead, but her short, plump body was starting to protest in a way that she could no longer ignore. In all of her years of working at the Windsor Hotel, she could count on one hand the number of times she'd called in sick, although during the last year she had struggled. Besides, the hotel catered to the wealthy, and she had not wanted to miss out on padding her salary with the generous tips they sometimes left on the bedstands, neatly folded bills slid under an ashtray. Occasionally, someone would also leave a thank-you note, saying how much they'd appreciated the extra clean room. Gizzy—that was what most people called her—was very good at her job. She had saved the notes over the years and kept them in a shoebox on the top shelf of her bedroom closet. Once a month on a Saturday night, she would take the shoebox down and reread them after listening to an episode of *Dragnet* on the radio (she would never miss one of those), reminding herself why she got up in the morning.

She pushed her cart down the hallway (which was much more difficult now since they put the carpet in) and stopped at room 311 on the same side as the last room. She reached for a small hand mirror that she'd slipped between the rolls of toilet paper on the cart and gussied up her hair a little just in case the guest was still in the room and opened the door when she knocked, which sometimes happened. Then she used the palm of her free hand to brush any lint from her uniform. She wanted to be presentable. She took pride in her appearance and in the work she did. A thought occurred to her. Perhaps she should inquire with the hotel management about whether they had any job openings that required sitting down all day. Maybe a phone operator. No, that wouldn't do at all. They were unlikely to train someone her age for a completely new job, when they already had an experienced housekeeper on the payroll. *Oh well, just a thought.* She set the mirror back in its proper place and knocked on the door, saying in a loud voice, "Housekeeping!"

At the same time she called out, she heard a loud bang from the other side of the door. But it wasn't exactly a bang. It was more like a small explosion, something like what she'd heard on some of the detective shows on radio, only much louder. That was it: it sounded like a gun going off. She froze in place for several seconds, staring at the numbers on the door, and then she turned around and hobbled down the hallway as fast as her painful feet allowed her.

⎯⎯⎯«(●)»⎯⎯⎯

Nigel Hughes, a retired Montreal police detective and, for the last five years, the hotel's chief of security—a.k.a. the "house dick"—sat at his desk in his office on the first floor, drinking his third cup of coffee of the morning and paging through a boxing magazine. He had done a bit of amateur boxing in his younger days and retained an avid interest in the sport. He always kept track of the local matches in Montreal. He rarely missed attending any of them. For recaps of previous fights south of the border, he relied on *Ring Magazine*. He had just finished reading about the Sugar Ray Robinson–Bobo Olson fight, in which Robinson had regained the middleweight crown by a second-round knockout in Chicago the month before. He had listened to the fight on the radio at the time but wanted to read the recap because the magazine always included some juicy gossip that never made the airways. He often thought about where he'd be if he had turned professional. He always concluded that it was a rough way to make a living and was glad that he hadn't gone that route. Putting criminals behind bars wasn't any less rough, but the odds where always in his favor. He was about to turn a page in this month's edition when he heard a commotion in the lobby and his name being called.

"Nigel! Nigel!"

He looked up toward the open door. He knew immediately who it was. What could she possibly want now? About once a fortnight, she would come rushing into his office with some imaginary crisis at hand. He would investigate, and it would never be anything serious. The old gal had quite an imagination. He stood up, slipped into his suit jacket that had been draped on the back of his chair, and walked toward the door as Gisele Lacroix came tumbling in.

"Nigel! Nigel!" she repeated, out of breath. "Room … room 311, Nigel."

"Slow down, Gizzy, slow down. Here," he said, sliding a chair to her, "get off your feet and take some deep breaths." He poured some water from a pitcher on his desk into a glass and gave it to her. "That's good, that's good. Now drink a little water."

She did so and then took several more deep breaths.

"That's a good girl. Now tell me all about room 311. What's all this brouhaha about?"

"I … I had just knocked on the door to clean the room when I heard a gun go off." She spat out the words like a machine gun spitting out bullets.

"Now, let me see if I understood you. You knocked on the door, and then you heard a gun go off," he said, towering over her. He stood over six feet and was in good shape for a man of his age. He grinned at her, smoothing down his mustache with his fingertips. "Now, Gizzy, when was the last time you ever heard a gun fired? Not on TV or radio—I mean in real life."

"But it sounded like one, Nigel."

"I thought as much. If you've never heard one in real life, how would you know it was a gun? It makes quite a bang, you know." He should know. He'd heard enough of them in Belgium in 1918 and his fair share on the streets of Montreal and at the gun range. "Maybe a vase dropped and broke. Maybe something else fell and shattered. Did you ever think of that?"

"It was a gun, Nigel, a gun. I'm sure it was." Her eyes were tearing up, and there was a tremor in her voice. Her body began shaking as if she were reliving the experience.

"If you say so, dear," he said, sighing. "Why don't you rest here while I go up and have a look-see? I'll figure it all out and come back and tell you. How about a nice cup of coffee? I made some fresh, just the way you like it."

Nigel Hughes poured some coffee into an extra cup he kept in the office without waiting for an answer, for he knew Gizzy would never deny herself a freshly brewed cup of joe. Once she had settled in and was sipping her coffee and warming her hands on the cup, he left the office, took the elevator to the third floor, and walked down the long hallway to room 311. He knew from past experiences that he had to check it out; she'd quiz him when he returned, and he'd have to have something to tell her, or he'd never hear the end of it. He didn't want to lie to her and concoct some story, not to Gizzy. He'd tried that once and gotten caught.

A gunshot, he thought. *At the Windsor. Now that's a good one!* That said, a few years back, some American gangsters had stayed at the hotel for an extended period—on the seventh floor, if he remembered correctly. They had rented out a suite and converted it into a gambling den behind the backs of management. They were pretty sly about it. Nigel had had his suspicions and kept track of the comings and goings. It had drawn in some pretty powerful people in the city, even the chief of police, which was why it had lasted as long as it had. The gangsters most assuredly had guns, but none of them had ever used them, at least not in the hotel.

He stood at the door and knocked with purpose, the way he used to do when he was in uniform on the force and called to domestic disputes. He had to knock with authority to be taken seriously; otherwise, he might as well have just thrown in the towel. "House detective," he said, his voice just above a conversational tone but falling short of a shout. There was no need to raise your voice too loud in the Windsor. Fancy hotels had the aura of a church. You could whisper or talk in a normal tone, but you never shouted. He waited about a minute and knocked again. "House detective. Is everything all right?"

When no one answered a second time, he thought for a moment about returning downstairs, but he'd get a good grilling from Gizzy. He'd have to have more than three cups of coffee to withstand that, so he took his passkey out, stuck it in the lock, and opened the door just a little. He put his face to the opening without entering and said, "Hello. House detective here. Is everything okay?"

Still there was no answer. No one was in the room, he guessed. Gizzy was listening to too many detective shows on the radio. The old girl indeed had quite an imagination.

He pushed the door open slowly and stepped fully into the room. Suddenly, a sharp smell stung his nose. It was familiar, and he didn't like it. "Hello," he called out again.

He was standing in a short hallway. On one side there was a suitcase on the luggage rack with the top opened. Leaning against the rack on the carpet was a leather briefcase. The bathroom was on the other side. The door was open, and the light was off. The hotel room still looked occupied, but no one was there. He sniffed the air again. The smell was stronger. "Damn it," he whispered. He knew the odor all too well and didn't like it. Gizzy might have been onto something after all.

"Hello," he called out for the umpteenth time. He couldn't see into the main room from where he was and didn't want to make the mistake of barging in on someone in bed. But there was the smell. As long as he was inside, he would check out the entire room. He slowly walked toward the main room. If he saw that someone was still in bed, he would leave quietly without disturbing the guest. The foul smell was urging him on.

The drapes were partially open, and light spilled into the room, creating shadows. As he approached the main room where the bed was, he saw the legs of a woman dangling off the edge, her high heels barely touching the carpet. She must be lying down on her back because that was all he could see. Strange. As he moved forward, the rest of her body gradually came into view. She was indeed lying down on her back. Her right hand was on her stomach, and in her hand was a revolver, her thumb in the trigger guard. Her head was lying in a pool of blood. He shifted his gaze, slowly, methodically, as his hand instinctively went under his arm for his own revolver. Behind her on the headboard and above it were blood splatters.

"Jesus Christ almighty" was all that Nigel Hughes could say.

Chapter 2
THE CASE

Three days later

PRIVATE INVESTIGATOR EDDIE WADE SAT behind his desk and carefully glanced to his right at his apprentice and wife of six months sitting at her own desk, pushed side to side with his. She'd been quiet for the last thirty minutes, emitting not so much as an "Mmm" or an "Aah." *Suspicious behavior,* he thought. Usually, when that much time elapsed without a word spoken or noise made, she was in the depths of thought and on the verge of an earthshaking pronouncement that she would be quite willing to share with anyone within earshot. He dared a second, longer look and wondered what was going through that beautiful head of hers. Was she having second thoughts about having gotten married? About leaving the bakery and going into business with him? No, he didn't think so. Those were his insecurities, not hers.

"A penny for your thoughts," he said, risking life and limb.

Josette snapped her head to the side and looked him directly in the eyes. The longer she maintained eye contact, the more important was what she had to say. He resisted looking at his watch and timing her. After an unreasonable amount of time had passed, the floodgates opened.

"Let's fly to Paris for the weekend. I heard that the show at the Moulin Rouge is particularly good. We could be back at the office early Monday morning."

"Have you seen our bank account lately? We can barely afford a taxi ride across the river to Laval."

"Party pooper," she said, pushing her lower lip out in a pout.

"One of us has to keep track of the finances and shoulder the responsibility." He cocked his head to the side. "You couldn't have been thinking about that all this time. You look serious. What's on your mind?"

"Things." She strung the word out for all that it was worth and sighed.

That was Josette's way of throwing up a roadblock in their conversation while providing a little space for him to maneuver around if he desired to pursue it. Eddie knew she wanted to say more, but he had to work for it. He thought he saw the corners of her lips turn up.

He leaned back in his swivel chair and placed his hands behind his head. "Aah, *things*! I should have guessed as much. *Things*! Those little damnable inanimate objects without a life or a conscious of their own, except what we give them. They stealthily creep into our subconscious and make pests of themselves like children until we acknowledge their presence. And once we do, they grasp and hang on for dear life."

"Very funny." She ran her fingers through her hair and then shook her head. When she was finished, she used her fingertips to swoosh aside several strands of errant hair from her face. "I was actually thinking about Gigi. You remember her, right?"

"I know only one Gigi, believe it or not. Gigi Bonnet. Engaged to a limey accountant. I think you introduced her to me once upon a time ago." He reached across his desk for his tobacco humidor and then snatched a Dunhill billiard out of his pipe rack. He usually had no problem whatsoever holding down a conversation and filling his pipe at the same time.

"That's her. She called last night, and we talked for a while."

"So that's who you were talking to. For a while, you say? I went to bed at the two-hour mark."

"You were timing me?"

"Not at all. The phone rang as the news came on the radio—two hours before I went to bed."

"She was pretty down and just needed someone to talk to."

"Why didn't she talk to her husband-to-be?" He put a match to the bowl and blew out puffs of smoke. Looking across his pipe, he said, "We talk all the time."

"She needed to talk to another woman, someone who could understand certain things. 'Girl talk,' it's called."

Eddie leaned forward in his chair. "Are you saying that there are things you talk to other women about rather than your own husband?"

"Yes, that's precisely what I'm saying, but don't take offense. I'm sure there are certain topics you wouldn't want to talk about. A girl's got to have her resources."

"I see." He puffed a few more times on his pipe, and then he wrinkled his eyebrows. "Like what?"

"Gigi is having an issue with her fiancé."

"You're right. I have no interest in exploring that aspect of humanity, unless I get paid to do it. Scratch that—I have no interest if the woman is known to me or my wife. Nothing good can come from being involved in pre-matrimonial skirmishes."

Ignoring his remarks, she continued, "They've been engaged for a year now, and every time she mentions setting a date, he avoids answering by changing the subject. She's getting tired of it, and I don't blame her. She's at a loss as to what to do."

"A year? We got engaged and married within four weeks." He looked at his pipe, then tamped the ash down with his finger. "His behavior is easy enough to explain. The guy's having second thoughts, that's all."

"Did you have second thoughts before we got married?"

"Of course I did, and so did you. Everyone should have second thoughts. That's the time to examine every reason why you shouldn't be married. If you can't think of any, or if your reasons are weak, then and only then you can pull the trigger. Marriage is a big step. You want to make sure you're going forward and not backward. If you remember, we talked through that like two rational human beings. They should do the same thing."

"Pull the trigger—jeez, you make marriage sound so romantic. But that was different with us. Gigi thinks he's cheating on her."

"Tabarnak!" he said. "Let me guess. She wants you to talk me into tailing him around town. Well, I won't do it."

"She did bring that up, though not in those words."

"And you quashed the idea, right? You told her that your husband doesn't work for people he or his wife knows, right?"

"Not exactly. I told her that I'd talk to you, and maybe you could give her some advice."

"My advice is this: tell her to look in the yellow pages under the *P*s and hire a private detective firm other than Wade Detective Agency. There are half dozen good firms in the city that would do a splendid job and another half dozen not-so-good ones that'll get the job done and are cheaper. She can have her pick."

Once again, Josette ignored what he had said and continued on. "She told me that he has some pretty strange behaviors—"

"My God, he's an accountant! Why wouldn't he? Besides that, he's British. There you go," he said, as if the matter were settled.

"Like telling her he was working late when the office was closed, not a light on, with only the night watchman there. She went there one night. And there were other things as well."

"Ah, the classic working-late routine! So why didn't she just ask him about it?"

"She thought about it but didn't know how to word it without it sounding like an accusation. She doesn't want a confrontation."

"Better to settle the matter now rather than after they're married. It'll be more expensive if she waits and finds out the bad news."

Just then, the phone rang on his desk. Eddie looked at his partner. "A prospective client! That means money!" He swiveled around and picked up the receiver. "Wade Detective Agency, Eddie speaking … Oh, hi! Yes … Yes, I'm free … Okay, right. See you soon."

He put the receiver down and looked at Josette. "That was Jack at police headquarters. Says he want to pick my brain on a matter."

"Tell him he's got to pay for the contents. Cash only. Tell him we have to finance a trip to Paris this weekend."

⸻ «•» ⸻

Homicide detective sergeant Jack Macalister sat behind his desk, twiddling a pencil in his fingers while looking at Eddie beside him, who was smoking his pipe. They had known each other since junior high school and had served in the war together in the same infantry unit. Eddie had even saved Jack's life once. Jack didn't look much different from those days, still slim and fit with a military-type haircut. Eddie had known Macalister long enough to know that the only time he twiddled a pencil was when he was frustrated about a case. After they had spent ten minutes dissecting the Canadiens' appalling ice performances in the last month and had agreed on no one particular remedy, Eddie asked Macalister which specific bit of information he wanted to pick from his brain. He didn't mention anything about charging for it.

Macalister tossed the pencil on his desk and got up to close the door. When he returned to his desk, he slid out the bottom drawer and took out a bottle of Johnny Walker Black Label and two glasses. He poured a couple of fingers in each and gave one to Eddie. They hoisted their glasses and together said, "To our brothers-in-arms who didn't make it home." That had become a ritual with them over the years since the war ended. They tossed half of their drinks back. Then they said, "And to those who did," drinking the remainder.

Then the police detective pulled a folder from his desk, opened it, and got down to business. "A woman was found dead in a room at the Windsor Hotel three days ago. Here's what we know. Her name was Anne Lovingate, age thirty-five. Date of birth is April 9, 1921. She checked into the hotel the day before her death, on Tuesday, January 2, using an American passport and a driver's license issued in the state of Minnesota." He paused a moment, looked up, and then said, "That's below Manitoba. They have a lot of lakes there."

"I know where it's at. Once upon a time, I went fishing in the Lake of the Woods on the Minnesota side."

"She lived in St. Paul." Macalister looked up again. "I suppose you know where that is too."

"St. Paul and its twin sister, Minneapolis, make up the Twin Cities, with the Mississippi River splitting them. More than half of the players on their hockey teams—the St. Paul Saints and the Minneapolis Millers—are Canadians, and half of those come from Quebec. The two cities are in the southern half of the state and about an hour's drive from the Wisconsin border. I fought a half dozen matches in St. Paul before the war. Did you know that a French Canadian bootlegger founded St. Paul? It was first called 'Pig's Eye' after Pierre 'Pig's Eye' Parrant before they renamed it. What else do you want to know?"

"No one likes a smart ass," Macalister said and then continued. "Her address was 987 Edgerton—" He stopped and looked up, expecting Eddie to chime in with something else. When he didn't, Macalister continued. "Which is on the east side of the city. The day after she checked into the Windsor, at approximately eleven in the morning, the maid knocked on her door, room 311, to clean it and change the sheets and towels, and she heard what sounded like a gun going off. She ran down to the main floor and informed the house detective, Nigel Hughes. I know him. He's a good guy; we worked homicide together for a while when he was on the force. He's a veteran of the Great War. Anyway, he went to the room and found Miss Lovingate lying on the bed with a gun resting on her stomach. Her thumb was in the trigger guard. The back of her head was blown off. Nigel called the police, and we got there twenty minutes later. It's my case."

He paused to sip the remaining drops of scotch in his glass. Eddie puffed on his pipe, wondering where this was leading.

"There was no evidence of a struggle. Nothing in the room was out of place. The chief says it's a clear case of suicide, so he wants to close the case. We have cases stacked up that are active investigations, and there's another stack waiting for us when we're done. On top of that, we're short of men. He doesn't want us to spend unnecessary time on something that can be written off as a suicide."

Eddie pulled the pipe out of his mouth and asked why Macalister was telling him all this.

"Simple," Macalister said. "I believe this is a homicide. I'd like you to do some nosing around—in St. Paul. I think it might have started from there. I talked to a homicide detective on the St. Paul police force, a Harry Haden. He won't be able to help much—he's as busy as we are—but he gave you free rein, as long as you behave yourself."

"What's the evidence to back up a homicide?"

"I don't have anything that's conclusive, but I do have a few things that I want to run by you. First of all, Lovingate's passport and driver's license are both missing from the crime scene. She used them to check into the hotel the day before. That's how we got the information on her. We couldn't find them in her room, and we tore the room apart. Detective Haden confirmed that there was such an address on the east side of St. Paul."

Eddie tamped his pipe and relit it. "Okay, that's interesting. The killer—if there is one—could have taken them. Anything else?"

"Plenty," Macalister said, repositioning himself in his chair. "The gun was resting on her stomach. The recoil of the weapon when it went off should have thrown it somewhere away from her. It's unlikely, but possible, that it would have landed where it did. We found two boxes of ammunition with twenty-five rounds in each inside her briefcase in a secret compartment. If you're going to kill yourself, one would do the trick. And before you ask, the ballistic test confirmed that that was the gun that killed her. Approximately fifteen minutes had lapsed from the time the maid heard the shot and when Nigel got to the room—plenty of time for someone to escape."

"So you're saying it was a setup."

"Possibly. On top of that, we also found that the labels on her clothes had been cut off. The shower had been used that morning. She was dressed as if she was going out to a corporate meeting. If she was going to commit suicide, why take a shower and get dressed up? Why go all the way to Montreal to do it? There might very well be simple answers to those questions. That's why I want you to go to St. Paul—to nose around. I think it started there and someone followed her here. You might be able to pick something up in St. Paul."

"And the chief still believes it's suicide? You told him all this?"

"Of course. I really don't think he believes it was suicide, but he won't say so. You could make a case of suicide if you ignored all the evidence, inconclusive as it is. He doesn't want to put any resources on this one because of the backlog. Besides, she doesn't appear to be Canadian. We checked everything in Canada, and believe it or not, there isn't a single woman in this country who's named Anne Lovingate." He tossed the folder to Eddie. "Crime scene photos. By the way, the serial number on the gun had been professionally removed."

Eddie opened the folder and flipped through the photos. Then he threw back what was left of his scotch and said, "Maybe she was Canadian and bought the documents from someone in the States and was hiding from her killer. That could account for the documents and the gun and ammunition." He puffed on his pipe a few times. "The passport and driver's license—she would have had to pay a hefty price for them. If she was in trouble and hiding from someone, it would have been something serious. This doesn't sound like a simple domestic dispute, although it could be."

"At this point, I'm not excluding anything. In St. Paul, you could talk to her parents and relatives. Find out something from her neighbors. See what kind of life she was living and if she was having a problem with anyone capable of murder." Macalister picked up the pencil and started his routine again. "Whether she was Canadian or American, if this was a murder, it happened in this city, and I have to do something about it, regardless of what the chief thinks. You want to fly to St. Paul? I'm afraid your pretty bride will have to stay put. My budget will only cover one person. You think you two lovebirds can be apart for a few days?"

"I thought you said the chief doesn't want to put any resources into the case. I assume that means men and money."

"He doesn't. I have a special little coffee fund set aside for things like this, but it'll only cover you."

Eddie continued to smoke his pipe and stared at Macalister. He was mentally calculating the time and expenses he would have to put into a case with no apparent leads. He knew how this would go down. The initial money would come out of his own pocket. When the case was over, he'd submit his expenses to Macalister. They—the police department—were cheap. He'd be reimbursed only a third of his going rate. In effect, Eddie would be paying to work an uncertain case. But it wasn't only Eddie now who would be making this decision; he had a partner to consider—his wife. He'd have to run this by her before he made a decision.

"I want someone to have a look at the crime scene first," he said. "It's still intact?" If the suggestion of a murder was confirmed by an expert, then he'd talk to his wife about moving forward. If the expert concluded it was a clear case of suicide, then there would be no reason to act on it.

"For the time being, I've got a guard at the door, so it's secured, but we're supposed to wrap it up soon. The chief gave me a week. Who'd you have in mind?"

"Roger Chapelton."

"He's a retired drunk."

"Yes, but he's still the best crime scene investigator around when he's sober. He's got a private license now, so he's not quite retired yet."

"Then get Roger sober. I'll need your answer tomorrow. If the answer is no, the chief is ready to close the case as a suicide. If it's yes, then we've got a week."

"I'll have an answer for you soon, maybe tonight."

"Before you leave, you want to wager on who's going to win the Stanley Cup this year?"

"The Canadiens are going to get their shit together and make the playoffs. Then they're going to take the cup."

"You've got a lot of faith in a team that's getting its ass kicked."

"Faith is what it takes, Jack. Faith and a lot of luck."

Macalister smiled and tossed the pencil on the desk again. "Faith and a lot of hard work."

"Yeah, there's that too," Eddie said.

Chapter 3
THE CRIME SCENE

EDDIE FINISHED PLACING THE CRIME SCENE photos along the edge of the dresser pushed against the south wall of the room and then turned around. The room was small but well furnished (all the rooms at the Windsor were, regardless of size). The crime scene team had been through it, done the necessary fingerprinting, and collected Lovingate's belongings. The coroner's office had taken the body to the Rose Cottage, where it would remain until a decision on what to do with it was made by the police, specifically by Jack Macalister. Eddie's possible involvement in the case would have a bearing on his decision.

"Anyone up for coffee?" he asked. He glanced at the bed's headboard and the wall behind it: the victim's blood splatter. If they could frame it, it would be a great piece of expressionistic art. Red paint splattered on canvas. It could sell for thousands.

Roger Chapelton looked at him as if he'd been offered poison. "Never touch the stuff after nine. Got anything stronger?"

"Not at the moment," Eddie said. He looked at Chapelton's assistant. "Candy? I could call down for some."

"No, thank you, Eddie. That was sweet of you to ask. Roger says he's taking me out on the town when we're finished here, isn't that right, Roger dear?"

"You bet ya, doll. The town's just waiting for us!"

Candy was a tall, voluptuous blonde who was young enough to be Chapelton's granddaughter. After "Roger dear" had retired from the Mounties, he had gotten a private license, opened an agency, put an ad in the papers, and hired her as his assistant. Since he was also a professional magician, she doubled as his partner on that front as well. Beyond that, it was anyone's guess. One thing that was certain about Candy, though, was that she could melt butter with her voice. Eddie could never understand the age difference between them, but obviously, they didn't have an issue with that. At least Roger didn't, because Candy was a double for Jayne Mansfield. Whenever Eddie saw them together, they were always pawing each other like a pair of felines in heat, so Eddie guessed that Candy probably didn't have an issue either.

Chapelton spent the next half hour examining the room. He went back and forth, grabbing photos off the dresser and comparing them to the walls and carpet and bed, holding them this way and that way.

Eddie and Candy stood off to the side in a whispered conversation. He wanted to know the trick behind taking a live bunny out of a top hat. She waved an index finger at him like a windshield wiper and whispered, "No, no."

"Okay," Chapelton finally said, replacing the photos. He then picked up the photo of the murder weapon and held it in front of him as if he were beginning a lecture with a new group of recruits at the RCMP academy.

Eddie and Candy went over to him.

"What we have here is a Smith and Wesson," he said, thrusting the photo at them, "model 22, six-shot, double-action, large frame revolver, chambered in .45 ACP."

"What does double-action mean, Roger dear?"

"I'll give you that lesson tonight, baby," he said with a wink. "It was designed in 1917 but didn't go into production until 1950. It weighs approximately 2.25 pounds with a barrel length of 5.5 inches. It isn't an ideal weapon to commit suicide with, but a gal who didn't know too much about firearms could certainly handle it. The muzzle velocity is 760 feet per second, not that that would mean much to a victim. It has a blade front sight and a notched rear sight, again something the victim wouldn't give a damn about."

Chapelton walked over to the dresser and set the photo down and then picked up several others. "Now, baby, what I want you to do is lie down on the bed." When Candy smiled at him, he added, "Don't get too excited now. This is all business. We're being paid for our time. Okay, that's it—hang your legs over the edge and just lie back." He glanced at the photo and then adjusted her position slightly to replicate the victim's.

Then he reached into his shoulder holster and took out his own gun. He dropped the magazine, racked the slide, and looked inside. "Here, baby, this will do. Hold it like this with your thumb on the trigger here," he said, demonstrating. He gave the gun to her, and she took it in her right hand. "Don't worry; it's not loaded, and the safety is on. Good. Now place it on your stomach like this. Good, good. Now just keep still for a while."

He turned to Eddie. "Look at this, Eddie. Have a good look. This is all wrong. I'm ninety-nine percent sure. The recoil of the Smith and Wesson when it was shot would have thrown it somewhere else, depending on how she was holding it. There are several possibilities, but this position isn't one of them. And there are a few other interesting things as well." He took off his jacket and draped it over a chair. Then he took the gun from Candy and straddled her. Talking to Eddie, he said, "There was a hole in the middle of her forehead, so she would have had to have held the gun like this." He placed the gun in Candy's hand with her right thumb on the trigger. Then he placed her left hand around the barrel and put the end to her forehead. "A woman, and maybe even a man, would hold the gun like this if she were going to shoot herself in the forehead—with two hands to steady it. It would be too awkward to hold it any other way, especially with one hand. She'd want to make sure she did it right. Now go get the photos of her hand holding the gun on her stomach and of her left hand."

When Eddie returned with the photos, Chapelton said, "Now what do you see?"

"Her right hand holding the gun with her thumb inside the trigger guard and her left hand resting on the bed beside her."

"Precisely! Now what don't you see?"

Eddie thought for a moment and then said, "Blood."

"Precisely! I've never seen a suicide with a handgun where there wasn't some sort of blood splatter on the hands." He demonstrated again. "I don't care how the victim shot herself. For example, like this." He took the gun and placed the barrel against Candy's temple. "Or like this." He moved the barrel under her chin. "There's always blood splatter on the hand holding the gun and on two hands if the victim used both. Can't get around that unless she wore gloves or wrapped her hand with a towel, which the pictures show that she didn't. Her dress didn't even have blood on it. How is that possible? I'll show you."

He raised his body up a little and then placed Candy's arms to her sides. He straddled her again, his legs pinning her arms down. "I could take the gun and shoot her in the head without worrying about her arms flailing around. My body is pretty much blocking any blood that might get on her, and her hands are covered by my legs. I might not get much blood on me if I had a towel over the gun. Now go get the other photos of the victim lying on the bed and tell me what's wrong with that scenario."

Eddie got the photos and returned. He looked at them and then up at Chapelton. "I don't know."

"You notice in the photos that the bed isn't disturbed? The spread is nice and flat, as if the bed had just been made. We can't be sure she even slept in it the previous night. If someone was trying to kill her, the lady would have been fighting for dear life. The bed would have been a mess. There's no evidence of that. So?"

"So she committed suicide."

"Perhaps. That's always a possibility. Or ..."

"Or maybe she was drugged."

"Precisely. Drugged or rendered unconscious by other means. Then that scenario suddenly makes sense."

Chapelton helped Candy to her feet and gave her a peck on the cheek.

"There's no doubt that this is where the lady's life ended." Chapelton pointed to the headboard, wall, and ceiling. "According to the police report that you showed me, that's her blood. But strange, unaccountable things often happen at crime scenes. I could write a book." He looked at Candy. "Maybe I will!" Turning to Eddie again, he continued, "But in my opinion, a second person was in the room with ... what was the victim's name?"

"Lovingate. Anne Lovingate."

"Yes, Miss Lovingate. Again, according to the police report, there was around fifteen minutes from the time the maid heard the shot and the time the hotel dick discovered the body. Plenty of time for a killer to escape." He stopped for a moment. "I thought I read something about her identity being in question."

"Maybe. We haven't confirmed it."

"So Lovingate isn't her name?"

"Possibly not. We just don't know. We have to look into it."

"Well, we had plenty of unidentified bodies when I was with the Mounties. Most of them remained unidentified. But I can say this much: Everything about a person, every scar or imperfection, contributes to the person's identity. When you spend enough time delving into the person, an identity will eventually emerge. 'Enough time' is the operative phrase here. But sometimes it's impossible. A dead body is just the starting point, but it's always trying to tell you something. That's when the hard work begins."

Chapelton put on his jacket and overcoat and adjusted his hat. Then he reached into the sleeve of his overcoat and pulled out a small bouquet of fresh, colorful flowers. Turning to Candy, he said, "Voilà—for you, my love. You are such a wonderful assistant."

"Oh, Roger dear! How lovely and unexpected."

"Just like magic! On that note, sweetheart, we have the whole town waiting on us!"

On their way out of the room, Chapelton said without looking back, "I'll send you my bill through Canada Post, Eddie. It's been a pleasure. Call us anytime!"

Eddie walked to the door and peeked into the hallway. Chapelton and Candy were walking hand in hand and giggling like teenagers. He shook his head. More power to them.

He closed the door and sat down in the armchair, making himself comfortable. He reached inside his jacket and took out his pouch of tobacco and filled his pipe. He puffed away, trying not to think, watching the smoke rise above him and then disappear. He had to give Macalister an answer by tomorrow about taking on the case. Not thinking was out of the question. He got up and paced the room, the smoke rising over his shoulder. He walked back and forth, from the door to the window.

A woman had lost her life in this very room just three days before. Whether it was suicide or murder might never be determined, but what was certain was that her end had been violent. Chapelton had made a very good case for homicide, but it wasn't conclusive. Did that matter? If so, to whom? It didn't matter to the chief who was about to close the case. But it would matter to Lovingate's parents and siblings if she had any. It would matter to her husband and children if they existed. Lovingate's death would matter to someone. The situation would be bad enough if she committed suicide, but what if she didn't? With the case closed, someone would be getting away with cold-blooded murder.

Eddie stopped in front of the dresser and gathered up the crime scene photos. He turned around and spread them out on the bed. One by one, he studied them again. Her face look peaceful in death, even with the bullet hole in her forehead. How could that be with such a violent and final act? Didn't she know she was going to die? He looked at her hands. Despite the fact that they were starting to discolor, they were beautiful— long, thin fingers. Had she played the piano? Had she taken lessons since she was a young girl? Had she spent hours every day practicing? Maybe she had grown up in New York and gone to Juilliard. Now that she was lying still and cold at Rose Cottage, did all that matter? She had been here on this earth for thirty-five years and in this city for an indeterminate time, and now she was no longer. Not even Chapelton's magic could bring her back to life again.

He gathered up the photos, shoved them into the envelope, and left the room. He needed a drink. He took the elevator down to the first floor and went into the lounge. At the bar he ordered a whiskey. He tamped the ash down in his pipe and relit it. A song was wafting through the lounge. He looked around and didn't see anyone he knew.

"Unchained Melody"—that was what was playing. Whenever he heard that song, he thought about his wife, Josette. He was a lucky man, and he knew it. He'd met her by chance. She was the sister of a client he'd worked for last spring. She wasn't the most beautiful woman he'd ever seen, but he'd felt a strong pull toward her during their first meeting. By the end of their second meeting, he'd been completely captivated. He'd fallen in love with her spirit, her spunkiness. She could match him intellectually and emotionally. It was by luck only that she had felt the same way about him. They had seen each other, off and on, for the next few months, taking it slowly, each of them growing inevitably, unavoidably more restless, hungering for something deeper than their present lives could provide them. At the beginning of summer, they had driven south to Upstate New York and into the Adirondack Mountains. There, in that enchanted wilderness of trees and animals, of cold, bubbling streams, of endless forest trails, of chirping birds and hooting owls, amid the wildflowers and the fresh mountain air, covered in blankets of pitch-dark nights, their spirits had joined and become one. Four weeks later, they were married.

The song stopped playing, and he took a sip of his whiskey. What if something terrible happened to Josette the way it had happened to Lovingate? What would he do? That was a stupid question.

Someone tapped him on the shoulder. He swung around.

"Eddie! I thought that was you."

He looked at her but couldn't come up with a name.

"Gigi. Gigi Bonnet. Josette's friend. We met a few months ago."

"Oh, yes, of course. How are you?"

"I'm fine, thank you. I was having a drink with a friend when I saw you come in."

"I'm usually not here, but I had some business to do in the hotel, so I stopped in for a quick one."

Gigi seemed nervous. Her eyes darted around, never focusing on anything in particular. Finally, they rested on Eddie. "Listen, I had a long talk with Josette yesterday," she said, "and—"

"I know," he said, interrupting her. "We don't have any secrets between us."

"I got to thinking after I put down the phone that it was wrong of me to have asked her to talk with you about my personal problems."

"No, no, not at all. I make a living trying to solve personal problems." He looked around, then back at Gigi. "Why don't we go over to that booth and sit down? We can talk easier. Would you like a drink?"

"No. Two's my limit, but thanks anyway."

She was a good-looking woman in her midthirties, brown hair, nice figure, but not Eddie's type even if he were free. Nevertheless, she was pleasant enough to look at. After they had settled into a booth, Eddie broached the subject he would have rather liked to avoid altogether. "Listen, I really don't know you very well, and I've never met … what's his name?"

"Symeon. Symeon Peters. He's originally from London but has settled down here in Montreal."

"Well, as I said, I've never met Symeon, so it would be difficult for me to give you any advice."

"I wasn't really looking for advice as much as I was thinking about hiring someone to look into his sometimes rather bizarre behavior."

"Can I ask you how old he is?"

"He's thirty-nine."

"Has he ever been married before?"

"No."

"Here's what I think is going on, Gigi. Symeon is going into middle age. He's been living a single life for nearly forty years. He's had only himself to worry about, and it's obvious that he was quite content with that; otherwise, he would have done something about it sooner. Then, out of the clear blue sky, he meets you and falls madly in love. Suddenly, his whole world is tipped upside down. He thinks ahead about his future with a wife and the possibility of children and all the responsibility that entails. Suddenly, he gets—"

"Cold feet?"

"Yes, he gets cold feet. He's not sure he wants to make a change. He's been comfortable and stable, and now he's facing the possibility of changing all that." He puffed on his pipe a few times. "You should know that most happily married men experienced that before marriage to one degree or another, especially if they married older. They're really little boys. They need to be reassured."

"Does that include you?"

"Absolutely. I had ice-cold feet."

"How did you handle it, if you don't mind me asking?"

"I talked to Josette about it. We talked it out. Turned out she had cold feet as well."

"And talking about it helped?"

"It did wonders. We set the date, and a month later, we were man and wife."

"You make it sound so easy."

"It's not that difficult. Listen, Gigi. Josette and I can talk about anything. Nothing is off-limits. I think that that's the way it should be between a husband and wife. If you can't do it before you're married, it's not magically going to happen after you're married."

"Well, you have certainly given me something to think about."

"I can only tell you what works with Josette and me, and it's made us closer."

Gigi slid out of the booth and extended a hand to Eddie. "Thank you, Eddie. I can see that Josette is a lucky woman."

Eddie stood up and shook her hand. "I'm the lucky one," he said.

Eddie sat down again after she left, pleased with the probability that he wouldn't have to do more in the continuing saga of Gigi and Symeon. *Gee*, he thought, *who would name their kid Symeon?* Anyway, if she wanted anything more from him, like tailing her fiancé, he would have to tell her that he didn't work for people he or his wife knew. Agency policy. That would put an end to it.

His mind suddenly flashed back to room 311 and the blood splatters on the wall. Jack Macalister would be expecting a call from him tomorrow. In other circumstances, he would have picked up the phone now and called him. He'd made a decision. But he had a wife and partner to consider now. How would she feel about him working on a case with virtually no leads and no money coming in? The idea was crazy for him to even consider. There was only one way for him to find out how Josette would feel about it; he had to talk to her.

———«●»———

Josette sat in the armchair by the fireplace that night and turned a page in the book she was reading. She sighed. Eddie glanced up from his own book.

Before they even got married, Eddie and Josette had decided that the back room of Eddie's office wasn't going to work for them. So they had gone on an apartment search. As luck would have it, Eddie knew someone who knew someone who knew someone who owned a building only about a half block from the office on Saint-Urbain. One of the apartments was going to be free at the beginning of the following month. They had grabbed it without even looking at it.

"What're you reading? That's the fifth time you've sighed in the last twenty minutes."

"You're keeping count?"

"I will if it continues."

"*The Second Sex* by Simone de Beauvoir, volume one of two ... in French."

"Sounds exciting. The French are always thinking about sex."

"It's not that kind of book. It's about how women were treated throughout history."

"Treated by whom?"

"Men, of course."

"I would have thought something like that would require a half dozen volumes at least."

"She argues that humanity is male and that man defines woman as relative to him. She thinks that women are merely baby-producers and that men run the world."

"She wrote two volumes to say that? Any taxi driver could have told you the same thing in a ten-minute ride across town."

"No, she says much more than that. I don't agree with her on everything, but she does make some good points."

"Listen, could we put our books down for a moment? There's something we need to discuss."

"Sounds serious. Does it have to do with your visit with Jack this morning?"

It did, indeed. Eddie proceeded to tell his wife the details of the Lovingate case that Macalister had imparted to him as well as the findings of Roger Chapelton at the crime scene. He left nothing out. The likelihood was great that they wouldn't be paid much if they took on the case. As a matter of fact, they would even have to spend their own money—in fact, they already had! Chapelton had to be paid for his time today. Eddie didn't want to influence her decision, so he remained neutral in telling her about the case. He ended by saying that he'd be okay with either decision, but that wasn't exactly true.

After he finished, Josette simply said, "Okay, let's do it," and went back to her book.

"Now wait just a minute. You do understand that we'll probably be working for free most of the time and that we'll be starting out with virtually no leads?"

"Eddie, this isn't the first time you've done an investigation for little or no money, and it probably won't be the last time. And as far as leads go, wasn't it you who told me that a good investigator finds his own leads? Besides, you just said that the police are about to close the case. If we don't take it on, what about the victim? The poor woman was murdered— probably. The police aren't sure if she's American or Canadian. She could be unidentified. Someone in North America is waiting for a phone call from her, but they don't know she's in the morgue. If you're undecided, then let's set a date. If we find nothing in a month, let's say, then we'll put it to rest. Anyway, you wanted my input, and that's it."

"What do we live on for a month? We don't have any clients right now. I forgot to tell you that Jack wants me to fly to St. Paul, Minnesota, on Monday for a few days to see what I can find out about her—on our tab. He said he'd reimburse us, but that's only going to be by a third."

"We're not broke. You've got your savings, and I'll be getting a third of what the bakery sells for when my parents retire next month. They already have a few prospective buyers. We're not going to be living in skid row. A month is just four weeks; it's not an eternity."

"I just want to make sure you know all the repercussions."

"There won't be any, Eddie, or at least not anything we can't handle. We could stand on our heads for a month, and things would be just fine. By the way, what are you reading?"

"*The Big Kill* by Mickey Spillane. It's about—"

"Stop," she said with her hand out like a traffic cop. "I think I know the plot already."

Eddie smiled, then said, "Oh, another thing I forgot to tell you. I bumped into Gigi in town this afternoon. We had a little chat."

"What did you say?"

"I told her that she and her husband-to-be better start talking to each other now before it's too late. Good thing they haven't eloped already. I wouldn't give them two months before one of them filed for divorce."

"They're a lovely couple, Eddie. You should see them together."

"Yeah, but they don't seem to talk about the serious stuff. I wonder how much they actually know about each other."

"How much did we know about each other before we got married?"

"Quite a lot. We talked nonstop."

Josette closed her book and set it on the end table. Then she got up and walked over to Eddie. She took his book out of his hand, put it on the floor, and sat on his lap.

"But it wasn't always about serious stuff," she said, mussing his hair. "If I recall, there were a few interludes between those *serious* discussions?"

"How about one of those now … if I'm not keeping you from Madame de Beauvoir?"

"I think she can wait."

Chapter 4
PIG'S EYE

LATE MONDAY MORNING, EDDIE BOARDED A Trans-Canadian aircraft at Dorval Airport for Chicago and then caught a connecting flight with Northwest Airlines to the Minneapolis–St. Paul International Airport/Wold-Chamberlain Field, arriving late in the afternoon.

During both flights, he'd been restless. He had tried sleeping, and when that hadn't worked, he'd opened the Spillane book he'd brought with him. After a few pages, he'd realized that he couldn't concentrate enough to follow the story, so he'd closed the book and stared out the window. He hadn't been able to get Anne Lovingate out of his head since he first saw the crime scene photos in Macalister's office. It had intensified when he was in her hotel room with Roger Chapelton and Candy. It was there, where she'd taken her last breath, that he'd met her ghost; he was sure of that. Now she followed him wherever he went. She entered his thoughts at will, possessing him, taking control of him.

Chapelton had confirmed what Eddie had already suspected, that the woman had been murdered, but he needed Chapelton's expertise in case he had to convince Macalister's boss. He still left the door open for the possibility that she had committed suicide, but only a crack. There was still a lot of evidence he didn't have. Strange things happened during investigations. Evidence collected toward the end of an investigation had the power to turn a sure case around 180 degrees.

To avoid the pitfall of acquiring evidence to prove a preconceived position—namely, that she had been murdered—and ignoring everything else, he would start off, at least initially, to prove that she hadn't been, to prove that she had taken her own life. He would, in fact, give full weight to both theories. Let Lovingate's spirit shift the evidence in one direction or the other as it came in. He would be there to observe and analyze it, arriving at a conclusion when there was nothing else to do.

Because he was somewhat familiar with St. Paul, he decided to rent a car at the airport rather than spend the money and waste time taking taxis around town. He drove the new two-tone Chevy Bel Air to the Ryan Hotel, where he'd made reservations over the weekend. The hotel was located in the center of town at the northeast corner of Sixth and Robert Streets. It was an impressive Victorian Gothic seven-story building, and the rooms were expensive. Eddie took few vacations, so he had decided to splurge on this work-related trip. He could use it as a tax write-off.

It was too late in the day to go to the police department to see Detective Harry Haden, so after he took a shower and put on fresh clothes, he stowed his .45 semiautomatic in the room safe that he'd requested when he made the reservation. Although he'd seen just a little of the city while driving in, so far it looked pretty much the same as it had fifteen years before. He'd been here a half dozen times for boxing matches. During each trip, there would always be a day or two after a fight for him to unwind, take in a few bars with some of the local fighters, or find a nice nightclub by himself and sometimes with his trainer to drink and listen to live music. He'd gotten to know the downtown area well, but not much more of the city. Just across the Mississippi was the bigger city of Minneapolis. It was only a twenty-minute drive from the downtown area of one city to the other, but he had never made the trip.

He got into his rented Chevy and drove down Sixth Street. He was hungry and knew where to go. It was only a five-minute drive there, but the weather in St. Paul was as vicious as the weather in Montreal: subzero temperatures and a nasty wind. Most of the streets in this area of town were like wind tunnels. Walking was out of the question. Since he had already rented a car, he might as well use it.

He pulled up to a narrow building on St. Peter Street with the same big letters on the window that he remembered, the words forming a semicircle: Original Coney Island Tavern. He let the car idle for a while. He hadn't driven far, and he wanted the car to warm up a bit before he turned the engine off. Anne Lovingate flashed in his mind. He couldn't forget her image from the crime scene photos—a hole in the center of her head, her eyes slightly open, her lips parted, the back of her head blown off. It wasn't as if he hadn't seen something like that before. He had, many times. In fact, he'd seen much worse than that during the war, unimaginable destruction to the human body. But there was something about Anne Lovingate that was different. He didn't know what, but there was something about her that wouldn't let him rest. If it turned out that she had taken her own life, what a waste. Maybe it was the way she had been dressed, the way he had imagined her if she were alive. She looked like a—for the lack of a better word—professional. Would he have felt the same about her if she had been dressed in rags and found dead in some cheap skid row hotel room? He couldn't say. The fact was, she hadn't been. She'd been found dressed as if she were going to a board meeting, found stone-cold dead in one of the most expensive hotels in Montreal. That was part of the known evidence; all else about her was speculation, even the images of her as she might have been that Eddie had created in his mind.

He turned the engine off, got out, and walked into the tavern. Not a thing had changed, not even the old Greek couple behind the counter. They didn't look a day older. Even though he had come in here every time he was in town for a fight, there was no reason for him to believe they would recognize him; it had been too long ago. But he recognized them at first sight. The place was somewhat crowded, but he found an empty stool at the end of the counter. Before he knew it, the old woman was standing in front of him.

"What I can get for you, young man?"

She must have stood all of five feet. A little on the heavy side, she wore a dark-brown woolen sweater that came down well below her waist. Her hair had been mostly black the last time Eddie saw her; now it was gray, pulled back into a bun. She was wearing wire-rimmed glasses.

"I'll have two, along with coffee, please."

The menu was simple; there was only one item on it. All that was required of the customer was to tell how many he or she wanted. The Original Coney Island Tavern kept life simple in a complicated world. She brought the coffee right away while her husband fixed the order. Before Eddie could even sip his coffee, she returned with a paper plate and set the food in front of him. Then she was gone again to serve another customer.

Of all the things Eddie associated St. Paul with, the Coney Island hot dog topped the list. But it wasn't just a Coney Island; it was the Original Coney Island! Had they invented it? He didn't know and didn't care. He hadn't had one of these in fifteen years. Oh, he had eaten plenty of Coney Islands in Montreal, but it wasn't the same. They even called them by a different name. He often dreamed about them and had even fantasized about them over the years, and now they were sitting in front of him, less than a foot away. He decided to take them in before going for them. They looked exactly the same: the warm bun, the skinny, succulent hot dogs, the out-of-this-world, one-of-a-kind chili sauce, the finely chopped onions, and the yellow mustard. He started to salivate. He couldn't take it any longer. You could never have just one; it was never enough. You had to have two at least. If you were really hungry, there was no limit. He picked one up, positioned one end strategically, aligning it with his mouth, and then—

Anne Lovingate, Anne Lovingate, Anne Lovingate. The hole in the center of her head, the eyes slightly open. The lips parted. The back of her head blown off.

He set the Coney Island on the plate. She was back again, haunting him—her spirit or ghost or whatever. He was being possessed by her, and he was unable to do anything about it. How long would this go on? When would it end? He had lost control of himself. How would he be able to function? What would happen to his investigation? Those were all good questions, but he had no answers for them. He ordered a shot of whiskey, then another.

"Sumpin' wrong with your Coney?" the old lady asked.

"No, no. Nothing at all." He didn't want to offend her. He ate the first one and then the second. He didn't enjoy them as much as he'd thought he would. Anne Lovingate made sure of that.

The old lady was sneaking glances at him, a confused look on her face. He gave her a thumbs-up. That might satisfy her. Finally, he gulped his coffee down and left, picking up a flyer from the counter by the cash register that had caught his attention.

Outside, he started the car and let it idle again. Sometimes he'd had a case that really affected him to the point that he'd lose sleep over it, but nothing like this. This was affecting his waking hours. Maybe he could do something to distract himself. It was worth a try. He picked up the flyer he had put beside him on the seat. It was an advertisement for a wrestling event at the St. Paul Armory that night. He looked at his watch. It had started already. Maybe he could catch the main event. He put the car into gear and drove off.

Twelve minutes later, he pulled into the parking lot of the armory. The lot was full, meaning they had a packed crowd, good for a Monday night. The building was red brick and looked more like a castle than anything else. It was primarily used for the Minnesota National Guard but was rented out for wrestling and boxing matches. Eddie himself had had his six St. Paul fights here, winning all of them. It would be nice to see it again, an old piece of his history.

He had to pay full price for the ticket even though most of the matches were done already. He found an empty chair in the back and was grateful he could sit down. A match had just finished, so the auditorium lights were on—a short break before the main event. Many of the spectators had gotten up to stretch or get something to eat. There was a lot of talking and arguing about the previous bout. Unlike boxing, professional wrestling was fixed in the sense that the winners and losers were already hashed out beforehand, but the fans didn't know that, or if they did, they didn't care. It was all legal because—well, because that was the way it was. It was more entertainment than sport. The wrestlers were paid well, and the fans got to see them beat each other up with the ringside chairs and tables. Everyone was happy, and no one took it too seriously—mostly.

This place, too, looked the same as it had fifteen years before—the chairs arranged in the same way, in four sections from ringside to the back walls on one level; the same concession stands selling the same things, mostly popcorn, pretzels, peanuts, candy bars, hot dogs, and cold beer. Eddie wondered whether it was the same ring he had fought in, because they used it for boxing as well as wrestling.

He checked the flyer again to see who had the main event. It was Kowalski versus Gagne, a big draw. Eddie had seen these two before at different times at the Forum in Montreal, a much larger venue. Killer Kowalski was six feet seven and carried 280 pounds of muscle. He was definitely the "bad" guy tonight. When paired with a relatively unknown wrestler, he was always the winner. But tonight, he was going against the hometown boy, Verne Gagne, a much smaller guy. Gagne was five eleven and weighed 215 pounds. He was the more athletic of the two and had "scientific" moves. He would be the winner tonight because this was his territory, and he was always the "good" guy. The fans all knew it, but they didn't care. They just wanted to see a fight; they didn't care if the fight was dirty or not. As a matter of fact, the dirtier, the better. Gagne was going to win regardless. The fans just wanted to see action. That was what they paid for.

Eddie stared at the ring and pictured himself in it. He wondered how far he could have gone if he had stayed in boxing. Boxing was fraught with uncertainties. The biggest one was injuries. An injury could put a fighter out for months or even a year or more. If that happened when the fighter was in his prime, it was devastating. Furthermore, a single punch could end a career. Eddie had been a good fighter—even more than just good. He'd been an excellent fighter. If he'd stayed in the ring, barring injuries, he most likely would have had at least one title, maybe more because he was tall and could have gained enough weight for another title or two. But the war had come, and he and Jack Macalister had decided to go south and join the US Army. At that point, Eddie Wade's boxing career was finished.

The lights dimmed, which meant that the main event was about to begin.

———«•»———

Eddie left the armory just before the bout ended to avoid being caught in the mad rush to the parking lot that was sure to come. He drove slowly in the general direction of the hotel, looking for a bar or a nightclub with its outdoor lights still on. He saw none. Unlike Montreal, St. Paul folded up early.

Gradually, almost imperceptibly, Anne Lovingate crept back into his brain. The dead Lovingate, the murdered Lovingate, the Lovingate who might have committed suicide. Anne, Anne, Anne. She wasn't after him as much as she simply possessed him. Why him? Why Eddie? She wanted something from him. Was it justice? If so, then she was telling him that she had been murdered. If she had been murdered, then her killer was out there somewhere. Had he followed her to Montreal, shot her in the forehead in her hotel room, and then staged the crime scene to look like a suicide? Was he back in St. Paul now? Was this the reason she was haunting Eddie? Was the killer in this city?

If she was in fact from St. Paul, then someone here in the city was waiting for a phone call from her, waiting for her to return. If Anne Lovingate was trying to tell Eddie that the killer was here in the city, then the killer was the only person who knew that she would never be making that phone call, never be returning to the people who knew and loved her.

Only the killer knew that—only the killer, a few other people back in Montreal, and Eddie Wade himself.

Chapter 5
THE ART OF PLEASING IS
THE ART OF DECEPTION

AT PRECISELY EIGHT IN THE MORNING ON
Tuesday, January 10, one week after the killer had put a bullet
through the head of Anne Lovingate—or after she had put the
bullet there herself—Eddie Wade had parked his car and was
walking toward the St. Paul Police Department headquarters,
freezing his ass off. The snow was piled so high that the streets
looked like tunnels. It was well below zero with what seemed
like a gale-force wind that could snap the limb from an oak
tree in a fraction of a second and toss it into the next county;
Hennepin County was having the same issues as Ramsey.
Eddie adjusted the collar of his overcoat with one gloved hand
while hanging on to his hat with the other. The wind was to
his back, which sped up his half-block expedition from his car
to the front door. If he seemed ungrateful for that, so be it.

The building was a six-story brick box with a rectangular
tower jutting out of the top, the only structure on that part
of Grove Street. A huge parking area full of prowl cars and
unmarked cars was located in the back of the building. Eddie

had parked in the visitors' section and made his way around the side to the front. He opened the door and went inside.

There were radiators on either side of the entrance, and he could immediately feel the warmth. He took off his gloves, unbuttoned his overcoat to catch some of the heat, and adjusted his hat. It had taken him only a few minutes to get from his heated car to the heated building, but he'd paid a terrible price; he was still frozen down to his bones. Directly in front of him and down the hall about ten feet sat the desk sergeant in what looked like a judge's bench, raised up a foot or so from the floor. He walked up to the desk and looked up at the officer. Now he knew what it felt like to stand before a judge who was about to pronounce judgment.

The desk sergeant looked down at him. "A little nippy out there, ain't it, son?"

Nippy? Eddie thought. *That's his judgment?* He wondered what this man would call a whiteout. "Yeah, just a little. I'm here to see Detective Harry Haden."

"And who might you be, laddie, if you don't mind me askin'?"

He had a watered-down Irish accent and looked to be retirement age, which meant he had probably been in this country for a very long time. He was relaxed and confident and spoke slowly, seemingly very much in charge of things and able to handle any situation that might come through the doors.

"Eddie Wade. I'm a private investigator from Montreal."

The older man looked surprised. "Montreal, you say now? So you know all about nasty weather. I used to go there a lot in me drinkin' days. The drinks were cold, and the little ladies were hot." He smiled and gave Eddie a wink. "And might Detective Haden be expecting you? He's a very busy man, you know."

"Sort of."

The desk sergeant angled his head slightly and gave him a look a teacher might give to a student who's trying to pull the wool over his eyes. Apparently, nothing escaped him.

Eddie continued, "He spoke to someone from the Montreal police headquarters last week, so yes, he's expecting me. He just doesn't know when."

"You wouldn't happen to be carrying a piece, now would you? If you are, you'll have to hand it over until you leave." His expression said that he was sorry he had to ask, but you know, it was policy.

"No gun, no penknife, nothing that could be misconstrued as a weapon." Eddie raised both arms at the elbows, palms out, to emphasize the point.

"Ah, that's grand now, laddie. The elevators are down this hallway by the coffee station," he said, pointing to his side, "and the stairs are off to the right. I'll give Harry a ring just now and let him know yer comin' up. Second floor, room 202, just off the landing."

Eddie took the stairs, figuring he'd warm up faster that way. Room 202 was indeed just off the landing. The door was open, so he knuckled the frosted glass lightly a few times and slowly pushed the door in. The office was large, with four desks in it, but only one was occupied. The man sitting behind one of the desks looked up from his paperwork but didn't say anything.

"Detective Haden?" Eddie asked.

"That's me." He threw his hands in the air. "You got me!"

Eddie stepped into the office. It felt like a tropical rainforest. "I'm Eddie Wade from Montreal. You talked to Jack Macalister last week."

"Yes, yes. He said you might be coming by. Come in, come in. Have a seat. Sorry it's so hot in here. Those damn radiators are either broken or going full steam, and you can't control them. Take off your coat and hat, or you're going to be sweating in no time."

Eddie took off his coat and hat, draped them over a chair, and then sat down in another chair in front of the desk. Directly behind and above Haden on the wall was a plaque with the Marine Corps emblem on it. Eddie couldn't help but see it.

"You served?" he asked. That question always meant "Did you serve in the war?"

"First Marine Division. Guadalcanal." The detective didn't elaborate; he didn't need to.

Harry Haden was in his forties. He was a short man with a slight build. He had long fingers like a surgeon's. He couldn't have weighed much more than 150 pounds. Yet if he had survived Guadalcanal, he must be one tough son of a bitch.

Haden cleared his throat. "Macalister laid out the case you're working on. I told him then, and I'll tell you now, that I'll help in any way I can, but I'm working my own cases." He pointed to the piles of folders on his desk. "So my participation is going to be minimal."

"That's fine, Detective. Macalister told me the same thing, so I'll be running with this on my own—I mean, with my partner in Montreal."

"Please, just Harry. I did some digging over the weekend. The name Lovingate is an unusual name, but I found two in St. Paul. None in Minneapolis." He slid a piece of paper toward Eddie. "Here are the full names and addresses."

Eddie picked up the paper and looked at it. "Two names. That's not bad. It narrows it down. Thanks! I'm glad I'm not looking for someone named Smith."

The phone on the desk rang.

"Sorry, I have to take this. I'm expecting a call." Haden was on the phone for only a minute before he hung up. "I'm afraid my presence is needed elsewhere. There's always something."

"No problem. I understand," Eddie said, getting up and taking his coat and hat off the other chair.

Haden stood up. "Listen, if you're free at the end of the day, I'll buy you supper. My wife's in Mankato visiting her parents. That's a couple hours south of the cities. Took the kids with her, so I'm free myself."

"Sounds good. Where?"

"Nothing fancy. There's a place in the center of town called Mickey's Diner, on West Seventh Street. They have good burgers. The only time I get to eat them is when the wife's away."

"I know where it's at. What time?"

"About seven?"

"See you then."

———«●»———

On his way to the first Lovingate address on the list, Eddie mulled over how he would handle talking to whoever was there. He first had to establish whether or not they were related to Anne Lovingate, and he had to do it in a way that left no doubt. And then there was Eddie himself. Would he tell them that he was a private investigator working for the Montreal police? That might scare them off. He had to come up with something that wouldn't tip his hand. Then a thought occurred to him. It might work if they didn't ask him for identification. He didn't want to lie to them, but he might not have a choice. He passed a filling station, did a U-turn, and then pulled in to ask for directions.

After getting directions, he continued to Summit Avenue for half a mile, then turned left onto Avon and drove another nine blocks to Osceola and turned right. There it was—second house on the left. He parked the car, jumped over a mound of snow, and walked up the shoveled path to the door. He pushed the doorbell. After he pressed it a second time, a man in his sixties opened the door.

Eddie eyed the man carefully. This could be Anne Lovingate's father. He scrapped his plan. He decided to be as straightforward with him as he was able to be. If the man's daughter had been murdered, he didn't want to play games with the poor guy.

"Hello. My name is Eddie Wade. I'm a private investigator from Montreal, Quebec. Are you Robert Lovingate?"

"I am. What's this about?"

"May I come in to talk with you?"

"Of course, son, come in. It's frigid out there."

Eddie stepped into the entryway where coats were hanging up and knocked the snow off his shoes. He was then led into the living room.

"Please sit down. I must say that my curiosity is aroused. Montreal is quite a distance from here."

Just then, a woman entered.

"This is my wife, Gloria. Gloria, this is Mr. Wade. He says he's from Canada."

"Canada? What's this all about?"

"Everyone, sit down please. Mr. Wade is about to tell us, dear."

Eddie sat in an armchair, and the couple sat next to each other on the sofa.

"I was hired to find someone who checked into a hotel in Montreal and then disappeared." There it was: the lie. She hadn't disappeared; she had been murdered. But he didn't want to tell them that, at least not at this point. If it turned out that they were in fact her parents, then at least he would have only one lie to correct instead of some wild, convoluted story he had made up.

"How does that involve us?" Robert asked, looking confused.

"When this person checked into the hotel, she used an American passport and a Minnesota driver's license. Both forms of identification had the name Anne Lovingate on them." His eyes went from Robert to Gloria and then back to Robert again. He saw a flash of recognition in both of their faces.

"Yes, go on, Mr. Wade. Is there more?"

"Well, my question to you is, do you know anyone with that name?"

They looked at each other for a long moment, then back at Eddie.

"I take it you're looking for a relative or someone who might know her," Gloria said. "Is that correct?"

"Yes, I am. That's why I came all the way to St. Paul."

They looked at each other again but didn't say anything. After an uncomfortable minute of silence, Robert spoke. "I'm afraid we can't help you, and I'll have to ask you to leave."

Eddie's mouth nearly dropped. Why the abrupt change? They had gone from being cooperative to nearly throwing him out in a matter of a few seconds. Did they suspect that he'd lied? Did they think this was some kind of con game? Were they hiding something?

Eddie took out his wallet and opened it. "This is my license," he said, giving it to Robert, "issued by the province of Quebec. I can assure you that the only reason I'm here is to find information leading to the whereabouts of Anne Lovingate. You could help me do that, if you know something."

Robert took the wallet, and he and his wife examined the license. After a minute or so, he gave it back to Eddie. "You have to excuse us, but for a moment we thought—Jesus, I don't know what we thought. You see, that's our daughter's name. Anne Lovingate."

"Do you know whether she traveled to Montreal recently? Lovingate isn't a common name."

Gloria spoke up this time. "That's impossible, Mr. Wade."

"Why is that?"

"Because our daughter died many years ago."

Eddie was stunned. When he didn't say anything, Gloria continued.

"When Anne was a year old, she contracted viral meningitis. The doctors did the best they could, but there weren't many options in those days. Maybe now would be different. She passed away only a few days after being diagnosed."

"I'm sorry," Eddie said. "That must have been quite a shock for you."

"That's an understatement," Robert said.

"Can you tell me what her date of birth was?"

"Yes, she was born on April 9, 1921, and passed on March 25, 1922. It was at 3:05 in the morning. We were there by her side."

"I'm really sorry to have brought this up." Eddie was indeed sorry, but he had a job to do. "Do you know of any other Lovingates in the area?"

"There's only one more," Robert said. "He's my older brother. Presently, he's in the hospital with a serious heart condition."

"And there's no one else by that name that you know of?"

"I'm afraid we're the only Lovingates around."

They talked for another hour. Gloria had made some coffee and served some homemade cookies. The Lovingates were fascinated that he was from Montreal and had appeared out of nowhere, so much of the conversation was about that. When it wound down, they shook hands all around, and the couple wished Eddie luck in his quest.

Outside, he started the car and let it warm up. He then jotted a few things down in his notebook. The last thing was the birth date of the Lovingates' daughter who had died of viral meningitis at the age of one—it was the same date of birth from the passport this Anne Lovingate had used to check into the Windsor Hotel: April 9, 1921.

———— «●» ————

Mickey's Diner was a fifty-foot-long, ten-foot-wide railroad dining car. It had red and yellow porcelain-enameled steel panels on the exterior along with art deco–style lettering proclaiming its presence. A row of ten windows ran from side to side. Inside, the counter ran nearly the length of the car, seating twelve customers on red plastic stools, with only two booths off to one side. But it really wasn't a genuine railroad dining car; it was just designed to look like one. It fooled most people, most of the time.

The diner had a large, twenty-four-hour, 365-day-a-year menu that included eggs, pancakes, hash browns, chili, mulligan stew, ice cream floats, milkshakes, malts, and donuts, plus all the coffee you could drink for a dime. The "house rules" were handwritten on a piece of cardboard taped to the cash register: "No Spitting" and "Cash Only." The rules kept life simple. Eddie and Harry Haden were sitting at one of the booths eating hamburgers and french fried potatoes.

"Goddamn it," Haden said. "I knew it was you when you walked into my office, and I put a face to your name."

"I didn't know I was known in this part of North America."

"Just before I came here, I swung around to my place. I kept every program of the fights at the armory. I found all six you had here in a box in the attic. The last one was with Al Hostak. You won on a split decision."

"That was a tough one. Al was good. That was his first fight after he broke his fingers with Tony Zale. I think he was holding back his punches a little, but he gave me a rough time anyway."

"I followed your career whenever I could. As I remember, you had quite a knockout record. You were moving up in the rankings and heading for a championship fight. Then nothing. I learned from one of the local guys that you hung up the gloves. I hope you don't mind me asking why."

"The war. After I got back, it just wasn't the same for me. A fighter's got to have an insane need to smash his way to the top. I didn't have that anymore. The war knocked that out of me, so I tried to get on the police force, but I didn't pass the physical because of a wounded knee. So I became a private dick."

The conversation segued to the war. Eddie talked about his time in Europe—something he rarely did with anyone—and Haden related a few stories about Guadalcanal, something, as it turned out, that he rarely did as well.

"What gets me, Eddie, is that after going through hell, killing and seeing others killed, I return to St. Paul after the war, get my old job back on the force, and see the same shit here. I can't figure it out."

"Well, when you do, tell me, because I'm trying to figure out the same thing."

"In the war, it was different. Goddamn it—it was a war. People were trying to kill you, so you got them before they got you. But it isn't all that different here, and I'm sure it's not that different in Montreal."

"It isn't, except the bad guys don't wear uniforms."

There was a long moment of silence. Someone dropped a coin in the jukebox, and Tony Bennett began singing "Stranger in Paradise." After a while, Haden asked Eddie how he'd gotten along today.

Eddie told him about his visit with the Lovingates and how the birth date of their daughter, Anne Lovingate, who had died thirty-four years before, was the same as the birth date on the passport that an Anne Lovingate had used to check into the Windsor Hotel a week ago, along with a St. Paul address.

"That can't be a coincidence," Haden said. "It stinks to high heaven."

"That's what I thought."

"It's easy enough to check out, though."

"I was planning on going to the hall of records tomorrow."

"You should be able to find what you're looking for there. What was your take on the old couple?"

"They seemed sincere enough—genuine."

"Don't let that fool you, though. Ma Barker seemed genuine too. But I can't for the life of me figure out what their racket might be, if they have one—saying their daughter was dead when she wasn't. And if the woman was their daughter, why did she turn up in Montreal?"

"Maybe they're trying to protect her. Maybe she was into something deep."

"Like what?"

"Now that's the question, huh?"

"You up for a couple of drinks?"

"Always."

"There's a little joint a few blocks away. It's quiet. My off-duty brethren go there to unwind."

"Sounds like it's a safe place to drink."

"Safe? With a bar full of cops? Hell, they're all packing rods! Who in their right mind would want to cause trouble there?"

Chapter 6
WHO WAS ANN LOVINGATE?

EDDIE HAD TOSSED AND TURNED FOR SEVERAL hours before falling asleep the night before. He'd been married for only six months but was already used to having Josette by his side. When she wasn't there, he'd found out, his sleep was disrupted. His wakeup call had come at six, followed by a quick shower and a breakfast back at Mickey's Diner.

Now he opened one of the heavy doors of the St. Paul City Hall and Ramsey County Courthouse on Kellogg, just a block away from where the Mississippi River made a bend on its journey starting at Lake Itasca in northern Minnesota. From St. Paul it would head south all the way to New Orleans before emptying into the Gulf of Mexico. He went inside and knocked the snow off his shoes on one of the doormats.

The building was a twenty-story art deco skyscraper completed in 1932. The entrance led directly into Memorial Hall. Eddie took a few steps in, stopped, and looked around in amazement. The white marble floor contrasted with three-story black marble piers leading to a gold-leaf ceiling. At the end of the hall in front of him was a massive sixty-ton, thirty-eight-foot statue made of creamy white Mexican onyx, called the "Indian God of Peace." Eddie marveled at its splendor.

There were murals on the walls to his sides, along with six bronze elevator doors, three on each side. He walked up to the Indian god, his heels echoing in the hall, and realized that it was a war memorial with 340 names, commemorating those from St. Paul who had died in the Great War. The statue sat on a revolving base that turned the figure 132 degrees every two and a half hours. At the base of the great statue, five American Indians were seated around a fire, holding sacred pipes. Emerging from the smoke of those pipes was the "God of Peace," who seemed to be speaking to all of the world. Eddie hoped that they were listening.

After standing there for a time, almost in a trance, he crossed over to the side and went up the staircase to the second floor, his shoes clicking on the floor all the way up. There was marble everywhere. He found the county records office and went inside. An older woman in her sixties was behind the counter, doing something with a stack of paper. She looked up as he entered.

"You look like a police officer on a mission. What can I help you with, sonny?"

Last night over beers, Haden had told Eddie where the records department was and that he should just introduce himself as a detective. They would assume he was on the St. Paul police force and wouldn't ask a lot of questions. They never asked cops for identification.

"I'm Detective Wade. I'd like to see the birth and death records of an Anne Lovingate—Anne with an *e* on the end."

"Not so fast there, Detective. You're not going to slip by me without first filling out the form. You think I was born yesterday?" She reached under the counter and produced a half sheet of paper and a pen. "You fill this here out, and I'll be right back."

Eddie filled out the form in ten seconds and then waited. The Lovingates were a charming couple, but Haden had been right. Trust but verify: that was what he was there to do.

The clerk returned. "Okay, what did you say your name was?" she asked. "Never mind. It's right here. Detective Eddie Wade. Never heard of you, but the department is big." She gave him a knowing look. "Now let's see, you want the birth and death certificates of an Anne Lovingate. Date of birth is April 9, 1921, and the date of death is March 25, 1922. Oh my! The poor child. She wasn't even a year old yet." She looked up at him. "So where's the justice in that, I ask you? She got cheated out of her life. It ain't fair, I tell you; it just ain't fair. Now the file cabinet is just over there"—she pointed to her right—"so it will only take me a jiffy."

As she walked away, Eddie felt as if the clerk was holding him personally responsible for the young life ending so quickly. Nevertheless, the old lady was correct: it wasn't fair, not in the least. Eddie looked behind him. There were some chairs lining the wall, so he sat down on one of them. He thought about what Haden had said last night. The experienced detective had concurred with Eddie that it was suspicious that both the child who had died back in 1922 and the woman who had checked into the Windsor in Montreal had the same date of birth. If the name had been more common, it wouldn't have raised as many red flags. But as Eddie had discovered, the name wasn't at all common either in Canada or in the Twin Cities. He looked toward the counter and saw that the clerk had returned. He got up and went over to her.

"Here's what I found, Detective." She laid the birth certificate in front of him.

Eddie read the certificate. It recorded the live birth of Anne Lovingate to her mother and father, listed as Robert and Gloria Lovingate, along with their ages and address. The document seemed to be in order. He looked up at the clerk. "And the death certificate?"

"There wasn't one. It would have been in the same file. In case it was misfiled, I also cross-checked it, and I didn't find one. Are you certain that the child died?"

"Yes, I just talked to the parents yesterday. She died on March 25, 1922."

"Are you certain that the death occurred in this county or even Minnesota?" She sounded exasperated.

That was a good question. The Lovingates hadn't specifically said, and Eddie hadn't thought to ask. "I'll have to find that out. I'm not certain."

"Well, you do that, Detective, and get back to me. You have to at least give me something to go on. I'm not a magician, you know? I just can't pick a death certificate out of a top hat."

"Eh, one more thing while I'm here. You have records of persons who changed their names, right?"

She gave him a look that said, *You're about to cross a line, buddy.* "I do, and that's going to require another form." She reached under the counter again and slapped down another half sheet.

Eddie filled it out and gave it back to her. He didn't bother to sit down this time, and she was back in half of a jiffy.

"I'm afraid you're batting near zero, Detective. I have no records of an Anne Lovingate changing her name, and there is no record of anyone changing her name to Anne Lovingate."

"Okay. I guess I'll have to do a little more homework then."

"You do that, Detective. I'm here from eight to five, Monday through Friday. If you return a few minutes before five, I will not be pleased."

"I'll remember that."

"You do that, Detective."

He went back down to the first floor and stood in front of the Indian statue again. Sixty tons. Thirty-eight feet high.

He looked up at it and wondered how anyone could sculpt such an immense piece of onyx. It made him feel small and insignificant.

Anne Lovingate. What in the hell is going on?

The birth certificate had listed the Lovingates' address as the same one he had been to yesterday, so they had lived in the same house when their daughter was born. They'd given no indication that their daughter had died anywhere else but St. Paul, in Ramsey County, but there was no record of the death. Officially, Anne Lovingate had been born but never died. What were Robert and Gloria Lovingate hiding?

And why?

———— «•» ————

It was a two-story, gray wooden house with a front porch whose winter windows were in place. It sat on Edgerton Street at the corner of Jenks Avenue, on the east side of St. Paul. The neighborhood was strictly residential, and a dilapidated red-brick elementary school sat catty-corner across the street from the house. The house was either a large one-family home or a duplex with two families living in it. This was the address listed on the driver's license Anne Lovingate had provided the hotel, and Eddie Wade was going to check it out.

He parked the car directly in the front of the house. The snow was piled high at the curb, so he walked around the car to the corner where it had been shoveled. His shoes crunched in the snow all the way up to the front door. There was no doorbell outside. The door leading into the porched area wasn't secured, so he opened it and went inside. He knocked on the inner door several times and waited. After a minute or so, he knocked on the door again, but harder this time. He peeked in and saw that the door opened into a hallway, with another door to the right and with stairs leading up to the second floor on the left. The building was probably a duplex with two families living in it. Just then, the door to the right opened, and a woman came through it.

The woman opened the front door. "Sorry. I was just baking," she said. "I heard your first knock, but I was taking muffins out of the oven. Are you looking for someone?" She looked to be in her midthirties. She was wearing a housedress with a red sweater over it and an apron tied around her waist. She had a nice, cute smile.

"As a matter of fact, I am," Eddie said. "I'm trying to locate an Anne Lovingate. This address was listed as hers."

"Anne Lovingate," she repeated. "Sorry, no one here by that name." She said it in a cheerful, giggly sort of way.

"Is there an apartment upstairs?"

"There is, but she doesn't live there. Never heard of her."

"Could she have lived here at one time?"

"I suppose she could have. Bobby Gates—he's a truck driver—lives upstairs. My husband and I and the kids moved in seven years ago, and Bobby was here before us. So if she lived here, it would have been before that. Never heard the name mentioned, though."

"Does Bobby live alone?"

"Not if he can help it. If you're asking if he's married, he's not. But he's got a different woman up there every other week. They come and go. It's okay with us, though, because he's pretty quiet."

"Does he ever introduce them to you?"

"Always, like this one is *the* one he's going to marry, but it never lasts. He never introduced me to a Lovingate, though. That's one of those names a person wouldn't forget. I would have remembered it. Now that you're here asking about her, I'm sure I'll remember the name when I'm a grandmother."

"Well, then, I'm sorry I took up your time."

"Not a problem. Listen, you seem like a nice guy. Would you like a muffin to take with you? They're hot, right out of the oven. I put chocolate chips and raspberries in them. The kids love 'em, but the husband has to lose some weight, so I hide them from him."

Eddie hesitated for a moment. "Yeah, that would be nice, Mrs. ..."

"Linda Meyers. Hang on a second, and I'll wrap one up for you. It'll warm you up."

━━━●《●》●━━━

Mrs. Meyers was right: the muffin was hot, and it did warm him up.

He sat in the car eating it. It wasn't quite as good as his wife's muffins, but it was delicious nonetheless. Josette was a wonderful baker, and he had gained five pounds in the six months they'd been married. He made a quick calculation. Five pounds every six months added up to too much weight over the next five years. He decided he'd better cut certain foods from his diet, or he'd end up a blob. Of course, he'd start tomorrow.

After he'd finished the muffin, he knocked on the doors of a half dozen houses in the neighborhood. No one was home in two of the houses, and he got the same answer he'd received from Linda Meyers at the others. No one seemed to know of an Anne Lovingate, the elusive Anne Lovingate.

His thoughts went to Robert and Gloria Lovingate again. They might have the key that could unlock this mystery. The only thing that he had been able to confirm without doubt was that an Anne Lovingate had been born on April 9, 1921, in Ramsey County in the city of St. Paul. The certified birth certificate confirmed that. Beyond that was a brick wall. He decided he would return to the Lovingates tomorrow and pump them for more information.

He put his car into gear and pulled away from the curb. He was heading to his hotel to think this through.

———«◉»———

The phone rang in his hotel room.

Eddie opened his eyes and looked at his watch. He'd been napping for over two hours. The phone rang again. He had been dreaming, and his head was foggy. Maybe it was Josette. He'd said he'd call her late each night while he was gone. Why was she calling him? He picked up the receiver on the third ring.

"Hello," he said in a low, muffled voice.

"Is this Eddie Wade?"

"Yeah, who's this?"

"Never mind who this is. You're looking for information regarding Anne Lovingate. I know all about her."

That got his attention. He sat up on the end of the bed, fully awake now. "How do you know her? What's your name?"

"Questions, questions. I bet you have lots of questions. Like I said, never mind my name. I knew Anne Lovingate, and I'm willing to share this information with you. That's all you have to know."

"I'm guessing you're not going to do that on the phone. Can I ask you how you got my name?"

"You cannot, and the information is going to cost you five big ones."

"I assume you want to meet somewhere."

"At Irving Park tonight at one o'clock. There are benches by the fountain. Sit on one of them. You know where that is?"

"I'll find it."

"Bring the five hundred smackers. If you bring anyone else with you, like your buddy Detective Haden, the deal's off, and I disappear forever. And I mean *forever*. What I got to say about Anne Lovingate is going to knock you off your feet. Got it?"

"Got it."

The phone went dead.

———«◐»———

At twelve thirty, Eddie swung around Irving Park. The street was a horseshoe cul-de-sac with older two- and three-story homes surrounding the small park. There were benches around the fountain, well lit with six pole lamps. The paths had been shoveled, probably by the city. He drove a block away from the area to the corner of Chestnut and parked by a ma-and-pa grocery store that was shut up tight. The sign above the door said "Cossetta's." He let the car idle.

He didn't like this. The park wasn't exactly isolated—there were houses there—but it would be one o'clock when he met this guy. People would be sleeping, and no one would be on the streets. It would be just them, alone, in the park. He reached inside his coat and pulled out his .45 semiautomatic. He chambered a round, made sure the safety was set, and returned the gun to his shoulder holster.

Under different circumstance, he wouldn't have met an informant for the first time late at night alone. He would have demanded they meet at a busy restaurant in the daytime. It would have been safer for him that way. The first time was always nerve-racking. He never knew what to expect. Anything could happen. If he had to meet the informant again, and if he could trust him, then anywhere would be fine, and the time of day wouldn't matter. But the first time, he had to set things up so the odds were in his favor.

He didn't like the odds tonight. The guy had called the shots, not Eddie. The only reason he had agreed to the meeting was that this might be his only opportunity to obtain some information on the unknown Anne Lovingate. After the guy hung up, Eddie had mentally gone down his list of questions. How did this man know Eddie was investigating the Lovingate case, a murder that had taken place fifteen hundred miles away and that had never made the papers? How did he know Eddie was in St. Paul and staying at the Ryan Hotel? How did he know Eddie had talked to Detective Harry Haden? These were all good questions with no answers. And because of that, Eddie was a fool for being here. But here he was.

He looked at his watch. It was six minutes to the hour. He would wait another two minutes. Then a thought flashed in his head: maybe this was Lovingate's killer. Maybe he'd followed Eddie to St. Paul to keep an eye on him and then decided Eddie was asking too many questions and needed to be bumped off himself.

He looked at his watch again. It was time to find out.

He shut off the engine and got out of the rental. He took his gun from his shoulder holster and put it in his overcoat pocket. He left his gloves in the car. He walked toward the park with both hands in his coat pockets, his right one holding his gun. His shoes crunched the snow. The weather was actually quite pleasant—no wind to speak of, and the temperature seemed to have risen. As he approached the fountain and the benches, he did a quick 360-degree look at the surrounding houses. They sat up a bit from the sidewalk with moderately sized front lawns, presently covered with snow. There must have been ten houses in the cul-de-sac, and he couldn't see one light on. Was that good or bad? He didn't know. He sat down on the third bench from the fountain. It was completely silent. The area formed a little nook. Maybe the houses acted collectively as a sound barrier, because West Seventh Street was just a couple of blocks away and had been somewhat busy just a half hour earlier. He should be able to hear the traffic from here, but he couldn't.

He was sitting out in the open like a goddamn fool. He was a target, and he knew it. He looked around for any sign of the person he was supposed to meet. No one was in sight. He was alone. Suddenly, he had second thoughts. Maybe he should leave. He could return to his car and then come back and wait for the guy. At least he'd be a little safer inside the car. Yes, that was what he'd do.

He rose, and just then, something whizzed by him. He heard it hit behind him. He looked back at the bench. There was a hole in one of the wooden slats that hadn't been there before; he would have seen it. It looked like a bullet had gone through it, but he hadn't heard gunfire. He took one step to the side and felt something graze the side of his coat sleeve. It was unmistakable this time; someone was firing a gun at him. There was a large maple tree five feet to his left. He made a wild dash to it. The trunk was wide enough to hide behind. He considered the path the bullet would have traveled to hit the bench. He peeked around the tree. The gunman had to be in one of three houses to his front; he couldn't have hit the bench from any other angle. Just then, a bullet whizzed by the top of his head, grazing the edge of the tree, knocking bark on him. He pulled himself in. Again, he hadn't heard the gunshot.

One thing was clear to him: the gunman was using a rifle with a sound suppressor. The snipers in his unit in the army had used them. He was a sitting duck where he was. The gunman could just wait him out. He had to get away from the area, or he would be pinned down all night. There was too much light from the pole lamps to make a run for it. He took out his .45 and looked to his rear. The closest house was approximately thirty feet away. He leaned against the tree, on the other side from where he thought the gunman was, and aimed his gun at the nearest light. He squeezed off one round, and the light went out. The sound was deafening. He shot out five more lights. It was now dark enough to make his move. He ran toward the house, hoping that the gunman no longer had the right angle from which to hit him or, if he did, that he couldn't see Eddie. He crossed the street and ran in between two houses. He was safe. He looked back. A few lights went on in some of the houses. No doubt, they'd heard the gunfire when he shot out the lights. Probably an equal number of people had kept their lights off but were looking out their windows as well. He made his way around the back of the houses. He would have to find a way back to his car.

The gunman was using a weapon that wasn't readily available to the average hunter or a criminal. It was definitely military grade; that much he knew. The Lovingate case had suddenly turned directions. This was no longer a case of a murder made to look like a suicide. It was now something much bigger than that—much more significant. But he still needed to do something that had started in room 311 at the Windsor Hotel in Montreal.

He needed to find out who Anne Lovingate was.

Chapter 7
CONSPIRACY?

ON THURSDAY MORNING, EDDIE WADE SAT IN his rented Chevy, warm air blowing in his face from the heater, musing, visualizing, calculating the odds.

He was reconstructing last night's scene at Irving Park. It had been a perfect setup, a perfect trap, and he'd walked right into it and nearly gotten himself killed. He'd gone back there earlier this morning to look for the bullet that had passed through the back of the bench. Most likely, it was buried in the earth, beneath the ice and snow and a fair measure of his pride. C'est la vie. It had to have come from a powerful weapon with a nightscope and sound suppressor—a military-grade sniper rifle. That, more than anything else, made him concerned, and he had every reason to be. Ordinary civilian killers didn't use that kind of weapon, not even professional hit men.

So who did then?

He had received a call in his hotel room. That should have been the first clue that something was wrong. Besides Josette and Macalister, only one other person knew he was in town working an investigation: Detective Harry Haden. Occam's razor: Haden had set him up for a kill. But that didn't make sense. Haden had been supportive of Eddie's investigation and had even given him the names of the Lovingates in the Twin Cities. Besides, he and Eddie had connected on a personal level; Haden was a war veteran like Eddie, and he was an ardent boxing fan. Anything was possible, but for Eddie it would be a hell of a stretch to suggest Haden could have had anything to do with what happened last night.

Furthermore, Occam's razor didn't say that the simplest answer was always the correct one. The rule maintained that the simplest theory was preferred over the more complex, with *preferred* being the operative word. The world was a far more complex place than it had been when William of Occam lived. Modern scientific and communicative advancements had been merely science fiction just fifty years ago, let alone centuries ago. While Eddie still held Occam's razor to be relevant in today's world, he would be foolish to consider that something more complex wasn't at play here.

No, Harry Haden hadn't set him up, but someone else had—someone with a connection to both St. Paul and Montreal, someone who knew Anne Lovingate, someone who knew Eddie was in town, someone who wanted him dead and the investigation stopped.

But he had no idea who that could be. The answers to the questions had to be complex.

He got out of the car, walked up the snow-covered path to the Lovingates' house, and knocked on the door. Robert opened it on the first knock.

"What a surprise, Eddie," he said. By the end of their meeting a couple of days before, they had been on a first-name basis. "I wasn't expecting to see you again."

"I wasn't expecting to be here again, but I have a request for you. May I come in?"

"Of course."

After knocking the snow off his shoes at the entryway, Eddie followed Robert into the living room. As they sat down, Gloria came downstairs from the second floor, said hello to Eddie, and then sat down next to her husband.

"I was just wondering whether you could take me to your daughter's grave site," Eddie said. "I want to have a look for myself."

There was a moment of brief silence.

"You want to have a look for yourself?" Robert asked. "It almost sounds as if you're questioning us. You don't believe that our daughter died?"

"It's not that way at all," Eddie said, realizing that he hadn't worded it quite right. "The people back in Montreal are going to want to know whether or not I actually saw your daughter's grave. They're used to verifying everything during an investigation, and they'd expect me to do the same thing. It will only take me a minute to see the headstone, and then I can truthfully tell them that I saw the grave."

"I see," Robert said. He glanced at his wife, who nodded slightly. "Unfortunately, we were about to leave soon. It's only by chance that you caught us here. We have a few appointments to go to, so we won't be able to take you there. I could give you directions, and you could drive there yourself. It's only about twenty minutes from here. Is that okay?"

"It is, and I'm really sorry about this. Sorry to bother you."

"No bother at all." He turned to his wife to say something, but she was halfway to the kitchen already. He turned back to Eddie again. "We just find this extraordinary that there is another Anne Lovingate from St. Paul with the same birthday as our daughter. Personally, I wouldn't have blamed you if you had thought we were lying."

"The thought never crossed my mind, I assure you," he said.

Gloria returned to the living room with a slip of paper in her hand. Both Eddie and Robert stood up.

"I assume you took Summit Avenue to get here," Gloria said.

"Yes."

"Then just go back to Summit and take a right. When you come to Dale, take a left turn. That's going north. Elmhurst Cemetery will be on your right side after about four miles or so. You can ask the people there to show you the actual grave site, but I wrote down the lot and the number in case you want to find it yourself. Lot H, number 147."

They said their goodbyes at the door. Eddie got into his car and let it warm up a bit.

He thought about not going to the cemetery. The Lovingates seemed quite open about his going there. They weren't hiding anything; he was sure of that now. But Macalister would want to know that he actually saw the headstone for himself—Eddie hadn't lied about that. He put the car into gear, pulled away from the curb, and started his twenty-minute journey.

———«◉»———

At nine o'clock that night, Eddie sat on the edge of his bed at the Ryan Hotel with the nightstand in front of him, writing out his notes on a legal pad he had bought earlier in the day. He had to check in with Josette in an hour, so he still had time to draft a report of his activities in St. Paul for Jack Macalister.

> Point one: (Fact) Anne Lovingate, the daughter of Robert and Gloria Lovingate, was born on April 9, 1921, in the city of St. Paul, Minnesota (Ramsey County), substantiated by a birth certificate produced at the records department at city hall. There was no record of her death on March 25,

1922, as stated by her parents. Additionally, there was no record of a name change involving Anne Lovingate. Investigator Eddie Wade had seen a headstone at Elmhurst Cemetery (Lot H, number 147) with the name of Anne Lovingate, date of birth April 9, 1921, and date of death March 25, 1922, engraved in it.

Point two: (Fact, but still needs verification) Anne Lovingate checked into the Windsor Hotel in Montreal on January 2, 1956, using an American passport and Minnesota driver's license. Her date of birth was April 9, 1921. The address on her driver's license was 987 Edgerton Street, St. Paul, Minnesota. Eddie Wade went to the house and talked to a Linda Myers, one of the residents. She had lived there for seven years and had never heard of Anne Lovingate. Neighbors in the area also had never heard of her.

Point three: (Speculation) The Anne Lovingate who checked into the Windsor Hotel in Montreal could have had some connection to the Lovingates in St. Paul. The exact date of birth in the same city is no coincidence. Either the Lovingates are lying, and their daughter never died (only way to find out for sure is to have the grave exhumed), or the dead woman presumed to be Anne Lovingate somehow got a hold of the real Anne Lovingate's records, stole her identity, and somehow destroyed the death certificate. Another possible theory is that the dead woman bought the identity from someone in St. Paul who had access to the records. If either is the case, the woman did an awful lot to hide her real identity. She would have had to spend a lot of time and money to conceal who she really was. I have no reason to believe that Robert and Gloria Lovingate are lying. Beyond that, there is still the possibility that the woman was Canadian. Either way, I would recommend the investigation move forward in Montreal.

Point four: (Fact) An unidentified caller phoned Eddie Wade at approximately eight in the evening on Wednesday, January 11, in his hotel room at the Ryan Hotel and stated that he had known Anne Lovingate and had important information about her "that would knock you off your feet." He said he would give me that information for five hundred US dollars. He set up a meeting for that night.

Someone with a military-type high-powered sniper rifle with a scope and silencer tried to kill Eddie Wade on Thursday, January 12, at approximately one in the morning at and around Irving Park (the meeting place), located approximately ten minutes away from the downtown area of St. Paul, Minnesota, in a residential neighborhood. The reason is a matter of speculation, but I'm confident enough to say it was to stop the Lovingate investigation from moving forward.

Conclusion: If the Montreal police continue to pursue the killer of Anne Lovingate (at this point I believe that suicide is not a viable explanation for her death), then it is imperative that the investigation into Anne Lovingate's true identity move forward. It is my opinion that this is not a simple case of murder, that there is something deeper and more sinister at play here that could involve many more people than just the killer himself. I am, of course, referring to a conspiracy. That's a strong word, and I don't use it lightly. At this point, that's what the evidence leads me to believe. I have left my schedule open should you want the continued assistance of Wade Detective Agency.

The draft didn't read exactly the way he wanted it, but that was fine. He'd revise it on the flight back to Montreal tomorrow. Macalister would want to see it right away. He looked at his watch. Time to make a call.

Josette would be waiting by their phone.

⟶⦿⟵

As Eddie was drafting his findings, a man not far away dropped a dime into the slot of a payphone and waited for the operator to answer. It was a bitterly cold night, but at least he was in a phone booth so the wind couldn't get to him.

"Operator," a woman said.

"I'd like to place a long-distance call to Ottawa, Ontario." He gave her the number.

There was a brief silence before she came back on the line. "That will be two dollars and twenty-five cents for three minutes," she said.

He had stacked nine quarters on the small shelf under the phone. He had already known exactly what it would cost. He dropped each coin into the slot and listened as they fell into the coinbox. The tips of his fingers were freezing. He stopped briefly to rub his hands together and then continued. When the last one was in, he heard the operator say, "Connecting," and then the phone started ringing on the other end, over a thousand miles away.

Christ almighty, he thought. He wasn't looking forward to this.

The call was picked up, but it was silent on the other end.

"It's me," he said. He thought about using the word *failed* but thought better of it. "It's a no-go. I think he's leaving tomorrow, so there's a"—he paused briefly to find the right words—"there is a lost opportunity." He'd finally gotten it out. He shook his free hand. It was starting to become numb. He was worried about frostbite, but he knew that was the least of his worries.

More silence on the other end and then: "You mean he's on the way back?"

"Yes, he'll be on his way back." There was no other way to put it.

This time the silence lasted much longer.

"Are you still on the line?"

"We'll take care of it on this end."

"You should know that—"

He wasn't able to finish the sentence because the phone went dead. Several coins fell into the coin return for unused time.

Chapter 8
WHO WANTS EDDIE DEAD?

Montreal
7:45 a.m.

"SO WHO WANTS YOU DEAD? I CAN THINK OF AT least a dozen people off the top of my head, but just in case I missed someone ..."

"Maybe it was the same person who murdered Lovingate and tried to phony it up as a suicide. Maybe it was the same person who tailed me to St. Paul because he was told to dead-end the investigation and me along with it. They might be one and the same, but I doubt it." Eddie thought for a moment while he took out his pipe and tobacco pouch. "I'm convinced this involves more than one person."

Eager to return to Montreal, Eddie had taken a late-night flight to Chicago the previous night. There he had taken a red-eye flight to Montreal with a brief stop at Idlewild in New York. He had arrived in time to go to his apartment, fill Josette in on the case, shower, and eat a quick breakfast before arriving in Jack Macalister's office at 7: 15 a.m.

"You're talking about a conspiracy then," Macalister said. He leaned back in his chair. "Tell me more."

As he thought about how to word what he was about to tell Macalister, Eddie filled his pipe, lit it, and took a few puffs to get it going. "There were only two people in Montreal who knew that I was running with the case: you and Josette. And only one in St. Paul: Harry Haden."

"You're forgetting the chief."

"Yeah, him too. That makes four."

"And then there's Roger Chapelton."

"Okay, Roger then. Five people, goddamn it! Someone on the inside must have fed whoever was involved in Lovingate's death that information. We can eliminate you—"

"Thanks. That's very kind of you."

"And Josette, the chief, and Roger."

"That leaves Detective Haden. What's your take on him? I only talked to him on the phone."

"Solid guy. If he were somehow involved in this and leaked it, he'd have to have connections in Montreal. That's possible, but it seems unlikely. That's why I believe there's more than one person involved, some sort of network with connections to St. Paul and this investigation. I'm convinced Haden had nothing to do with it."

"The mob?"

"That's what I'm thinking. They have their nasty fingers everywhere. Maybe no one followed me to St. Paul. Maybe someone here just picked up the phone and ordered my hit. But there's one thing I can't figure out. The guy who tried to kill me used a silenced sniper rifle, military type. I'm absolutely certain of that. That doesn't sound like the mob."

"Something like the De Lisle carbine?"

"Right. Not even the mob would have access to something like that, especially on short notice. If the mob came after me, they would have had a dozen different ways to do it, but not with a De Lisle."

"I agree." Macalister paused a long moment. "Okay, so the case might be going in another direction. It's becoming more dangerous than either one of us first thought. I won't be surprised or hold it against you if you want to step aside."

"Step aside? You gotta be shitting me, Jack. I'd take out a bank loan and pay you to keep me on this. This is something big. I don't know what it is, but I want to find out. Lovingate's murder is only the tip of the iceberg. Anne Lovingate was someone special, someone important enough for her killer or killers to go to the effort of trying to stop the investigation and me. I tell you, Jack, this isn't just an ordinary murder investigation. It's going to lead to something big."

"Okay, but one more incident like in St. Paul, and I'll shut it down and hand it over to the RCMP. I should do that now as it is."

"Fair enough," he told Macalister, but he had no intention of stopping the investigation until the end, with or without Macalister's blessings.

"I want a daily update, and don't argue with me about that. Where are you going to start?"

He tamped the ash down in the bowl of his pipe and puffed several more times before answering. "Where the murder took place, the Windsor. Then I'll move forward like a game of chess, one move at a time: make a move, reassess, and change directions if it's called for. Then make another move and another and another, until I get the bastards behind this."

"If you need some resources, let me know. Don't ask for any manpower, though; it ain't going to happen. Money either, outside of your normal fees, minus two-thirds. Needless to say, you're going to have to watch your back."

"Then don't say it."

"One more thing."

"What?"

"I don't see how it's possible, but if the leak came from inside this building, I'm not sure where to plug it. I just don't see who could have done it. We've been playing our hand close to our chest."

Eddie puffed on his pipe. "Yeah, I don't see how it's possible either. So maybe whoever was involved in Lovingate's murder is also set up to keep an eye on us—like I said, a conspiracy. Their operation would have to be widespread to know I had gone to St. Paul and talked to Haden. The only ones I know who could do that are the mob. They have people on the inside everywhere. But killing Lovingate the way they did— it just doesn't seem like them. Neither does the guy who tried to kill me in St. Paul using a De Lisle or something like it. We're missing something, Jack. There's something we're not considering. Do me a favor, will you?"

"It's already on my list. I'll have someone sweep my office for bugs today, the telephone lines included."

"Good."

"In the meantime, like I said, watch your back."

"You too."

<hr>

The doorman at the Windsor, dressed in a long empire-red overcoat and black top hat, used a small handheld whisk broom to brush the snow off Eddie's pantlegs and shoes. There wasn't much, but the doorman's fastidious attention to standards established long ago compelled him to at least make a show of it. The hotel was clean, and he wanted to keep it that way. Eddie himself was indifferent.

Whether the hotel was crowded or not depended on the space the crowd occupied. In this case, there was a goodly number of people milling about, but the lobby was so mammoth that it seemed as though a few errant ants were scattering around, trying to find someplace to nest. The opulent hotel had been built at the end of last century to symbolize Montreal's growing prominence and wealth in North America and to serve visitors arriving by train at the Windsor Station. Eddie always felt ill at ease when he was here. He was the odd man out.

He walked straight ahead, his shoes clicking on the marble floor, to the long mahogany reception counter, where he stood under a chandelier. The clerk, a middle-aged man impeccably dressed in a pinstripe suit with a waistcoat (no doubt required by the management) and gold chain attached to a pocket watch, greeted Eddie like royalty, as if he were the only guest in the hotel and it was the clerk's duty to make certain that his stay was as pleasant as possible. When Eddie flipped open his wallet and showed him his private license, the clerk sobered up, like Eddie had stepped in some fresh canine droppings outside and still had some of it on his shoe.

"I'd like to talk to the guy who checked Anne Lovingate into the hotel on Monday of last week. That would be January 2."

"Yes," he said with a dour expression, "Miss Lovingate. How unfortunate, taking her own life as she did. I might be the one."

"Might be?"

"Was. I *was* the one," he said in a tone suggesting that the correction really had been unnecessary, but he'd done it anyway for the benefit of someone with less grace and class than he himself.

"Good. Could I ask you a few questions? I'll pay you for your time, of course."

The man's face changed expressions again. A little cash always helped, even at the Windsor. "How may I help you? We at the Windsor are always at your service."

"First of all, was she alone when she checked in?"

"There was a gentleman with her, but he himself didn't check in."

"What was Miss Lovingate's state of mind?"

"I beg your pardon?"

"How did she act?"

"Oh, act. I see. Well, she acted as if she wanted a room. That's what people come here for—a room."

"Was she happy or sad or—"

"Ah, yes. She was friendly enough, quite pleasant and cheerful even. Both of them."

"What sort of identification did she use?" He knew the answer, but he wanted to verify it—to see whether the clerk's answer would be consistent with his previous account to the police.

"A passport and driver's license. She was an American, you know." He paused briefly, as if he were troubled. "I'm not sure I should be talking to you like this. You're not with the police, you know."

"I'm working the case with the police. Pick up the phone." He impatiently jerked his head to the right. "Call police headquarters. Ask for Detective Jack Macalister. He'll give you the lowdown. But he won't be pleased that you questioned his authority. Go ahead—make the call."

The clerk paused a moment as if annoyed. Fluttering his eyes at a furious rate, he said, "That won't be necessary."

"Did you check the passport and license yourself?"

"I did. I wrote down the numbers as well as all the other pertinent information, like her foreign address. That's standard."

"I see. The guy who was with her—could you identify him if you saw him again?"

"I only glanced at him, so I'm not certain. He had a mustache and black-framed glasses, that much I know. They stood out. We were quite busy when Miss Lovingate checked in, you see. We had a big wedding reception here that day, and the guests were arriving, so the lobby was quite chaotic. A photographer was here, taking pictures of the guests as they arrived. It was quite hectic, you see."

"Do you know who he was—the photographer?"

"I'm afraid not. The wedding party hired him, not the hotel."

"Can I get the names of the happy couple?"

"We're not supposed to give out that information. It's private, you know."

"I can have Detective Macalister come down and ask you that question, and he won't pay you a wooden nickel for the information. He has a budget; I don't." Eddie was beginning to dislike this guy.

"One moment then," he said, the dour face returning, and he disappeared through a door to the right of him.

It was a long shot. But if the photographer had inadvertently caught Lovingate and her gentleman companion in one of the photos, Eddie might have a lead, something to identify the guy. Photographers usually just snapped away at wedding guests, ending up with many more pictures than the wedding party wanted. Maybe Eddie would luck out.

The clerk returned and gave Eddie a piece of paper.

"Thanks for your time, buster. You were helpful." He reached into his pocket for a tram token and then flipped it to him. "Here's your wooden nickel. Don't spend it all in one place."

Eddie hated spending money when he didn't have to.

———— ◉ ————

The happy couple must have been rich. The first clue was that they'd had their reception at the Windsor. The second one was that they lived in the classy part of Westmount. Eddie pulled up to a three-story house in the middle of the block, got out, and knocked on the door. A tall, fat man with a gray mop of hair on his head opened the door. He was wearing a bathrobe over his shirt and pants and wool-lined slippers on his feet. He stood there without saying anything, holding a cup of hot coffee. Steam rose from the cup and was snatched outside by the cold air.

"Excuse the intrusion, sir, but I'm looking for Samuel and Lorraine Beaverton. I believe they just got married last week." Eddie could be polite if the occasion called for it.

"If you're selling something, they're not interested."

"Actually, I'm not selling anything at all. I'm with the police, and I'd like to ask them a few questions." Technically, this was a lie, but he felt it would move things on a little.

"The police?" The man drew back a little, spilling some of the coffee.

"No need to be concerned, sir. They're not in any kind of trouble. I just want to ask them about some of the photos that were taken at the Windsor Hotel before their reception. I'm working on a case that they could help me on."

"Oh, I see." He relaxed and took a sip from his cup. "My daughter used this address, but she and her husband actually bought a house a few weeks ago not far from here. They're in Cuba at the moment for their honeymoon."

Eddie reassured him that he only wanted to look at the photos taken at the Windsor that day. "Do you have access to them?"

"I'm afraid the photographer still has them. They're planning to sit down with him when they return to select the ones they want."

"Do you by chance have the name of the photographer?"

"I do indeed."

"I'll have to have your permission to see them."

Of course, Eddie could have his permission, the man said. He was glad to cooperate with the police. He gave Eddie the address and told him that he'd call the photographer right away and give him his okay.

——«●»——

Marchand Photographie was located about six blocks west of the father's house on a busy avenue. There was a "Closed" sign on the door, but Eddie could see someone inside the shop. He knocked on the door, which caught the person's attention. The door swung back.

"You must be the police officer that Fred just called about. Come in." He stepped aside to let Eddie in and then locked the door again. "You want to see the Beaverton photos. My name is Jules Marchand, by the way, and I'm the owner."

They shook hands. The photographer was about the same age as Eddie and had a short beard and slight frame. He wore an Irish-knit sweater, which gave more bulk to his upper body. He seemed friendly enough and willing to cooperate.

"You did a job for their wedding Monday of last week at the Windsor and shot pictures in the lobby. If you don't mind, I'd like to see those. I'm looking for a particular person who wasn't a wedding guest but whom you may have caught in one of your pictures."

"Let's go in the back room. I finished developing them yesterday, but the Beavertons aren't back from their honeymoon yet, so I still have them."

As they went into the back room, Eddie said, "I hate to bother you with no notice, but the case is pretty important. I won't take any more of your time than what's necessary." Marchand was cooperating, and Eddie wanted him to continue. A little politeness went a long way.

"I'm usually open now, but I have to catch up on some developing for other customers. I work here alone and do everything myself. When you're in business for yourself, the customer is always the boss. Some of them think that the photos magically develop themselves. Glad that I'm here to help." They stopped at a long worktable. "Here they are. Please touch them only on the sides, if you will. They're not in any particular order, but most of the ones I took in the lobby are here in this pile."

Eddie started through them carefully, putting them down one at a time, creating a second pile. "You do nice work, Jules."

"I'll give you my card if you ever have the need."

"I just got married myself last year, but I know a couple who are engaged. They haven't set a date yet, but I'll pass on your card."

"Most appreciated. I do much more than weddings, you know, and I pride myself on customer service."

"I'll keep that in mind."

Eddie continued through the photos, carefully examining each one, especially those taken by the reception counter. After a few minutes, he stopped. "This is what I'm looking for." He showed the photo to the photographer.

"Yes, I wanted to get these people you see up front, but these two people to the side of them popped into the frame. I didn't realize it until I developed it."

"You see this guy here with the mustache and glasses?" Eddie asked, pointing. "Could you isolate just him and enlarge it?" The image showed the full length of the man behind Lovingate at the reception counter. He was crystal clear but a distance away from the camera.

"If you've got a little time, I could do it right now. Always happy to help the police. Is he in some kind of trouble?"

"We just want to ask him a few questions."

"If you'll have a seat out front, I'll do it right away."

"However long it takes."

———— «❖» ————

Later that night, Eddie and Josette sat at the bar of the Lion's Den next door to their office, each drinking a Molson, Josette from a glass, Eddie out of a bottle. Bruno leaned on the bar between them. He owned the bar as well as Eddie's office. He was short and bald and built like a brick shithouse; any uninformed customer might mess with him once, but never twice. Notwithstanding, he and Eddie were like brothers together, or more accurately, like father and son.

"Yeah, I thought all last night," Bruno said, "about not opening up today."

"Why?" Eddie asked. "You almost never close up."

"Are you forgetting what day it is today?"

Eddie and Josette looked at each other.

"It's Friday!" Bruno said.

"I know," Eddie said. "There's one of them each week."

"The thirteenth!"

"Don't tell me you're superstitious, Bruno," Josette said, trying to suppress a giggle.

"Listen, I had every reason to stay in bed today with the blankets pulled over my head. Terrible things have been known to happen when Friday meets and greets the thirteenth. You two may think this is a joke, but I'm telling you, bad things go down on this day."

"Like what?" Josette asked, looking over at Eddie with an expression that said she was egging Bruno on.

"Like what, you ask? The history books are full of awful things that happened on Friday the thirteenth."

"Full of awful things, eh?" Eddie said. "You can't even give us one example."

"Example? You want an example? I'll give you one. For example," he said, chopping the air in front of him with his hands, "Buckingham Palace, the place where the king beds down with the queen, was bombed during the war on Friday the thirteenth. How's that for an example?"

"But it was bombed eight other times not on Friday the thirteenth," Eddie said.

"Okay, you want a better example? How's this? On July 13, 1951, which happened to be a Friday, the state of Kansas was hit with twenty-five inches of rain. Oil tanks caught on fire and exploded, and passengers on a train were stuck for four days."

"How do you know about that, Bruno?" Josette asked.

"I was there on that train, going to a heavyweight championship boxing match, the only one I missed in a decade."

"You never told me about that," Eddie said.

"I couldn't talk about that nightmare for years." He paused a moment, clicked his fingers together, and then shouted, "Jesus Christ!"

Eddie and Josette exchanged looks. Was Bruno starting to relive the experience?

"Jesus Christ!" he said again. "He invited twelve guests for supper one night, making the total number thirteen. The next day, Friday, he was crucified!"

"Well, I can't argue with you on that one," Eddie said.

"So that's why I thought about not opening the bar today."

"What stopped you?" Josette asked.

"I thought about how much money I'd lose."

Chapter 9
A PLAN TO GET THE KILLER

EDDIE LOOKED OUT THE FRONT WINDOW OF their apartment and saw gray clouds overhead. He turned around to Josette, who was sitting on the floor, entertaining the two cats with a ball of yarn.

"Do you think the weather can influence the mood of a person?" It wasn't just a frivolous question. Eddie was in a reflective mood and wanted to know what Josette thought.

"I know it can," Josette said. "I can get very moody in the winter, sometimes even depressed. You better get used to it."

It was their first winter together.

"You should have told me before now. I could have prepared." He paused a moment, then added, "How bad does it get?"

"Truthfully?"

"Of course."

"Bad." She paused a moment as if to let that sink in. "The best strategy to use with me when I'm really down in the dumps is to let me have my way. You'll avoid a big scene that way."

"Let you have your way with what? Can you narrow that down a little for me?"

"With everything," she said, throwing her arms above her with her fingers splayed. She sometimes used her hands to emphasize what she was saying, like Italians. Eddie was used to that. He'd grown up surrounded by Italians. His mother had been Italian, and he himself was half Italian. "For instance, like now." She sliced the air in front of her with karate chops, then fanned her hands to the sides in a gesture of openness. "You could give me a little more responsibility with the agency. Let me handle some cases alone."

"You don't look particularly down right now. Are you trying to pull a fast one on me—take advantage of my good nature?"

"No. I'm just giving you an opportunity for a little practice before my forthcoming moods become unbearable for you." She rolled the ball of yarn across the living room floor and watched Antoinette and Henri run after it. Then she got up and sat on the couch.

Eddie joined her. "It's out of my hands," he said. "You're going to be licensed by the province in another six months. Until then, there's only so much you can do. If I gave you free rein with a client and the province found out about it, you'd lose your chance for a license, and I'd be fined or even lose mine. That would be the end of the Wade Detective Agency. We'd both be baking croissants and éclairs for a living."

"Yeah, I know all that," she said, sighing. "I'm just getting impatient."

"Listen, you're going to be a great investigator, but you're still learning the ropes. Just continue answering the phone, drumming up a little business, and scheduling meetings. And the research you do is vital to our operation. Be patient, and in no time, you'll have your license and all the clients you want. Speaking of research, what did you find out about Lovingate when I was away?"

"There's no record of an Anne Lovingate arriving in Montreal by any of the commercial or private airlines on January 2 or anytime in the past month. She could have crossed the border by car or train, if she even came from the States at all."

"Did you lie to get that information and tell them that you were with the police department as I asked you to do?"

"Yes, I did, but I don't like having to do that." She made a face at him. "That's just a little thing I've got—lying. I don't like doing it."

"Neither do I, but you better get used to it if you're going to be a private investigator. It's for the greater good." He said this in a joking way, but he meant it.

"I suppose we all have to make our little sacrifices."

"Now you're talking, sister. That puts you one step closer to that license you want."

They both looked down at the photograph in front of them on the coffee table.

"Who do you think he is?" Josette asked. "Maybe he was her lover."

"Yeah, and maybe he was her killer too. The prisons are full of lovers who killed their spouses and girlfriends."

"I don't get it. She was cheerful when she checked into the Windsor on that Monday. The next day, she's shot dead."

"I saw the other pictures with Lovingate and the guy," Eddie said. "They didn't look particularly tense. As a matter of fact, they looked pretty happy."

"Maybe she decided to break off whatever they had going between them, and they argued. The guy loses it and decides to kill her and make it look like a suicide—a spur-of-the-moment thing."

"That's one theory, but the hotel room hadn't been disturbed in any way. You'd think that there would have been some evidence of a struggle in that scenario. She looked physically fit. And the theory doesn't account for all those rounds the police found in her briefcase. And why were all the labels on her clothes removed? Why weren't her passport and driver's license found?"

"Okay, she or he or both of them had a secret. The question is what was it?"

"Fine, she wanted to keep the bullets secret, and whatever she had planned to do with them was also a secret. But what could one broad—" He stopped in his tracks, glanced at Josette, and then continued. "What could one woman do with that much ammunition? You don't need all that for self-protection. Even I don't carry that many rounds on me. And there's another thing. We're assuming that the guy in the photo was in her room. There could have been someone else there."

"The obvious answer to all the rounds she had is she wanted to kill someone. That fits in with her phony documents. And you're right—there could have been someone else in the room, but right now, this guy in the photo is our only lead."

"If he was in her room, then either he was an accomplice to what she was going to do, and maybe things went haywire and he killed her, or he was there to specifically stop her from doing whatever she had planned."

"In either case, she obviously knew him, as the photos show. Any way we look at it, we should focus on finding this guy."

"If he's still in Montreal." Eddie paused briefly and stared at her. "I'd bet money that he is. The police have kept this out of the papers, so the guy probably thinks they think it's just another suicide. They're not looking for a murderer. He'll feel comfortable staying put. There's no rush for him to leave the city."

"If he's still in Montreal, how do we go about finding him?"

"That's a good question. He might be curious about what's happening behind the scenes. Some criminals are like that. They want to know what's going on, so they can make their next move. We have to do something to draw him out."

"Like what?"

"I don't know. Let me think. I wish I knew what they were up to. Having that many bullets with her could mean only two things; either she was terrified for her life, and having that much ammunition gave her a sense of security, or she herself was after one or more persons. You wouldn't have that many bullets stashed away in a secret compartment of your briefcase if you were going to commit suicide."

"I thought we had eliminated that possibility," Josette said.

"We did." He paused a moment to think, and then he said, "If I didn't know better, I'd say she was a hitman. I'd say *hitwoman*, but that doesn't sound right."

"You mean a professional killer?"

"I know—it sounds silly, doesn't it? But yes, that's what I mean. I still think there's some kind of connection to St. Paul even though I haven't found any evidence of her ever being there, except for having the same name and date of birth as the child who died." Eddie hadn't told Josette about the attempt on his life; he didn't want her to worry unnecessarily.

"Maybe she was reading Simone de Beauvoir too. Maybe she was about to go on a rampage and start knocking off men, one by one."

"Did de Beauvoir say anything about women killers in that book you're reading?"

"Not yet, but hey, you draw inspiration from where you can."

"Are you saying that I should keep an eye on you?"

Henri suddenly darted past them, batting the ball of yarn like a hockey puck. Antoinette sat off to the side like a spectator, swooshing her tail back and forth, enjoying the show.

Eddie stood up and stretched, then went into the kitchen to make a pot of coffee. "I was thinking about your friend Gigi this morning," he said over his shoulder. "She seemed like a reasonable person. I hope she decided to talk things out with her fiancé. What was his name again?"

"Symeon Peters."

"Oh, yes. How could I forget that name? I've never known anyone called Symeon before. What kind of guy is he?"

"I don't know him that well, but he seemed decent enough. Gigi is obviously very much in love with him. They seem happy."

"I'm sure he has a perfectly good explanation for his behavior, but if they don't talk it out, Gigi will never know. That's how things fall apart in a relationship: lack of communication. They could have a happy life together, but if they don't learn to talk things out, they're not going to have anything together but hardship and pain."

"You sound like a philosopher. You'd make a great marriage counselor or a priest. What other little secrets are you hiding from me?"

"I can't tell you all of them in our first year of marriage together. You'll get bored with me and throw me out in the street." He swung around in her direction. "Did I ever tell you I have a good friend who's a priest?" he asked, walking toward her and sitting down again. "We grew up together in Little Italy."

"Did he save your soul?"

"No, but I did save him from getting beaten up when we were kids. He was a target of bullies because he never fought back."

"You were a fighter even then?"

"Hey, I was always a fighter," he said and then raised his fists to his face, playfully throwing a few punches at her. "My fans told me more than once that I could have been the world's middleweight champ—light heavyweight and heavyweight too, if I'd gained some weight. I had the height for another ten, fifteen pounds. You have no idea who you're living with!"

"Okay, champ, what do we do about the Lovingate case?"

"I need to see Jack Macalister first. I want to run a few things by him and show him the guy in the photo. I won't be long. When I come back, what say we go to Schwartz's Deli for a bite to eat?"

"Sounds good. I'm starving. But it's Saturday. Isn't Jack off work? Maybe ice fishing or skating in the park?"

"He practically lives in his office these days, so he'll be there. I'm sure his wife isn't thrilled. Homicide has a backlog of cases and a shortage of men, so everyone's working overtime. That's for the greater good too!"

"But not for marriages," she said. "Okay, I'll stay put and continue to read Simone until you get back. Maybe I can get some tips on how to become a professional killer and take my rightful place among men."

———— «●» ————

A bottle of Johnny Walker Black Label sat on Macalister's desk with the top off. Macalister reached for it and poured some more into their glasses.

"This is good, Eddie," he said, staring at the photo between them. "It's clear and crisp. We can use it. Goddamn it, how'd you get it?"

Eddie explained how he'd chased it down yesterday.

"Gee, pal, I wish I had your ass on the force."

Eddie sat back, filled his pipe, and grinned. "I wouldn't be of any use to you now, Jack." He lit his pipe and blew smoke across the desk. "I'd be dead meat. I've been my own boss for too long. We'd have back-alley brawls. Our friendship would take it on the nose."

"So we'd make you chief, and you could give the orders. You'd be calling the shots."

Eddie grinned at that, as if the idea were viable. "Now that we have his face," he said, "how're we going to find him?"

"First of all, we don't know for certain if he's the killer. We don't even know whether or not he's involved in any way. The only thing we know for certain is that he was with her when she checked into the hotel. We have to talk to him. And we can't let on that we're looking for him."

"Okay, all hush-hush. Any suggestions?"

Macalister took a sip of his whiskey and set the glass down again. He ran his tongue across his lips. "I've got an idea. If I'm full of shit, just tell me."

"When haven't I?"

"I have a guy here on the force, Constable Cousineau. He's our sketch artist and a very good one, a real Leonardo da Vinci. Actually, that's what we call him. What do you say I have him do a sketch of Lovingate today and run it on the front page of the major newspapers tomorrow? I know all the city editors; they'll love the idea. I don't want to put a picture of her dead in the papers. Cousineau can sketch one out with a smile on her face as if she's alive. If she's from Quebec, maybe someone will recognize her and come forward. Also, there's a good possibility that this guy will see it. If he's the killer—and that's still an *if*—he'll obviously know that she's dead. After all, he put a bullet in her forehead. I'll tell the papers to write that she's simply missing. This may or may not throw off his game if he's the killer, but if it does, he might become curious about what's going on. He may want to see what we're up to. It's happened before with criminals. Sometimes they want to get close to the action to keep one step ahead of us. If he does, he could make a mistake. He doesn't know that we have his picture and can identify him. He may feel comfortable showing his face; he may do something really stupid like contact us."

"Sounds like something I might try if I were running the show. But it's a real long shot."

"Of course it is, but we've captured criminals before on long shots. Besides, you have something better to suggest? Speak up! Don't be shy."

"Actually, I have absolutely nothing, better or otherwise."

"Okay, I'll get the balling rolling. I'll feed you the leads as they come in, but I want you to know that we'll get calls from every lunatic in Montreal and environs. Half of them will confess to murdering her and burying her body up in Saguenay. The other half will give us detailed descriptions of kidnapping her, chopping her body up, putting her through a meat grinder, and feeding her to their dogs. There are a lot of sick puppies out there."

"Let's just hope that the real killer is curious enough to make a move." Eddie picked up the photo and stared at it. "The thick mustache and black glasses are pretty identifiable. You could walk down Sainte-Catherine on a busy day and pass by only a few who look like that. That could be our break."

"Only if he takes the bait. And if he doesn't? He could lie low or shave off his mustache and get new glasses and walk around carefree without us ever knowing about it."

"In that case, we may never find him."

"There's that too."

"You're forgetting something: the chief. Do we have enough time? He wants to close the case."

"I'll take care of him. I'll spin a tale so convincing that he'll start polishing his badge and shining his shoes for his press briefing when this is finished."

Driving back to his apartment, Eddie had a sick feeling in his stomach. Was this all going to be worth it? Jack thought so— he was enthusiastic. So did Josette. Eddie himself also had thought so as recently as leaving Macalister's office minutes before, but now he was having second thoughts.

He'd worked cases like this in the past. They started off small. He remembered the tram case from a few years before. It had been a murder case as well, and the case had been closed after only a few days. But he'd decided to investigate it on his own because he'd witnessed the murder, and no one else was doing anything about it. It hadn't taken long before it ballooned into something big, putting his own life at risk as well as that of the woman he'd been dating. She ended up in the hospital with a gunshot wound that had been meant for him.

Was he doing the same thing with this case, only this time putting his wife at risk? She was working primarily in the office and should be safe enough there. But there were no guarantees even then. There was always the possibility that things would get out of hand, exposing him and her to things he couldn't control. He had already been shot at in St. Paul; would that happen again in Montreal, only this time with her at his side? He wasn't concerned about himself, but was it fair to expose Josette to danger?

He thought about that as he made a left turn off Dorchester onto Saint-Urbain. The traffic was light, so he sped up. After about a half mile, he crossed rue Milton. This was where the tram murder had happened. The intersection had become a constant reminder to him that the world could change on a dime. As if he needed to be reminded.

Josette had freely decided to become an investigator. He hadn't twisted her arm; she'd brought up the subject herself. Maybe, however, had he never been one himself, she'd still be baking pastry in Notre-Dame-de-Grâce. But that was water under the bridge. He'd never know for sure. Nevertheless, he bore some of the responsibility for her decision. He could have vehemently dissuaded her; instead, he had encouraged her by saying that she'd make a great investigator, a position he still held. The horse was out of the barn now, and he couldn't very well put it back without causing irreparable damage to their relationship.

Was there something else he could do to lessen the risk for her? Maybe he could change the direction of the agency itself. He could take on easier, safer cases and still make a decent living. He was doing that now, at least part of the time. There was always insurance fraud. That was pretty much a safe bet. London Life had been feeding him plenty of cases, including some that he'd had to pass on because there were too many. And there were plenty of divorce cases and suspicious spouses who wanted him to get the goods on their husbands or wives. And there were also plenty of companies that wanted him to do background checks on prospective employees before they hired them.

Those were always viable options that would increase the load enough for two investigators, although he wasn't thrilled with the idea. He didn't have to go after killers—that was his choice—especially when he wasn't being paid for it. But he hadn't gone into the business to get the goods on cheating husbands, as lucrative as that was. From the very beginning, he had wanted to chase after the killers and hard-core criminals. It gave him a certain satisfaction, taking them off the street and making the city a little bit safer. How willing would he be to give those cases up? He didn't know.

Yet the Lovingate case was staring him in the face now. Could he abandon ship? Macalister would understand, but would Josette?

Josette had been adamant about taking on the Lovingate case. Could he come up with enough reasons to stop the investigation? He had mentioned one of them to her already—the time they'd have to spend on it without being paid. But he had been half-hearted about that concern, and Josette had countered with her own reasons to stay on it. Now he could make the case again, more forcibly. He could tell her that based on his experience, the case would go nowhere, that they'd be wasting their time and money pursuing it, and he wouldn't be lying. He couldn't afford to work cases like this, he could say. Would that be enough to persuade her? It might be with most people, but he wasn't certain it would do the trick with Josette. She was as relentless as he was once she made a decision. Furthermore, he wasn't convinced that he could make the case forcibly enough.

If that failed, as a last resort, he could tell her about the gunman in St. Paul; her brand-new husband had almost been murdered. It was true, and she might even agree to end the case, but she'd also know that Eddie was playing on her emotions, manipulating her decision. She would resent that; over time, she might even hate him for it. He wouldn't risk their marriage.

He was at a dead end; he had no choice but to back up and find another route to move forward with Lovingate. He didn't know for certain whether he could find her killer, but he damn well was going to do everything he could to try. He was already committed.

Chapter 10
GATHERING THE EVIDENCE

ACCORDING TO THE HEBREW AND CHRISTIAN calendars, Sunday was the first day of the week. However, according to the International Organization for Standardization, Sunday was the seventh day of the week. In spite of the lack of agreement, English speakers had in our lexicon, handed down for generations, the following terms: Passion Sunday; Low Sunday; Palm Sunday; Mothering Sunday; Sunday clothes; Sunday best; Sunday driver; Sunday-go-to-meeting; bloody Sunday; and Sunday punch. It was a simple, two-syllable word—Sunday. The modern word had been derived from the Old English *Sunnandæg*, which meant "the day of the sun."

But today was anything but sunny.

Eddie and Josette had a light breakfast of toast and coffee, having stuffed themselves the night before with smoked meat sandwiches and french fried potatoes at Schwartz's Deli. Josette would be going to the office to man the phone and to continue studying *The Canadian Manual for Private Investigators* that Eddie had bought for her. It had been written by a retired private investigator out of Toronto, and Eddie thought it covered most topics well. What it didn't include,

Eddie would fill her in on himself. He had been particularly impressed with the author's emphasis on the need to gather evidence. There were many different kinds of evidence, but ultimately, they all served one purpose: to link a criminal with a crime. Evidence proved that a particular person stole the diamond earrings or pulled the trigger, but it wasn't synonymous with truth. That was a different matter entirely. By and large, criminal courts weren't as concerned with truth as much as they were with evidence. It was the evidence that sent someone to prison or to the hangman's noose. Truth was a by-product to be either used if the occasion demanded it or discarded if it got in the way of a conviction.

After feeding the cats and making sure they had water, Eddie and Josette said their goodbyes. He drove south on Saint-Urbain into town and parked across the street from Notre-Dame Basilica. He walked the block to the Rose Cottage.

The wind was nasty, and he had to hold his hat in place at the brim so it wouldn't take flight. He opened the door and walked down the stairs and through a tunnel until he got to another door. It was rarely locked, so he opened it and walked in.

Rose Cottage was a slightly more acceptable term for the city morgue. The man in charge was the chief coroner, Cecil Becket, a tall, lanky man of indeterminate age with frizzy white hair. He was sitting behind his desk doing paperwork and smoking his pipe when Eddie entered.

Becket looked up when the door opened. "Well, look what the wind blew in," he said out of the side of his mouth, puffing out the words.

"I'd like to see Anne Lovingate," Eddie said. It was a simply worded statement, politely and directly stating his desire—no fuss, no bother.

"What? No 'hello, how are you'? What's the world coming to?"

"Hello, Cecil. How are you? Can you show me Lovingate?"

"And hello to you. Hope you're fine, and yes, indeed, I not only can but will." He got up and walked toward Eddie, heading for the coolers behind him, leaving a trail of smoke. "You seem tense for a newly married man. Hope all's well on the home front."

"The home front's dandy. Just got a lot on my mind."

"Don't tell me the police dumped the Lovingate case on you."

"Okay, I won't."

"I suppose they want to cut down on their budget. I hope they're paying you something." Becket slid out a chamber drawer with the body in it and then pulled back the sheet to the waist. "I suspect you don't think it's a suicide then," Becket said.

"I'm looking into it."

They stood in silence for a moment, looking at the face of Anne Lovingate.

"Macalister wants me to keep the body for a while," Becket said, "for identification purposes." He puffed on his pipe a few times and then said, "Unidentified bodies are pretty common in the city. It's a shame, really, dying and then being buried without the name you were born with and used your whole life. At least she's got an alias."

"Hmm," Eddie said.

"I saw the *Gazette* this morning with her sketch on the front page. The likeness is great."

"Macalister had da Vinci do it."

"Ah, Bobby Cousineau. He's the best. He's in the wrong business, if you ask me. He showed me his paintings once. They were magnificent—ought to be in a museum."

"He likes being a cop … apparently."

"That's what he told me."

"Do you buy the suicide bit?"

"Not in the slightest. I could give you a host of reasons, starting with the fact that there wasn't any blood or gunshot residue on her hands, but I won't bore you. What's the chief thinking? Someone plugged her, probably a boyfriend. That's common enough. Either she tried to break up with him, or he caught her cheating and went ape. We get a few of those cases every month or so. Sad stories, all of them. And the victims aren't always women. The gentle sex isn't always so gentle. You've got to be careful with the people closest to you. A sad commentary on human existence, eh?"

"You better watch it, Cecil, or you'll become a cynic."

"I've been around the block with that several times. I was a cynic for the first twenty years. When I was pretty far into the rabbit hole, I figured I'd better change my attitude if I was going to survive. I'm not a bloody idealist now—the war took care of that—but I no longer look at dead bodies as merely masses of organs that stopped working. These were living and breathing human beings who were once celebrated and loved by someone. They all have a story to tell, even the unidentified ones."

"What's her story?" Eddie asked, nodding at the corpse.

"I play a little game with the John and Jane Does and try to create a life for them. It humanizes them, gives them a little life. It's good for my soul as well." He puffed on his pipe as he thought for a moment. "Well, she never had children; I know that for a fact from the exam. With what she was wearing, I'd say she was a professional. Maybe a lawyer, maybe worked for a corporation. She seems more Slavic than American or Canadian. Look at the face. She seems a bit Baltic to me. Fair skin, blonde, round face, slight swelling of the upper eyelids. But people move around the globe these days with frightening speed, so maybe indeed she's American or Canadian, and her ancestors came from one of the Slavic countries.

"I studied the official report on her. It said that the shower had been used that morning. So she gets up, takes a shower, puts her makeup on, gets dressed in some pretty expensive clothes, and then hears a knock on the door. She opens it, knows the person, and invites him in. Either they continue a conversation started some time before, or she decides to break off the relationship right then. My guess is that they continued a conversation; it hadn't been resolved, or she might not have let him in. Regardless, it doesn't go down well for the guy, and somehow, he renders her unconscious. He looks around the room, finds her gun, and shoots her, making it look like a suicide. He hears the maid knock on the door and freezes. Five minutes later, when the coast if clear, he takes off. Good luck finding him."

"You should be a detective, Cecil. The police would solve more crimes."

"I am in my own way, but the police fail more often than they solve crimes. That's just the hard reality. If a person wanted to kill someone and planned it out well—I mean really well, looking at the crime the way the police would—then eighty percent of the time, the killer would get away with it. Like I said, that's the hard reality. The ones who don't plan it out, who murder on the spur of the moment, they get caught because of some stupid mistake they made. Killing someone and not getting caught is rather easy to do. All it takes is a bit of planning." He looked down at the face of Anne Lovingate again. "This one was well planned, Eddie. It wasn't really done on the spur of the moment as I just suggested. The killer entered the room with the murder weapon with the intention of killing her. In covering it up, he planted the box of rounds in her briefcase. And she let him in freely, which means that she never considered being murdered—a fatal mistake on her part."

"The evidence does seem to point in that direction."

"You're going to have a dickens of a time finding him."

"Yeah, I know."

"This woman had a deep secret."

"Yes, I think she did."

"Don't destroy yourself trying to find it. Don't let this be your winter of discontent."

"I'll try not to, Cecil."

"You're a married man now. That's something to keep in mind. You've got to back off once in a while for your own sanity, and for Josette's. You're not used to doing that."

"I'll keep that in mind."

———— «●» ————

Eddie pounded the pavement for the next few hours, going to bars and restaurants around the Windsor Hotel, handing out the picture of the man who had been with Lovingate when she checked in at the hotel. Whether or not he was the killer remained to be seen. If he wasn't, he might be easier to find. He could work downtown; maybe he frequented one of those establishments; maybe someone would recognize him. If he was the killer, maybe he was already in Winnipeg or Vancouver by now, or in any one of a thousand different cities across North America. In any event, Eddie told the barkeeps and restaurant managers (he knew them all personally) not to advertise that he was looking for the guy. He didn't want to scare him into hiding if he was still around.

The temperature had dropped a few notches from the morning, and the wind had picked up, so he decided to drive back to Mile End and warm up at the Lion's Den. Bruno was sitting behind the bar, reading the morning's edition of the *Gazette*. He looked up when Eddie came in.

"Well, if it isn't my favorite gumshoe. What brings you here on a Sunday afternoon?"

"Your warm personality," Eddie said, sitting on one of the barstools. "It's cold outside."

"How 'bout a hot toddy to warm your inners?"

"No, just some coffee with some juice."

"Brandy okay?"

"That's fine."

Bruno moved to the side to make the drink. Grabbing the coffeepot, he said, "You look down, Eddie. Married life not suiting you?"

"My marriage is fine. Why do people keep asking me that?"

Bruno set the spiked coffee in front of him. "How could it not be, being married to Josette? She's a doll, Eddie. I have to hand it to you, buddy—you know how to pick women. What's the secret in case I decide to get hooked up in my old age?"

"Open communication, Bruno. A couple has got to be able to talk to each other without throwing pots and pans at one another."

For some reason Gigi and Symeon popped into his head. He didn't know whether they threw pots and pans at each other (they probably didn't), but they sure didn't have any open communication, which led him to believe that they were hiding something from each other, something that wasn't good for a relationship. He decided to tell their story to Bruno without mentioning names. He ended by saying that the guy might be cheating on the woman, and they weren't even married yet.

"If the guy is pushing forty," Bruno said, "he's got to have a few secrets under his belt. And some of them might not be too good, if you know what I mean." He stopped briefly to run a hand across his bald head. "You know, working behind the bar here, I hear all kinds of stories from the jokers who come in. One in particular I remember. He tells me about this guy he once knew. Actually, they grew up together. The guy gets married. He's a traveling salesman, you see. He and his wife buy a nice little house, and after a while, they have a couple kids. Nice little life in the suburbs. But because of his job, he's gone a lot, maybe even for a week or more at a time. But the wife knew that before they got married, so that isn't a problem for her. They've both adjusted to that kind of life.

"Here's the kicker, Eddie. It turns out that this guy had another wife and kids in a town fifty miles away. He was living two separate lives in two separate towns, and neither family knew about the other one. Can you beat that? How's that for a secret?"

"How did he get caught? You can't pull that off for very long."

"One weekend, the guy decides to take family B to a lake midway between the two towns. Wife B sits sunning herself while the kids splash in the lake. The guy's sitting next to his wife in a beach chair, smoking a stogie, a Molson in his hand, enjoying life, not a care in the world. All of a sudden, wife A is standing over him, looking like some banshee. As it turned out, wife A had brought her kids to the same lake because it was their favorite one. The wives both filed for divorce, and the guy is doing time for bigamy. A very sad ending for everyone concerned."

"So what's the moral of the story?"

Bruno threw his head back and thought about that as if for the first time. Then he snapped his fingers together. "If you're going to keep a secret, you better make sure it's kept a secret, or your world will come tumbling down."

Eddie smiled at that, but he was thinking about Anne Lovingate. Had she been leading two separate lives as well when her world had come tumbling down?

—●(●)●—

Josette sat at her desk in the office, reading her manual. She could have done this in her apartment, but she had forgotten the manual on her desk and had decided to stay in the office once there. The phone hadn't rung all day, so she'd gotten a lot read. The only thing she didn't like about the book was that the author used the word *evidence* in about every other sentence. It was overkill. She got the point! Move on.

She wasn't trying to second-guess him. She agreed with what he'd written. He was saying that evidence was vitally important to convict someone charged with a criminal offense. Too many criminals walked free because the evidence against them was weak. In those cases, the author stated more than a few times, the investigators weren't good enough; they hadn't done their jobs. If a person committed a crime, there was always evidence of it—somewhere. Sometimes it was right there in front of the investigator's face; other times, he'd have to take a shovel and start digging for it until he hit China. The investigator's job, plain and simple, was to find the evidence.

She closed the book. Her head was spinning. She needed a break. She got up, stretched, and then poured herself a cup of coffee. She walked around the office several times to get the circulation in her legs going and then sat down again. She began thinking about her friend.

Gigi had been visiting the bakery for years. Early on, Josette had struck up a friendship with her and had begun seeing her outside the shop. Usually, they had met in a restaurant or for a movie. They both liked bingo, so they'd played once a week for several years. Josette had even invited Gigi over for family meals. She was sweet and enjoyed life. When she met Symeon and started to go out with him, Josette couldn't have been happier for her. And now Gigi believed he was cheating on her.

If he was in fact cheating on her, maybe there was something Josette could do. It was apparent to her that Eddie wasn't interested in doing anything. But that was okay. He had his own reasons. However, Gigi was her friend, and maybe she could help. Gathering evidence would be good practice for her, and at the same time, she'd be helping Gigi from further entanglement if it turned out that Symeon had indeed been cheating on her. Gigi wouldn't want to marry someone she couldn't trust. On the other hand, maybe Josette could provide evidence that Symeon hadn't been cheating on her, that it was something else, something innocent that Gigi had been misreading. Josette could clarify the situation for her so the two could get on with their lives, together or apart. At the moment, the relationship seemed to be at a standstill. All it might take was the evidence, one way or another.

She picked up the phone and called Gigi at home. She didn't want to discuss the situation over the phone, so she asked Gigi if she'd meet her for lunch on Tuesday. Gigi accepted the invitation. Josette put the receiver down, bound and determined to become the best female investigator in Canada, maybe even in North America. Gigi would become her first unofficial case.

She sipped her coffee and then opened the manual again. She had much more to learn about gathering evidence.

Chapter 11
FOLLOWING LEADS

"YOU LOOK LIKE SHIT."

"I feel like shit. I must have caught a cold from Molly. She's home in bed, dying. Kept me awake all night. When I got up this morning, I had the chills, fever, runny nose. You name it, I have it."

"You should have called in sick."

"What can I say? I'm a dedicated employee of the city. Besides, the telephone's been ringing off the hook. Sit down. It makes me tired just looking at you standing there."

Eddie sat down. Macalister reached over his desk, picked up a file, and slid it over to him.

"You should have a little of that Johnny Walker you keep stashed in your drawer," Eddie said. "You'd feel better. It's good medicine."

"I've had three shots already since I got here. It's not working." He sniffed and then blew his nose. "You want some?"

"I'm fine. What's with the folder?"

"We've got people calling in on that sketch of Lovingate—names, addresses, phone numbers." He blew his nose; it sounded like a foghorn.

Eddie opened the folder and skimmed the names.

"I have to tell you, Eddie, most of them are going to be loony-birds who won't know shit from shinola, but they'll all have to be checked out. It's unavoidable work, but we may luck out and find someone who knew her. I took most of the names for my men to check out. I'm making a few of my guys available for the case for now; you can thank me later. The rest are yours—not many, since you're not being paid much, but enough to keep your interest in the game. We can expect more calls. The sketch will attract every asshole in the city."

"I've interviewed a few assholes in my time."

"Good, because there'll be more. They'll be coming out of my ass."

"That's a lovely thought."

"I thought you'd like that."

"The more, the merrier, I suppose."

"Someone somewhere knows her."

"North America is pretty big."

"Yeah, but she was murdered here in Montreal. She must have rubbed shoulders with someone other than her killer."

"She wasn't here that long before getting knocked off."

"How do we know she's not from Westmount or Outremont or some other neighborhood in the city? Everyone who stays at the Windsor isn't from out of town."

"She had luggage."

"Maybe she wanted a change of scenery for a few days and brought some extra clothes and a toothbrush with her. And a gun. The point is, Eddie, we know little about her, so we can't fall in a trap and start making assumptions."

"If she's from Montreal, someone is bound to know her and come forward when they see the sketch. She doesn't look as if she was a hermit."

"I've got a guy keeping tabs on the missing persons reports in Canada and the States just in case. It's a big job, but we might luck out. In the meantime, we should just focus here locally."

"I still think that our best shot is to find the guy who was with her when she checked in at the hotel. He could settle all our problems."

"Or create more."

"Jeez, you're rosy today."

———«●»———

Eddie pulled up to 5768 Avenue Westluke in Côte Saint-Luc. The house was a small split-level bungalow that looked fairly new. The neighborhood was well cared for. Professional people lived here—doctors, lawyers, corporate accountants. You didn't have to be rich to live here, but you did have to have a solid, steady above-average income. He noticed a new black Cadillac in the driveway.

He glanced at the first name on his list, got out of the car, and walked up the short cement path. He climbed a few steps and then knuckled the door. It was opened immediately by a short well-dressed man.

"My name is Eddie Wade. I'm working with the police. They received a call from a Myron Berku yesterday concerning the sketch of the woman in the newspaper."

"Ah yes, yes, that's me. I'm Myron Berku. Please come in. That was fast, I must say. Fast indeed. You people don't let grass grow under your shoes for very long, now do you?" He smiled. "Silly me. I should have said, you people don't let snow melt under your shoes for very long."

Eddie followed him into the living room.

Berku was a short, thin man in his early fifties with a pencil-thin mustache. He wore a three-piece suit with highly polished shoes. The tip of his nose seemed to converge with his upper lip, giving him a weasel-like appearance. He carried himself well, enunciated his words impeccably, if not too fast, and appeared to be a little fussy in his mannerisms.

"Please sit down, Mr. Wade, please sit. Now would you like something to drink? Something hot, perhaps? It's a cold one out there today, it is. Ah, you just came in, so you'd be quite aware of that, now wouldn't you? Coffee, tea? Maybe something stronger? Oh, but of course you're on duty, and I wouldn't want to tempt you—wouldn't want you to get into trouble."

"I'm fine, thanks. I don't want to take any more of your time than necessary, so I'll get right to the point." He took out his leather-covered notebook and a pen. "You told the constable who talked to you when you called that you know the woman in the sketch."

"Oh yes, I did indeed. Yes, I did, yes," he said, nodding his head.

"What's her name?"

"Elizabeth McDonald," he said, lowering himself into an armchair. He paused slightly after each syllable. "I call her Beth—at least I used to. She was of Irish extraction, you see. Her parents, rest their souls, were from Dublin. North side of the city, I believe Beth said."

"What do you do for a living, Mr. Berku?"

"Oh, please just call me Myron. Now what do I do for a living? Well, let's just say that I'm self-sufficient. I'm not a rich man, you see, but I'm not poor either. You might say that I'm somewhere in between the two."

Eddie jotted down a few notes and then looked up. "Tell me how you know Beth."

"It was quite by chance, you see. We met on a bench, of all places, in Mount Royal Park—Parc du Mont-Royal, if you will—one sunny day at the end of last summer. Late August, if my memory serves me. She looked lonely, terribly lonely, you see, so I struck up a conversation with her. I took pity on her. What else could I have done but say a few kind words to her?" He stopped a moment, as if expecting a response. When it didn't come, he continued. "As it turned out, that was the best thing I could have done, for her and me. We hit it off immediately. We must have talked for hours that day. It cheered her up, you see. I knew I *just* had to see her again, and I think she felt the same, so we exchanged phone numbers."

"What did you talk to her about?"

"What did we talk about? Well, everything under the sun. Small talk, you see. Small talk can go a long way, and it did. There's nothing *small* about small talk."

"Did you see her again?"

"Oh yes, I did. We saw each other often for the next few months. We went out to movies and restaurants. Took in some concerts and a few plays, and we strolled in the park on sunny days. Golden memories! That's what they are. Golden memories! Of course, I didn't know it at the time. Looking back at it, though—and I have, there's no doubt about that— looking back at it, it was love at first sight for the both of us on that park bench." He paused briefly and stared over Eddie's shoulder, as if lapping up the past.

"Go on."

"Go on. Yes, yes, of course, I'll go on. We actually got to know each other very well, to the point I asked her for her hand in marriage."

"And ..."

"And of course, she accepted. For the next week, we planned out our wedding ceremony, in detail—you know, the guest list, the reception, even the menu. We were both looking forward to it. The ceremony was to be the following month." He paused once again to take a breath.

"Then ..."

He looked over Eddie's shoulder again, out the front window this time. His demeanor seemed to fade away. "Then she just disappeared." He spoke slowly now, in a dreamlike trance. "I never saw her again. I looked everywhere, everywhere there was to look, but there was no trace of her."

"Does she have relatives? You seemed to imply that her parents were dead."

Suddenly, Berku snapped out of it. He redirected his eyes to Eddie. "That's quite right. Her parents were dead, so she was alone in this world, alone except for me, you see."

"Was she from Quebec?"

"Oh yes, from a small village up north. I forgot the name. She came to the city to look for work."

"Her disappearing just like that must have come as a shock to you."

"Oh, it did. It did indeed."

"What did you do?"

"What any red-blooded Canadian man whose fiancée had just disappeared would do. I went to the police, of course, to file a missing person report, but they didn't take me seriously. Now that she's dead, I bet they regret that, regret that badly."

"The paper didn't say that she's dead, only that she's missing."

"Oh, they can't fool me." He rose from the chair and became animated, gesturing with his arms and hands. "She's dead all right; otherwise, why put her picture in the papers? Answer me that!"

"As I said, she's just missing."

"Oh, they can't deceive me. Beth was kidnapped by the government because they wanted to punish me. You see, I know certain things, and they wanted to punish me because of that. So they kidnapped her and then killed her so they could deprive me of the happiness she brought into my life. They spied on us. They did, yes indeed. I didn't know it at the time, but now I know it must have been them. Who else could they have been? When the time was right, they grabbed her. I know all about how they work. She's dead, oh yes. She's dead all right." He stood over Eddie and bent down a little. "But please don't tell them that I know, or they'll come after me too. Promise me that, will you?"

"I promise I won't mention it, Myron," Eddie said, exasperated, as he put the notebook and pencil in his pocket. He stood up and walked toward the door, Berku following behind.

"A promise is only as good as the man making it. Are you a good man, Mr. Wade? *Are* you a good man? Answer me that, why don't you, Eddie Wade?"

"I'm a good man, Myron. My lips are sealed," he said, pulling a zipper across his mouth with his hand. Then he left.

Before Eddie got more than a few steps away, he heard the man behind him say, "I'll hold you to that, Eddie Wade! Yes, indeed, I'll hold you to that!"

Outside in the car, he got out his pen again and then reached for his list of names lying on the seat. He sighed and then scratched through the name of Myron Berku. From there, he drove to the *Gazette* to talk to Jake Asher.

In any newsroom of any big-city newspaper, there was always a cacophony of sounds so unique as to distinguish it from any other human activity. The sounds were easy enough to isolate with a modicum of concentration, but it was the combined effect that separated this set of sounds from all the others and made it truly distinctive. Reporters coughing, arguing with each other, murmuring to themselves, laughing aloud together, clicking Zippos to light their cigarettes and cigars, sliding coffee cups across desks, and shouting, "Copyboy!"— all against the backdrop of typewriters pounding away and the incessant drone of teleprinters. The *Montreal Gazette* was no exception.

"How can you stand all that racket?" Eddie asked, standing over Jake.

Jake looked up from his desk. "What racket? This is sweet music to my ears. It means that the paper is doing what it's supposed to be doing, that it won't go out of business next week, that I'll get paid another check. You know what they say about a quiet newsroom."

Eddie sat down beside Jake's desk. Jake had been a crime reporter for nearly as long as Eddie had been alive. He was short and fat and usually had a cigar stuck in his mouth. Eddie was there that afternoon to pick Jake's brain, so he explained the story behind the sketch of the woman on the *Gazette*'s front page.

"I was about to do a little investigating myself," Jake said, "but Macalister asked the editor to keep it out of print. I got all the dope, though. Don't ask me how, and I won't have to lie to you. I thought it was a simple suicide, but you're telling me now that it's a homicide case."

"It seems that way. You think the mob might be involved in this?" Eddie had his doubts, but he wanted to run the idea by Jake before excluding it.

"First of all," Jake said, "a gun with that many rounds could have been a plant. Ordinary people who keep firearms for protection usually don't have the serial numbers removed, and they don't carry that many rounds with them. That's suspicious. You were right to question a suicide. However, if the mob had been involved in knocking this broad off, they wouldn't have been so obvious about it. They don't like the publicity. In the old days it was different; they wouldn't have cared less. But not today. Oh, they make an exception now and again, but generally, they want to knock someone off, they do it on the QT. They just make the person disappear. The police might find the body fifty years down the line when some farmer is plowing his field."

"Does she look familiar at all to you? Maybe a girlfriend of a local gangster?"

"She doesn't. I would have remembered that face. But that doesn't mean she wasn't. However, whoever killed her wanted her to be found and wanted the authorities to believe it was a suicide. They wanted to send a message to someone. Now it could have been the mob. They've been known to operate like that when the occasion calls for it. But those cases have usually involved a member of a rival gang—you know, another gangster, a guy, not some beautiful broad. So nix on the mob." He thought for a moment, then added, "What I think you've got here, Eddie, is something bigger than just a mob hit—something much bigger."

"Like what?"

"That's the sixty-four-thousand-dollar question, isn't it?"

"I might take out a bank loan to find out."

"If you do, let me know. I'd take a vacation from the paper for that kind of money and work the case."

"What's bigger than the mob when it comes to murder?"

"Murder?" Jake asked, pulling the cigar out of his mouth. "Maybe that's the wrong word. Maybe we should be using the word *assassination*. That takes it to a whole new level."

⸺»◉«⸺

Eddie had something to think about. *Assassination?* He could only remember that word being used to describe the murder of some high-profile person, a politician or a diplomat, not an ordinary person. But Jake was rarely wrong when it came to crime. It warranted further consideration.

From the *Gazette*, he drove back to Mile End to an apartment building only a few blocks from his own. He buzzed the superintendent and was let in. He walked up a short flight of stairs, stopped at the first door, and knocked. The door opened immediately, and a tall, balding man in his forties stood in front of him. He had a massive stomach that protruded over his belt. His sweater was ripped in several places, and his jeans were stained with motor oil and grease. He smelled of cigarettes and body odor. His sleeves were rolled up to his elbows, revealing a tattoo of a naked woman on his right forearm.

"I'm looking for Jean Petit. My name is Eddie Wade, and I'm working with the police."

"Is this about the picture in the newspaper?" the man whispered, looking over his shoulder.

"It is."

He turned around. "Honey, I'm just going to show this man apartment 203. I'll be right back."

As they climbed the stairs to the second floor, he said, "My wife is a very jealous woman. I don't want her to know about this. We'll just go up on the landing where we can talk."

When they got there, Eddie asked, "So you know the woman in the sketch?"

"I don't exactly know her, but I met her last week."

"Tell me about it."

"Well, it's this way. I was over on the Main two Wednesdays ago to pick up some supplies at the hardware store. It was nearly noon when I finished, and I was getting a little hungry, so I went to Schwartz's next door. Know where that is?"

Eddie nodded. "Go on." Everyone in Quebec knew where Schwartz's was.

"I got my sandwich and a black cherry soda and went to find a seat. It was busy, so I sat down at the only table with an empty chair. It happened to be beside this beautiful broad with long blonde hair. After I started eating, I noticed that she was staring at me. I mean, she was really staring at me. If she were a guy, I might have said, 'Hey, bud, what are you staring at? Give me a break.' But I'm a polite guy, so I looked over and smiled at her. Well, that's when it happened."

"What happened?"

"She started talking to me, and pretty soon she was telling me how handsome I was, that we should meet up that night and go out for some drinks. Now, Eddie, you gotta understand—I'm a happily married man. It was hard for me to listen to all that. She actually became aggressive, wanting to know where I lived and what my phone number was. I didn't want to be impolite to her, but I couldn't listen to her anymore. When she started pawing me, I got up, took my sandwich to the counter, and asked the guy for a paper sack. Then I left. Don't get me wrong now—if I were single, it would have been a different story. She was gorgeous, if you know what I mean. Really class A stuff."

"And you're sure it was the woman in the sketch?"

"No doubt about it. It would be hard to disremember that face."

"And you're sure it was two Wednesdays ago? That would have been January 4."

"Absolutely. I only go to the hardware store on Wednesdays, and I know it wasn't last week. If you start off the week short of something, Wednesday is a good day to get it. Then you've got a few extras days to boot if an emergency comes up, but it almost doesn't. Yes, it was Wednesday, January 4."

"Okay, Jean. Thanks for your time. I won't keep you anymore. We'll be in touch if we need anything further."

"Don't you want to know what happened after I left? She ran after me to my truck and tried—"

"If I need more information," Eddie said, interrupting him, "I'll be sure to contact you."

"Listen, don't mention this to the wife if you call back. Like I say, she can be pretty jealous."

"It'll be our little secret."

"Jeez, thanks, Eddie. You're a great guy for a cop."

"Don't mention it."

Back in his car, Eddie scratched Jean Petit off his list. Anne Lovingate had already been laid out on a slab at Rose Cottage on Wednesday, January 4. Petit must have been one of the loonies Macalister had warned him about.

Chapter 12
SECRETS

JOSETTE HAD KISSED EDDIE GOODBYE BEFORE eight on Tuesday morning and had smiled as she remembered Eddie telling her about two interviews the previous day. She had stopped short of laughing and refrained from cracking wise about them. They'd been funny all right—even Eddie had thought so—but mostly they were pathetic. There must be a lot of lonely men out there, she had told him, married or not, doing their best to create a little excitement in their fantasy worlds. Were there women who did the same?

She would be meeting Gigi for lunch at noon today, so she had gone to the office for a few hours to answer the phone (which hadn't rung) and to study her manual (which she'd done diligently) and then returned home to change clothes. The purpose of the luncheon wasn't simply "girl talk," although there would be a fair amount of that. She wanted to squeeze Gigi for information, without her knowing she was being squeezed. She hated being deceptive; it wasn't in her nature. Now she found herself lying not only to Gigi but also to Eddie. Eddie had told her to "get used to it" if she was ever going to be an investigator. It was as if he'd given her his permission. She was certain Eddie hadn't intended to include himself in the people she should lie to. But if she had to get used to it, she might as well start today.

La Tour Eiffel was a fancy restaurant on Stanley near Sainte-Catherine. The food was good, but Josette liked the atmosphere even better. It was where the artsy crowd hung out—the writers, painters, and poets. She went about once a month and never knew anyone there—the bohemian scene was about as far away from her everyday reality as it could possibly get—but she was always entertained by their showy, pretentious, and often spurious public displays. Sometimes she would just sit at a corner table and watch them talk to each other in their sometimes eccentric clothes, flashing cigarette holders and gesticulating with their arms flying every which way—always with serious expressions, always solving the problems of world. They were the postwar offbeats, the experimentalists, the radicals, the unorthodox, the avant-garde of art, culture, and society. Ignore them at your own risk. There wasn't a nickel's worth of humor in any of them. They were, if nothing else, amusing.

Josette and Gigi had had a light lunch of salad and a sandwich and were finishing it up with coffee.

"Yes, of course," Gigi said. "I still see your parents every day."

"That's more than I do," Josette said. "It's been three weeks, at least."

"Your mom says that you're terribly busy these days. It must be quite a change for you, going from the bakery to being an investigator—a real private eye."

"I'm not one yet. I'm just a student of the trade. I'm an apprentice, as Eddie likes to call me. It'll be another six months before I get my license. In the meantime, I study and answer the phone. It can be quite boring at times."

"Well, knowing you the way I do, I'd say you're getting antsy."

"Just a little bit," she said, laughing.

When Josette told her friend that her parents were selling the bakery and retiring, Gigi was shocked. Their shop was a landmark in the neighborhood. Josette told her that they were looking forward to relaxing and doing some long-overdue traveling. When there was a lull in the conversation, Josette asked whether there had been any progress on Gigi's own home front.

Just then, there was a ruckus at the table behind them. A small group of artists had been arguing over the state of art in the Soviet Union. One side maintained that socialist realism was superior to American expressionism. The other side claimed that Russian artists were merely slaves who were told what to paint by the state and how to do it. When someone exclaimed, "Capitalist swines!" all hell nearly broke loose. The manager, who was quite used to their bizarre ways, rushed over and calmed them down.

"Ladies and gentlemen, this isn't a debating hall. This is a public restaurant with other guests to consider. Please conduct yourselves with proper etiquette!"

Looking over Gigi's shoulder, Josette said, "They obviously have too much time on their hands."

"Far too much!"

"Anyway, so how's it going with Symeon? Any progress?"

"If you're asking if I've talked to him yet, the answer's no. When I start to bring it up, I get so embarrassed about it that I just clam up."

"So things haven't changed between you two."

"I'm afraid not."

"I'm not being nosy, Gigi, but what exactly is he doing that you're concerned about?"

"Like I said before, I think he might be cheating on me. He's been acting very strange, and it's gotten worse since the beginning of the year. He's been making excuses not to see me. Says he's got to work late. When I call him at work, at his desk, he never answers."

"Maybe he's in another part of the building."

"I thought so too. I drove there one night and went to the front door. The night watchman told me that no one was in the building. They have to sign in and out with him after hours. But it's not only that. He's just been very preoccupied whenever he's around me, like his body is there, but his mind is somewhere else. I sense he always wants to leave and go somewhere else when we're together."

"And you think it's another woman."

"I don't know what to think anymore, Josette. Just last week, we were supposed to have lunch together. He canceled it that morning because he said he had to drive to Ottawa for a last-minute meeting. I saw him that afternoon downtown, going into a lounge."

"You think he was meeting a woman there?"

"I was too afraid to go in and find out."

"Have you brought up setting a date lately?"

"I'm afraid to do even that, afraid of what he might say."

Josette couldn't see their relationship going on like this for too much longer. Gigi needed some help, and soon. Josette had to do something, but what? Maybe if she saw them together, she'd get a better idea of what was going on.

"Listen, I've got an idea. Maybe Symeon just needs to be around a married couple to see how they act with each other in a home setting. Maybe he's having second thoughts about getting married."

"Eddie mentioned that to me when I saw him."

"Both Eddie and I did before we got married. That's perfectly normal. Most couples go through that."

"He told me that too."

"Listen, find out if Symeon's free tomorrow night. If he is, come over to my place for dinner, all four of us. It might be good for him to see Eddie and me together in our apartment. We've been married for only six months, and we're very happy. Maybe he just needs to see that there's life after the marriage ceremony."

Josette's eyes caught movement behind Gigi. One of the artists, wearing a red beret and a lime-green sweater, rose from his chair, grabbed his coat, calmly stated to those at his table, "I shan't suffer communist-sympathizing fools any longer," and walked out.

⸺◉⸺

Eddie wasn't having any luck today. A few of the people he had visited had said that they'd made a mistake about identifying the woman in the paper. Others had provided information that was so vague as to render it useless. The next guy on his list was Angelo Mancini, who lived on Rue de l'Alverne in Saint-Leonard. Maybe Eddie would have better luck with him.

He pulled up to a wide-set semi-detached brick triplex. Along with Little Italy, where Eddie had grown up, the area was heavily populated with Italian immigrants and their descendants. Generally, the neighborhood was run-down. Saint-Leonard had more prostitution and gin joints than any other part of the city and all the street crime that came with them. But there were also a lot of decent families there who were just too poor to move away. Eddie knew many of them. He also knew Angelo Mancini.

Mancini lived on the second floor of the building. Eddie climbed the outside stairs, packing down the unshoveled snow with each step. He took off a glove and rapped on the door. He knew he'd have to wait a bit for Mancini to answer, but after a few minutes, he knocked again. He could see his breath—the minuscule droplets of water, the fleeting, misty cloud in front of him that disappeared and repeated itself with each breath he took. The door was suddenly pulled back, and he was staring at a cocked revolver.

"Angelo, it's me, Eddie!" he said, his arms up at the elbows, his palms out, as if they could stop a bullet.

"Eddie? Eddie Wade?"

"Yeah, it's me."

Mancini lowered the gun slowly. "Oh," he said. "Come in, come in. It's a bastard out there today. Sorry, you can't be too careful these days."

The door led directly into the kitchen. Eddie went in and took off his overcoat and draped it over a chair. He left his hat on. His mother had once told him that it kept the body heat in.

"I wasn't expecting you, Eddie. I've got some coffee in the pot. How 'bout a nice hot cup to warm the bones?"

"Sounds good, Angelo."

No one in the neighborhood knew exactly how old Angelo Mancini was. Eddie himself could only guess, but he must have been in his late sixties or early seventies. He was frail now, but surprisingly, he could still get around. Eddie thought it was because of his decades of working as a mailman. He had white unruly hair that he almost never combed, and he wore thick lenses in wire-framed glasses. Like many people who lived alone (his wife had died nine years before, and they'd never had children), he would talk up a storm when someone visited him.

Mancini poured two cups of coffee and brought them over to the table, and then both he and Eddie sat down.

"You always greet your guests with a six-shot revolver?"

"Not always. You still in the detective business? I haven't seen you since Mackenzie King's third term of cheating taxpayers out of their money."

"Aw, it hasn't been that long, Angelo. Remember last summer when we went barhopping and ended up sleeping in La Fontaine Park?"

"Now that you mention it, I wonder how I forgot. That constable woke us with that goddamn contraption of his. Scared the shit out of me—you too, as I remember. Thought there was an air-raid warning that German bombers were overhead."

"Speaking of the police, Angelo, you called them yesterday about that sketch of a woman in the paper. I'm working with them to identify her. Do you know her?"

"Never saw her in all my years."

"Then why did you phone the police?" He took a long sip of his coffee.

"Saw sumpin' else. The police never take old fogies like me seriously. They think we're all senile. I figured if I could get one of them to come out to me, maybe I could convince him. Never thought in a million years they'd send you." He stopped speaking and sipped his coffee. Then he stared at the cupboard behind Eddie.

"You want to tell me about it, Angelo?"

He looked at Eddie again. "That's why you're here, ain't it?" He paused a moment, as if organizing his thoughts. Then he reached over to the revolver in front of him and uncocked it. "Sorry about that, Eddie. I wouldn't have shot you. But when it's a stranger at the door, looking into a cocked gun is usually good enough to scare him away. Anyway, I was downtown two weeks ago. On Tuesday, to be exact. Must have been around ten forty-five, eleven in the morning, sometime around then. I had some errands to do, but I needed to sit down and rest awhile. So I sat down by the delivery door in the back of the Windsor Hotel. When there's no delivery there, it's peaceful, and nobody bothers you. You can't just sit down in a restaurant or bar anymore and not buy sumpin'—not even in the wintertime. The bastards won't let you. It was cold, but not like it is today, so I got my pipe out and fired her up. You still smoke a pipe?"

"I do."

"Okay then." He took another sip of his coffee.

After a moment, he continued his story. As he'd puffed away, the door next to where he was sitting had suddenly flung open and banged against him. A man came barreling out and ran down the alley. He never looked back, so he didn't see Angelo sitting there. As he was running away, he pulled a wig off his head as well as his glasses, plus something else from his face, and shoved them in his coat pocket. Then he disappeared around a corner.

"I thought that looked very suspicious. You don't see that every day."

"Tell me the day and time again."

"Tuesday, two weeks ago. I wrote it down when I got back here, so I wouldn't forget it. Around eleven in the morning, give or take."

"That would have been January 3."

"If you say so. I don't keep track of dates anymore. I'm too old for that. It was two Tuesdays ago. I know that because that's when I did my errands. That's what I wrote down."

"Did you see his face?"

"No. He was running away from me, and he never looked back. Now you have to admit that's sumpin' strange, sumpin' the police might be interested in, huh?"

"Yeah, I think they would be, Angelo."

"Whaddya think he done, Eddie? I mean with that disguise and all? Bet he was up to some kind of mischief. That's why I called the police."

"I'll be sure to tell them. Listen, with your eyesight, are you sure you saw him take off a wig?"

"Sure, I'm sure! Ain't nothing wrong with my eyes. I just take off my glasses, and I can see like an eagle—distance, that is. Up close is when I need them. I put them on to fill my pipe.

When the guy came running out, I took them off to see what all the fuss was about."

"I see." Eddie's eyes slid across the table to the revolver. "The police know you have that gun? They're not going to like it if it's not registered."

"Don't really care. It can't fire anyway. The firing pin is screwed up. I haven't fired it in three decades. Like I said, I just keep it around to scare off intruders. It looks menacing, no? An old codger like me has got to keep sumpin' handy."

———— ◖◕◗ ————

Eddie opened the door to his office and walked in.

Without looking up from her manual, Josette said, "You know, it says here that it's against the law to break into a building, home, or car for the purposes of acquiring evidence." Now she looked up. "Is that true, even if you know for certain that there's incriminating evidence in a building, home, or car, enough to convict someone?"

"Yes, dear, it's against the law. You can be fined, lose your license, and go to jail. You need a warrant to enter someone's private property. But only the police are issued warrants. We aren't."

"Don't you think that's unfair?" She cocked her head.

"There's a lot in this world that's unfair, Josette. You can add that one to your list. Besides, would you want some private dick breaking into our apartment?"

"That's different. We haven't committed a crime, and we don't have any incriminating evidence in our apartment that proves we did." She paused a moment, then said, "Have you ever broken into a building, home, or car to acquire evidence?" She followed the question with a little grin.

"So many times that I can't even remember the number."

"And isn't that hypocritical of you? Or maybe it's just plain reckless behavior?"

"Both. I promise I'll never do it again, and under no circumstance are you to ever try it. Besides, that's what the police get paid for. They're the ones with the warrants. And when they have one, they're not breaking in; they're entering legally, whatever method they use."

"Am I to believe that promise and accept it like a nice little wifey and say, 'Yes, dear'?"

"Is that a rhetorical question, or do you want an answer?" He took off his overcoat and hat and hung them on the coatrack, then threw his gloves at the base of the rack. "I need a stiff drink," he said.

"Make that two if you're pouring."

He sat down at his desk, opened the bottom drawer, and pulled out a bottle of Canadian Club. He poured two fingers in each coffee cup and gave Josette one. He still had a little coffee in his own cup.

"Here's to Lovingate," he said, raising his cup. "May her killer be found soon."

"Preferably by us," Josette added.

They tossed back their drinks at the same time.

"Gee, the whiskey tastes a little different." He picked up the bottle, held it up to the light, shrugged his shoulders, and then set it down again. "I just had a nice chat with an old friend of mine. His name is Angelo Mancini. He was one of the people on my list."

"Isn't he the old-timer you got drunk with last summer, and then you both slept in the park and nearly got arrested for vagrancy?"

"That's the guy!"

"Was the chat worthwhile, or was he just let out of the looney bin and wanted a little excitement in his life?"

"Worthwhile, but there's good news and bad. Which one first?"

"Always the good news first. It's scarce. Bad news always comes in abundance. It's never-ending."

"He actually saw the killer running from the loading dock area in the back of the Windsor Hotel about the time Lovingate was murdered—ran right past him. Angelo didn't know he was a killer, though. He just thought something was fishy. That's why he called the police."

"So he can identify him, right?"

"Here's the bad news. The guy's back was turned to Angelo as he ran by. But as he was running away, he pulled off a wig and glasses and probably a mustache. He had a disguise on."

"If I were prone to cussing, I'd do it right now. That means the picture we have of him is useless. We have no idea what he looks like."

"I'm sure he's Lovingate's killer. The question is, if he's still in the city, how are we going to find him?"

"Hmm," Josette mumbled.

"Well, I *am* prone to cussing. Goddamn it!" he shouted, pounding the desk with his fist.

"Do you want to run that by me one more time? I didn't quite hear you."

"We're back to square one—worse than that. At least before we had a peg to hang his hat on. Now we don't even have that."

Josette was characteristically calm. She rarely got her feathers ruffled, which was one of the many things he loved about her.

"Remember you told me that a good investigator creates his own leads? Maybe we should start doing that."

"Jeez, you're no fun. I was just about to wallow in my own self-pity."

"While you're wallowing away, I had lunch with Gigi today. I invited her and Symeon over for dinner tomorrow night. We do have a social life, you know. I hope that's okay with you."

"Actually, that sounds great, baby! We need a little diversion right now. I'm all for diversions, especially if a case is particularly hard. You go back to the case feeling refreshed. It's like taking a shower. Gets the blood flowing to your head. You feel invigorated. You feel that spark in your brain. What time are they coming?"

"I didn't say they accepted the invitation, just that I extended the offer. Gigi will call me tomorrow morning if Symeon is free."

"Diversions, baby! That's what we need right now. They'll kickstart the case again. Did I ever tell you about my theory of diversions?"

"I thought you just did. You're telling me there's more? Hand over the bottle of whiskey, bud. I think I'll need another drink."

Chapter 13
COMPLICATIONS

THE ELLIS DETECTIVE AGENCY WAS LOCATED A few doors down from the Montreal Forum on rue Sainte-Catherine, where the Canadiens played their home games. The Ellises, Sully and Angie, were a husband-and-wife team of investigators whose research skills put all the PhD candidates at McGill to shame. They were also great hockey fans. Eddie and Sully had gotten into the business about the same time, after the war, and had maintained a close friendship over the years. On occasion, they would help each other out on cases, but money had never crossed their palms; bottles of whiskey were always the medium of exchange.

It had been Sully and Angie who had encouraged Eddie to think about taking on Josette as a partner, not by words as much as by example. Josette had already expressed interest in becoming an investigator, and watching the Ellises in action together had only made Eddie's decision easier.

It had been a few months since Eddie last saw the Ellises, so when he arrived at their office on Wednesday afternoon, they chatted away, catching up on their lives in the world of misfortune and deception. Angie related a story of a case she'd brought to a bizarre conclusion, and they all had a good laugh. Then she asked Eddie how Josette was doing on the job. He explained that she was going to make a great investigator, but patience wasn't one of her virtues. She was eager to get into the field and catch criminals.

Sully looked at Angie and then at Eddie, as if to say, "This one too."

Eddie glanced at his watch; he wanted to get back to his list of people who had called the police about the Lovingate sketch in the papers. He had nearly forgotten why he had stopped in, so he explained the case to them.

"If you could show the sketch when you're out and about, I'd appreciate it. Don't go out of your way, though. It's a long shot, and the sketch is already in the papers, but you never know who you may come across."

"You know, Eddie," Sully said, leaning back in his chair. He had a head full of curly brown hair, a thick mustache, and a granite jaw and was taller than Eddie—quite the contrast to petite Angie. "We had a case like this a few years back. An unidentified body had been lying in one of Becket's coolers at Rose Cottage for a few months, and the police were going to tell Cecil to bury him."

He went on to say that business had been a little slack at the time, so Sully asked Cecil to hold off a week and let him see what he could do. The police had no idea who the guy was, and no one had reported him missing. After the week went by, Sully decided to hang it up and call Cecil so he could bury the body. As he was about to pick up the phone, a woman came in and wanted to hire him to find her missing husband. He asked her whether she'd filed a missing person's report with the police. She said she hadn't. Turned out the guy was the missing husband of the woman. He was an American wanted in five states for armed robbery, mostly banks. He had had a heart attack one night and died on a street corner near the port. He never carried any ID with him.

"The point is—"

"The point is," Eddie said, interrupting him, "I could sit back in my office and wait for someone to come in and break the case."

"Her picture is out there in the papers. It could happen."

"It could, but I don't think her murderer is going to wander in someday."

"No, but if you knew who she was, you'd be a step closer to finding him."

"I'll take that into consideration. On that note," Eddie said, getting up and putting on his overcoat and hat, "I have to push on."

"Tell Josette I said hi," Angie said, "and to hang in there. She'll get her license soon enough. Tell her after I got my license, this lunkhead here"—she thumbed her husband and smiled—"wouldn't give me my own cases for years. Be nice to Josette, will you, Eddie? She's got a good head on her shoulders. Tell her I'll give her a ring."

"That good head on her shoulders is what I'm afraid of. She'll be running my agency before I know it." He glanced over Angie's shoulder and saw his wedding picture hanging on the wall in a silver frame: Eddie and Josette together, dressed to the nines, big smiles on their faces. The Ellises had been witnesses to their marriage. Sully had taken the picture.

Good people, these Ellises.

———— «•» ————

Eddie's culinary skills were limited to making spectacular bologna sandwiches with mayonnaise and sliced garlic dill pickles. Since they were having guests over for dinner that night, the kitchen belonged to Josette exclusively. Fortunately, her cooking skills matched her baking skills. Her favorite dishes were French, and since her ancestors had come from

Normandy, she had decided to cook filets of sole Dieppoise, poached sole served in a white wine sauce and garnished with mussels and shrimp, with steamed vegetables on the side.

"Scrumptious!" Symeon Peters declared. As if to reinforce the assessment, after taking a second bite, he added, "Absolutely scrumptious!"

Gigi nodded in agreement.

Eddie thought Symeon's English accent sounded pretentious. But he thought all Brits sounded fake, so it was nothing against Symeon personally. He glanced over at Josette. She was the one who had done the cooking, not him. He couldn't very well say anything in reply; it would look as if he were taking credit for the meal.

"Thank you. I'm glad you're enjoying it," Josette said, almost shyly.

What was this? Josette had never been shy about anything since he'd known her. Maybe it was that accent of Symeon's. Canadians as a rule tended to bow down and quiver in its presence; it made men feel emasculated and women submissive. Eddie could never figure that one out. Maybe he had too much American in him to bend at the waist.

They ate in silence for a minute or two. Then Symeon looked over the table. "So how did the pair of you meet, if you don't mind me asking? Gigi tells me that you're newly married." He glanced at his watch.

Eddie didn't know whether the question was for him or Josette or both of them. When Josette didn't say anything, he stepped up to the plate. He certainly wasn't shy. "We got married about six months ago. Only knew each other a few months before that."

He went on to explain that he'd been working a case when they met. He didn't go into details because it was personal and none of Symeon's business anyway. The purpose of having them over, as Josette had explained it to him, was to show

Symeon that they had had doubts about getting married but had worked their way through them by talking things out.

"We spent hours talking about whether it was the right time. Should we wait? Were we rushing into an unknown future? You know, that sort of stuff."

"You must have reached a satisfactory conclusion," Symeon chimed in, "because here you are!" He glanced at his watch again.

"We decided we could talk about it forever," Josette added, "so we did like most couples do—we took a chance. And it was the best thing we ever did, right, Eddie?"

"You bet ya, baby." He reached over and caressed her shoulder with the palm of his hand. It was all true, but Eddie hoped they weren't laying it on too thick. He decided to change gears in case they were. "So how did you two meet?" Eddie asked. "You're from London, right?"

Gigi remained on the sidelines, eating and taking everything in.

"I am indeed, old man. Highbury, Islington, to be exact. Canadians don't know where that is, so it's plain London to you folks." He took a forkful of food, put it into his mouth, chewed for an eternity, and then spat out the rest of the answer. "The bank that Gigi works for does business with my accounting firm. Well, it's not mine. I should say, the one I work for. On the odd occasion they have a social gathering. We met at one of those." He looked to his side at Gigi. "That must have been a few years now, right?"

"Yes, almost two years exactly," Gigi said and then offered him a smile.

"Well, how time flies when you're having fun!" Symeon said to no one in particular.

They talked for a while longer. It was all quite pleasant, with everyone mostly contributing their share. Gigi, however, seemed a bit reticent. Eddie thought that the rest of the evening would proceed as well as it had been going. The diversion had turned out to be a good idea.

When everyone was finished with their meal, Josette got up and started for the kitchen. "I'll put some coffee on. I made some tarte aux pommes. We can have that after our meal settles a little."

This time Symeon made a point of looking steadily at his watch, holding his wrist out longer than what was necessary. "I'm afraid we'll have to call it a night. I have an important client coming in bright and early tomorrow morning, and I still have to prepare for him. Can we take a rain check on the coffee and dessert?"

Eddie looked back at him, surprised. Gigi looked shocked. Josette looked like an angry she-wolf.

"Couldn't you stay for a while longer?" Josette asked with more politeness than the situation called for. "It won't take long for the coffee, and the dessert is already made."

"I'm afraid we'll have to put it on the back burner. My client, you see?"

Eddie studied him for a moment. It wasn't Symeon's accent that irritated him; it was something less tangible but there nonetheless. He just couldn't put his finger on it.

————— •《•》• —————

They drove a full three minutes without saying a word.

Three minutes wasn't a very long time; it really wasn't. But it seemed like an eternity to Symeon. Gigi was obviously miffed about something. It was probably his insistence that they call it an early night, but what could he do? He'd used his work as an excuse: he had to work late and get up early. It was true; it hadn't been a complete lie. The situation did involve work, but not as an accountant and not tomorrow. He had to meet someone tonight. Okay, it was a last-minute thing, but he couldn't very well tell Gigi that, now could he? After all, he'd taken the time and made the effort to squeeze in both the meeting and that stupid dinner engagement. That was something, wasn't it? He'd gone out of his way for her.

"Lovely couple," he said, glancing at her out of the corner of his eye.

She stared ahead through the windshield at the road in front of them and said nothing.

Another three minutes dragged on before he decided he better apologize. "Listen, I'm sorry we had to leave so early, and I know you're angry, but—"

"Angry?" she said. "I'm not at all angry. I'm embarrassed and frustrated. They went through all the trouble of preparing for a fine evening, and Josette slaved in the kitchen to cook us a delicious meal, and we ended up throwing it in their faces."

"That's putting it a little too harshly, isn't it?" He was trying to concentrate on his driving, but the conversation was a distraction. "Don't you think?"

"Not harsh enough, if you ask me." She turned her head in his direction for the first time. "I don't understand you, Symeon. For the last two weeks you haven't been acting like yourself. You've been avoiding me and seem preoccupied when you're with me. We're supposed to be a couple, engaged to be married, but every time I mention setting a date, you change the subject. You won't even talk about it. Sometimes I feel like a piece of lint on your sleeve, waiting to be brushed off when you notice it." She paused a moment, looked down at her hands, and then looked back up at him. "What's happening to us, Symeon?"

The real question for Symeon to answer was how he would continue on with his secret life and maintain a semblance of normality. At the moment, he had no idea.

"Gigi, don't you think you're overreacting just a tad bit?" he asked, pulling the car to the curb in front of her apartment.

"After all, it was only a meal and a bit of socializing. I'll invite them over next week to my place, if you'd like. We'll spend more time with them. I'm quite a good cook myself, as you know."

"Don't bother yourself," she said. "And don't bother walking me to the door. I'm quite capable of getting there on my own." She got out of the car and slammed the door behind her.

Well, that hadn't gone down very well, now had it? He waited until she had taken her keys out of her purse and opened the door, and then he drove away.

She was right, though; he had been avoiding her. He hadn't thought he was being so obvious about it, but apparently, he had been. And now he found himself in this mess, a mess of his own making. It wasn't as if they hadn't warned him about avoiding entanglements. They had, and on a number of occasions to boot, so he had no one to blame but himself. But enough of that—he had been summoned, and he had to go.

He drove for another twenty minutes and then pulled up outside the Greystone Lounge on the east end of the city. He walked in and sat at the end of the bar alone. There were only a few people there, and the atmosphere was relaxed and low-key. The barman walked over to him. He was a tall man and built solidly. His face was neutral, as if facial expressions were a foreign concept to him.

"Hey, bud. What'll it be?"

"A beer. Something on tap, anything."

"You got it!" He went to the taps and poured a half pint, then brought it to Symeon. "How 'bout those Canadiens?" he asked in a loud voice, sliding the beer in front of him. "They lost again tonight to the Rangers. Heard the whole game on the radio. Five to one."

"Good for them," Symeon said. He took a few gulps.

"They keep that up, they won't even get in the playoffs."

"Serves them right," Symeon said, not the least interested in hockey.

The barman looked around in front of him to see whether he was being watched. When he decided he wasn't, he leaned forward, looked at Symeon, and lowered his voice, nearly to a whisper. "You heard about the fire in Ottawa?"

Symeon nodded his head.

"A file went missing. They don't know if it went up in flames or it found its way into someone's hands."

Symeon jerked his head up, alarmed, but didn't say anything. This was news to him.

"Our names might be in it. We've got to be extra careful. Don't take any unnecessary chances. They'll contact me when they know more. I'll send you a message the usual way. That's it."

Symeon nodded and felt depressed. First Gigi, and now this. Was there anything else coming his way to make his life more complicated than it already was?

The barman raised his voice loud enough for those who were sitting at the tables to hear. "If they start winning again, they might have a chance. But I'm putting my money on Boston taking home the cup this year."

Symeon couldn't care less who won the Stanley Cup this year or any other year. He was thinking about the missing file and the possibility of being exposed. Could there be any other graver threat to him than that? This was what he'd feared the most in the last five years.

And then there was Gigi. What was he going to do about her?

Chapter 14
A TARGET

EDDIE HAD SPENT THURSDAY MORNING following up on his list of names from Macalister, while Josette stayed at the office, studying her manual and jotting down notes, mostly questions to ask Eddie later. By eleven thirty, he had run out of steam and so drove back to the office to have lunch. He'd mostly skipped midday meals in the past, but since he'd married Josette, she had persuaded him that he'd have more staying power with something in his gut. Fuel was important. Could he expect to drive his car on an empty tank? Of course not. She made a good argument; however, he hadn't seen any difference. He had never told her so, though. He looked forward to stopping what he was doing and being with her in the middle of the day whenever he could. He didn't want to spoil that.

He sat at his desk, leaning back in his chair with his feet propped up, half of a bologna sandwich in one hand and his Spillane paperback in the other. He lowered the book and stared at Josette sitting at her own desk.

"Symeon Peters is a real asshole; you do know that, don't you? After being privileged with a spectator's view of the grand event last night, I have a great deal of empathy for Gigi,

141

not to mention sympathy. Peters is a sniveling, self-centered British toad. Your friend deserves better."

Josette looked up from her manual. "Well, he certainly had me fooled. I always thought he was a nice guy." She took a bite of her own sandwich.

"Just standing up like that and announcing they were leaving, when the evening wasn't half over. Now that takes chutzpah. A guy who can do something like that will cheat on his fiancée." He paused a moment, then added, "You can quote me on that."

"Chutzpah, now is it? That's the Jewishness in you dribbling out."

"Do I detect a tone of criticism in your voice?" Since discovering last year that he was half Jewish, he'd become a little sensitive.

"Cool your heels, Moses," she said. "It's merely an observation. Did you see the look on Gigi's face when he said they had to go? She wasn't pleased. She looked like she could have sliced him up and thrown him out the window."

"I can imagine the conversation on the way home."

"I've known Gigi for years, and she's usually calm and dignified. But I have seen her let loose on occasion, and it has never been very pretty."

"I hope she gave him a verbal thrashing. He deserved it."

Eddie went back to his book, and Josette continued to educate herself on detective work. After a few minutes, he put his book down and finished his sandwich.

"I forgot to tell you, I saw Sully and Angie yesterday," he said, rubbing his hands together to get the crumbs off. He picked up his cup and gulped down some lukewarm coffee. "Angie's going to call you for a girly chat. She told me to say that you should hang in there, that you'll be licensed up before you know it."

"Is that what she told you now?" she asked, closing her book harder than what was necessary. "Did she also tell you that after she got her license, she continued to answer the phone and make coffee for the next five years?"

"She did mention something about that, but I don't think it was quite five years."

She wagged a finger at him. "Don't you get any bright ideas in your head, buster. I didn't leave the bakery to answer the phone and take your messages for the next thirty years."

"How about the coffee?"

"You're a real comedian."

"So how many years did you have in mind then?"

She picked up a pencil from her desk and threw it at him. "I want a case of my own the day I get my license."

"You can have all of mine." He thought for a moment. "I plan on retiring when you get your license and managing you in my spare time. I have to catch up on my fishing, you know."

"You'd like that, wouldn't you, sitting with your feet up, smoking your pipe, your line in the water?"

"I could sit in a boat all day at Lake George and dream about Paris." He threw his head back and his arms up. "Aah ... *Paris!*" he said, using the French pronunciation.

Then they both said together, "We'll always have *Paris!*" and laughed for the next minute.

"I asked Sully and Angie to show the Lovingate sketch around town, see if they could come up with something."

Josette picked up the photograph of the guy with the mustache, wig, and glasses. She studied it for a moment. "I wonder what this guy would look like without the disguise."

"He'd look like my uncle Giovanni."

She turned her head toward him. "You don't have an uncle named Giovanni. As a matter of fact, you don't have any uncles at all."

"If I did, that's what he'd look like ... without the disguise."

"Be serious. Can a photographer change the photo? I mean, could he take out the mustache and glasses and do something different with the hair?"

"That's not a bad idea. I don't know if that's possible, but maybe a sketch artist could work something up. We'd have a more accurate idea of what the guy might look like."

"How about the guy who did the Lovingate sketch? Could we get him to do it?"

"That's da Vinci. I'll have to check with Jack on that, but that's another good idea. I'll call him today. Keep the wheels spinning, baby! You're going to do great things in this world."

"Tell me something I don't already know. By the way, I brought what was left of our dessert from last night with me. It's in the icebox. Want a slice?"

"Sounds good, but let's keep it for after supper tonight. Care to go next door and bend the wrist with Bruno for a while? He's always good for a laugh or two."

"Now he's a real comedian! He just doesn't know how funny he can be."

"If he ever finds out, Bob Hope better watch out."

"Give me five minutes to do my face."

"You don't need that much time, baby. You don't need any time at all."

They said their hellos at the bar with Bruno and talked about nothing in particular for the time it took him to pour a couple of Molsons from the tap. Just before they left the office, Josette had suggested to Eddie that they grab a table in the back of the Lion's Den because she had something to discuss with him. It wasn't crowded at all, so they carried their drinks to an empty table, took off their coats, and sat down. Josette immediately brought up the topic of courtroom evidence.

"There are all kinds of evidence," Eddie said, "some more important than others."

"Some more important than others," Josette repeated. "For instance?" She sipped her beer and listened intently.

"For instance, the photograph of the guy who was with Lovingate when she checked into the Windsor. It shows only that the guy was with her when she checked in. That's an undisputed fact. But you'd have to make a deduction to prove that he killed her. If a lawyer tried using only the photograph to prove his case, the argument would be pretty weak. No lawyer would do that. In court, it would be considered circumstantial evidence. The photograph would certainly be useful for an investigator, as it is for us, but alone, it doesn't carry much weight. A lawyer could certainly use it in court, but he'd have to have something more substantial to support it."

"So if this guy did kill Lovingate, what sort of evidence would be needed for a conviction?"

"Ideally, direct evidence. That would be a witness, for example, who actually saw him shoot her. But that's no good, because as far as we know, there were no witnesses. Then you have forensic evidence. That would be fingerprints of the killer on the murder weapon, the killer's hair or own blood left at the crime scene, or blood on his person from the victim—those sorts of things. That's also called physical evidence. There seems to be little or none of that. In crimes of passion, there are usually all kinds of evidence left behind. But professional killers, those who plan out a murder well, that's another story. They mostly leave a clean crime scene. They know what the police will be looking for. Unfortunately, that seems to be the case with Lovingate. Professional killers are usually harder to get. That's why they're called professional."

"What if the killer took something belonging to the victim, and later the police found it in his possession? Would that be considered direct evidence?"

Eddie took his pipe out of his jacket pocket and filled it from his tobacco pouch. He lit it with a match and blew smoke over his shoulder. "Maybe. If the killer had some ongoing relationship with the victim, he could say that she had given him the item sometime before the murder occurred. But if the killer had something of hers that he could have gotten only from the crime scene, and that there would be absolutely no reason for him to otherwise have, then that would probably be considered direct evidence."

"How would that play out in the Lovingate case?"

He puffed on his pipe, tamped the ash down with his finger, and puffed some more. "I've got to think about that now. Let's see. If the killer took something personal from Lovingate that should have been at the crime scene, the hotel room, something that he shouldn't have—ah, I've got it. Lovingate's passport and driver's license were missing from the crime scene. It's already been substantiated that she had them when she checked into the hotel. There would be no reason why someone else would have them. If they were found on the killer or in his home, I think most prosecutors would consider that direct evidence of the crime. The killer would have a lot of explaining to do, and a clever defense attorney could weave a credible story, but I still think it would be damning evidence that would convince a judge or jury."

"What if the killer said that Lovingate had given those to him for safekeeping?"

"That's always a possibility, but there would be no way for him to prove it because the victim is dead. The prosecutor would maintain that he stole them after he killed her, and that would have more weight with a judge or jury."

"I see," Josette said. She seemed to be in deep thought.

"Just remember that circumstantial evidence is fine for an investigator because it could be linked to something more important, like direct evidence of the crime. It's good for the case, but alone, it usually doesn't lead to a conviction."

"Usually?"

"Yes, usually. I won't say it never leads to a conviction, because some very strange things sometimes happen in courtrooms, especially when a jury hears a case. You can never predict them for certain. Judges either. Several independent pieces of circumstantial evidence could land—and have landed—a person behind bars. Personally, I think it's unfair, but that's the way the cookie crumbles. However, it's unlikely to happen in a capital murder case. A prosecutor needs hard evidence for a conviction ... usually."

Josette remained silent, taking in everything.

Eddie puffed away on his pipe and then drank a mouthful of his beer. "That's enough for one lesson," he said. "A person can take in just so much at a go."

"Thank you, Professor Wade. That was very kind of you to remind me of that."

"Don't mention it. I'll give you another lesson tonight in our bedroom, under the sheets. It's on an unrelated topic."

"You don't say. Will I have to take notes?"

"Not if I can help it."

Just then, the jukebox came to life, and Elvis Presley began singing "That's All Right, Mama."

Suddenly, Bruno was standing over them. "I hate to interrupt this little lovefest you two have going here, but I thought the lovely lady here would like some instruction on the proper way to boogie-woogie, since I know for a fact that her husband, handsome as he might be, has problems just walking."

Josette looked up at him, beaming. Eddie just smiled and shook his head—not another one of Bruno's bright ideas.

Josette stood up and took his outstretched hand. "Why, thank you, kind sir. I would love to partake!"

They moved several feet away from the table and began to kick up a storm. Eddie leaned back in his chair and watched them dance—and dance they did, as if there had been no yesterday and would be no tomorrow.

⟶«◉»⟵

Ottawa
The same day

He sat in his claustrophobic makeshift office and was disgusted by the thought of even being there. He hadn't worked all those years, dedicating his life and achieving success, to end up in this hovel more suitable for vermin than for human beings. It was only temporary, though, so he had to make the best of it. He didn't have a choice. That was the hardest part for him to digest, because he was supposed to be the one calling the shots—was and had been for a very long time. But even at the highest levels, there was always someone else above, eyeing you, jotting down little notes, always an arm's length from your file.

Across the small table from him was a subordinate. The lighting in the office was so bad that the man's face was half-shadowed. Between them sat a bottle of vodka. He reached for it and poured some into their glasses. The two men raised the glasses in a silent toast and drank. When they finished, he poured some more.

"You've been brought up to speed?" he asked the man.

"I have. Yes, sir."

He was irritated that he couldn't see the man's full face. Of course, he knew him well, maybe even better than the man knew himself, if that was possible. Nevertheless, whenever he was speaking to a subordinate, he always wanted to see his unobstructed face and look him in the eyes. That way he would know whether or not he was being understood. This too would be temporary, but for now, he was still irritated.

"So you know there was a failure in St. Paul." It wasn't a question. He knew that the man knew about it, but he left nothing to chance. He wanted a clarification. Clarity was important to him.

"Yes, sir. I was briefed."

"Good then. Drink up."

They lifted their glasses at the same time with a nod that substituted as a toast and emptied them.

He poured some more. "I'm sending you to Montreal to do the job. Do you know why?"

"Yes, sir."

"Why, then?" He wasn't being sarcastic or pedantic. He wasn't that kind of man. Again, he simply wanted clarification—the words spoken aloud. That way nothing could be misconstrued.

"Because I'm the best man you have."

"Good. You are correct. You are the best man I have; that's why I am absolutely certain you will not fail. Am I wrong to believe that?"

"No, sir. You are not wrong; failure is not an option for me."

"Good. That's what I want to hear. Drink up. It's good stuff, no? It's from the motherland."

"It's very good, sir." And once again they tipped their glasses.

"If I could have sent you to St. Paul in the first place, we wouldn't be sitting here now, because, as you say, failure is never an option for you, and the job would have been done already. But since I could not, well, here we are."

"Yes, sir."

"You're a professional, so I'll leave the method to you. I have only one request." He suddenly stopped—how stupid of him. "No!" He slapped his hand on the table, as if reprimanding himself. The bottle of vodka and the glasses jerked but didn't spill. "Request" was the wrong word. "I have only one *demand* of you. You must do it in such a way as to make it look like an accident. That is paramount. So a bullet to the forehead is obviously out. The idiot in St. Paul did not follow orders and failed, so he paid the price. Do you understand what I'm saying to you?" He tried to look into the man's eyes but had a difficult time because of the shadows.

"Yes, sir. I fully understand."

He slid a folder across the table. "Everything you need to know for the job is in this folder. Memorize it tonight, every detail. Do not take notes. And then return the folder to me tomorrow before you leave. Understand?"

"I understand, sir. May I ask the name of the target, sir? I want to start memorizing it immediately."

He poured more vodka into their glasses. "Yes, you may. His name is, of course, in the folder, but I'll tell you now." He stopped to drink some more. When his subordinate saw him, he did the same. *He's a good man*, he thought. *The right one for the job. He wants to start memorizing the name right away.*

He set his glass down and said, "The target's name is Eddie Wade—W-a-d-e."

Chapter 15
THE GAMES PEOPLE PLAY

SYMEON PETERS ROSE LATE ON FRIDAY morning, which was uncharacteristic of him. He usually allowed himself an extra hour in bed on weekends, but today was a workday. After the terrible news on Wednesday night, he'd gone to work the next morning as usual but hadn't been able to accomplish much, so he'd told his boss that he had some personal business to take care of on Friday and wouldn't be in. That, too, was uncharacteristic of him, so his boss hadn't questioned him. The truth of the matter was that he needed a three-day weekend to sort things out.

He'd had a rough time of it last night, tossing and turning, unable to shut off his mind. He would fall asleep, and then twenty minutes later, he'd find himself sitting up in bed wide awake. At three o'clock, he had decided to get up. He read a book by some unknown Canadian author in the living room under the torchère floor lamp until four o'clock, when he returned to bed and the cycle began again. It was around seven when he finally fell asleep and stayed that way for more than an hour. It was probably out of pure exhaustion that he had done so, since his mind had still been spinning. Symeon had problems with no resolutions. Christ almighty, that would keep anyone up at night.

His first problem was his fiancée, Gigi. He didn't know what to do about her. He had put her off now concerning setting a date for their marriage to the point of embarrassment. It wasn't that he didn't love her; he did, or at least he thought so. He had never been romantically in love before, so he had nothing to compare it to. And then there was the fact that he had to work around her with his other duties that he couldn't very well tell her about. That too was placing him in an awkward position. He did have to cut his time short with her at times, and she was right when she accused him of always being preoccupied with something else whenever they were together. Guilty as charged. But what was he to do? My God, he was only human; he wasn't some kind of robot.

He poured some coffee and took it into the living room and sat down. Gigi was a beautiful woman. She was intelligent, charming, and witty, always brightening up his day. He loved being with her; he really did. At the beginning of their relationship and until this month, they would go out to restaurants and concerts or rent a boat and explore a new lake outside of the city in Boucherville or Drummondville or some such place. They would even take hikes through the gentle, rolling mountains in the Laurentians. Just last month, he had begun teaching her how to downhill ski. And now suddenly, he found himself avoiding her; she had become a bother to him, an obstacle who needed to be circumvented. In plain words, she had become a problem—a big problem. *And I created it*, he thought, sipping his coffee.

And what made matters worse, as if anything actually could, was that they had warned him about steering clear of unnecessary entanglements. They'd said he wouldn't be here that long, that Montreal was only a temporary assignment. He'd taken them at their word. He'd expected a few months, a year at the most, and he had been quite prepared for that. But it had been five years now, and there had been no indications that they were going to move him anytime soon. It was becoming clear to Symeon now that he'd made a mistake in getting involved with Gigi, but it hadn't been entirely his fault. They had to bear some of the responsibility themselves for keeping him in one place for so long. But of course, that didn't matter; they never bore responsibility for anything they did. Why would they, when they could shift the responsibility to someone else?

Maybe he should just break the engagement with her and end their relationship completely. It certainly would solve his problem. It would be awkward, no doubt, but it would get the job done. She would be devastated, but she'd get over it. There were other fish in the lake for her, plenty of men who would find her a treasure. She was still young enough. But if he were to do that, how would it impact *him* emotionally? *Emotions*, he thought. Apparently, they didn't believe he had any. He chuckled at the thought. Oh, they knew he had emotions all right; otherwise, why would they have given him all those warnings? They expected him to keep all of his feelings under control. It was good for the job, and it was good for them, but it certainly wasn't good for Symeon himself. It would have been easier for him to control his emotions if he'd had short-term assignments; he was certain of that. He would have been content with one-night stands. His job would have kept him busy enough to prevent him from establishing long-term relationships. But he'd been here for five goddamn years! He was still young and healthy and had his looks. What did they expect from him?

And then there was the other issue that had kept him awake last night, a far more important issue—a potentially deadly one. He'd of course known about the fire in Ottawa—it had been front-page news in all the papers in the country.

The fire itself was no concern of his, really. What was his concern was the file that had gone missing. He wished to God that it had been destroyed in the fire. His contact had said that Symeon's name was in it, along with his own and all the details of the operation. That last part was, of course, implied, but if his name was in the file, then so was the operation. If the file ended up in the wrong hands, it would be over for him—for both of them. There was nothing he himself could do about it, except wait it out and see what happened. He didn't expect to get much sleep until the file turned up—or until he knew for certain that he had been exposed.

He took another sip of coffee, then put the cup down on the end table. He picked up the folded *Gazette*, spread it out on his lap, and stared at the large sketch of Anne Lovingate. She stared back at him. Then, for the umpteenth time, he read the article, trying to figure out why the authorities had said that she was missing when in fact she was dead.

What kind of game were they playing?

———«◑»———

Eddie had received a call that morning from Angie Ellis with a lead on the Lovingate case, from one of the "eyes and ears" the Ellises had used for years. She vouched for the man—he was a straight shooter. His name was Leo Lemaire, a taxicab driver who lived in Griffintown at 378 Rue Saint-Martin in an apartment house. After talking with Angie, Eddie had called Lemaire to make arrangements for an interview after lunch. Lemaire had been upfront with him; he needed to be paid. "I'm not running a fricking charity here," he had told him.

Now Eddie showed him the newspaper sketch of Lovingate. "So you saw this person?"

"Yeah, I seen her. I picked up a couple from the Dorval Airport and drove them to the Windsor Hotel. Actually, they wanted to stop about a half block from there. They said they wanted to do something, as if they needed to make an excuse for me. I could have cared less where I left them off, as long as I was being paid for the trip. That was her all right, just like I told Angie. She was a babe; you don't forget a face like that. By the way, this is going to cost you a double sawbuck."

"That's fine, Leo. What day was that?"

"Monday, January 2. It's right there in my logbook. See for yourself." He held it out for Eddie to see.

"You said you picked up a couple. Tell me about the man."

"Whaddya want to know? He was a normal guy."

"What did he look like?"

"Tall, clean-cut. Fancy dark-blue overcoat. What can I say?"

"Was he wearing glasses?"

"None that I could see."

"Mustache?"

"No. I would've remembered that. I'm good at remembering faces."

"Were they both carrying luggage?"

He thought for a moment. "Let's see now. I put two cases in the trunk. One was a briefcase, and the other was a suitcase a lady might have. So no, only the woman had luggage. I've been picking people up at the airport for eons and never seen a guy with just a briefcase. Besides, she looked professional to me, the kind of lady who would carry a briefcase. A lawyer or something like that." He paused a moment. "Are there lady lawyers?"

"I'd imagine so. On the way into town, how did the couple act? What kind of mood were they in?"

"That's the thing. I'm always chatty with the customers. What can I say?" He shrugged his shoulders. "I like to talk to people."

"Go on."

"Anyway, after about five minutes or so, I stopped being so chatty. I could tell they didn't want to talk. People are like that sometimes. They didn't want to converse, so I shut my trap. No cause to get someone wrapped around a wheel for nothing. These two, they were serious, like they'd just had a fight or something. I just shut up and drove them into town. They didn't say a word to each other all the way in."

"Anything else you can tell me?"

"Hey, you're the one asking questions and paying for the answers. I don't have anything else if you don't."

Eddie gave him a twenty and then went out to his car. He started it and turned on the heater. Then he looked at his notebook. What he had was worth the twenty bucks.

Lovingate had flown into Montreal on Monday, January 2, but she must have done it under a different name, probably another alias. Josette had checked with all of the airlines for a Lovingate and had come up empty-handed. The guy with her either had flown in with her, or more likely, had taken a cab to meet her, because he didn't have any luggage. And he wasn't wearing a disguise. However, when Lovingate checked into the Windsor a short time after she was dropped off, the guy was wearing a wig, a mustache, and glasses, and both of them were seen to be in a good mood. The next day, he killed her, if it was the same guy.

Lemaire said he dropped them off a half block from the Windsor. They must have gone in somewhere so the guy could put on his disguise. That meant that Lovingate knew about the disguise. Had they been in on something together, something that then went wrong? Had he been forced to kill her the next day and make it look like a suicide?

Were the killer and the victim both leading double lives?

Eddie pushed the gear into place and drove off.

——«•»——

That night, the professional from Ottawa arrived at the Windsor Hotel in a rented black Ford Fairlane Town Sedan. He hadn't rented it himself, of course; someone else had rented it for him. He, however, was one the who had changed the license plates from Ontario to Quebec before he left Ottawa.

The drive hadn't taken that long, but he was tired. He'd been on the go all day before making the drive, preparing everything he needed for the job and memorizing every last detail in the folder. Now he was more mentally than physically exhausted. A couple hours of sleep would do him well. Then he could proceed unimpeded with his task. He didn't require much sleep to function at the top of his game. As he'd told his boss, failure was never an option for him. He didn't want to consider what would happen to him if he failed, so he didn't.

He walked up to the check-in counter, carrying one suitcase. "I'd like a room, please," he said.

"Certainly, sir. Can I get a driver's license from you? How long will you be staying?"

He took out his wallet and placed his license on the countertop. "Let's say a week, but I may be checking out sooner. I'm a salesman, and you never know when the boss is going to call and send you somewhere else."

The clerk picked up the license and looked at it. "I quite understand ... Mr. Jacobson, Mr. Henry Jacobson. Oh, I see you're from Cincinnati. I had a guest who checked in a couple of weeks ago from there. I can imagine you have the same winters there as we have here."

"Yes, of course. It's cold with a lot of snow." He hated small talk.

The clerk wrote down the pertinent information and had Mr. Jacobson sign his name in the guest book.

"Here are your key and license, sir. Would you like a bellboy to carry your suitcase up?"

"No, thanks. I'll do it myself."

"Well then, I hope you enjoy your stay with us. Please call the desk if you have any requests. Room service is available until midnight and starts again at five in the morning for the early birds. The elevators are off to your left."

The man found his room on the fifth floor and took a long, hot shower. He was more awake now than he had been during the drive to Montreal. Now that he was getting his second wind, he ordered a sandwich from room service. When it came, he sat down at his hotel room's small desk, and while he was eating, he mentally prepared himself for the next day. He had everything in his head. He was forbidden to jot down notes in case he slipped up and left one in the room or somewhere else. That would be amateurish; he would never do something like that, because he was a trained professional.

The job had to be done as soon as possible, but he couldn't rush it and make mistakes. Even the best could slip up when pressed for time. Tomorrow he would survey the landscape, see where the target lived and worked, and get a sense of the target's work schedule. That in itself would be the most time-consuming part of the job and might take two or three days. This had to be done right. During that time, he would also be looking for the appropriate place where the accident would happen. If everything went as planned, he could be back in Ottawa on Tuesday or Wednesday—maybe even on Monday if he could pull it off in that time frame. His boss would certainly be impressed by that. He might even get a promotion out of it. If not, most assuredly he'd get a brilliant writeup in his folder, which he knew was as good as a promotion.

Notwithstanding, whenever he arrived back in Ottawa, Eddie Wade would be dead. From an accident.

Chapter 16
THE TICKING CLOCK

IT HAD BEEN NINETEEN DAYS SINCE ANNE Lovingate had been found dead in her room at the Windsor Hotel by the house detective, Nigel Hughes, and sixteen days since Eddie and Josette had taken on the case. Eddie had been doing the legwork—the analysis of the crime scene, the travel to St. Paul, some of the interviews, and keeping in touch with Jack Macalister. Josette had studied, answered the phone, and held the fort down. Both needed a Saturday diversion with absolutely no talk about work.

They were both engrossed in their books, Eddie lying on the couch, Josette sitting in the armchair, the two cats sleeping on top of the bookshelf.

Josette looked over her book at Eddie. "Still reading that Spillane novel?" she asked. "What was the name of it again?"

"*The Big Kill*." He shifted his position slightly, turning on his side. "I haven't picked it up in over a week, so I had to start all over again. Forgot what I read."

"What's it about?"

"Someone big got killed, something like that. I'll tell you when I find out."

"Hmm."

"You still reading about sex?"

"About women," she said, correcting him. "You should try reading it sometime. It might broaden your horizons about women."

He lowered his book and looked at her. "My horizons are too broad as it is. Eighty percent of my cases in the last eleven years have involved women in one way or another. They can cheat, lie, and kill as well as any man. How's that for equality of the sexes?"

"You're keeping score? Your mind has become tainted, dear husband. You ought to get out more and see how the other half lives."

"It's the job. If you're a private investigator for more than a day, your mind becomes tainted. Didn't I tell you that? I'm sure I did."

"All the more reason to get out and mingle with normal people."

"Show me a normal person, and I'll show you a criminal in the making. Who do you think criminals were before they were criminals? Just everyday normal people. That's why society will always need police departments, the Mounties, and private dicks. There's a steady supply; we'll never go out of business. You've entered a field where job security is so obvious that you don't even have to research it."

"You're making my point, lover boy. Most people are law-abiding citizens and never get in trouble. Those are the people you should mingle with more."

Eddie put his feet on the floor and sat upright. "Oh yeah? And just how do we tell them apart? Just when you lower your guard, just when you say this person is super-duper, or that person is a terrific guy, he hits you in the jaw with a right cross, followed by a left uppercut to the solar plexus."

"You can't go through life believing everyone is a potential criminal."

"Oh yes, I can, and I do. It keeps me one step ahead in the game. If I find out I'm wrong, well, that's fine and dandy. But if I'm right, I get to live another day to tell the story."

"What about me? Do you think I'm a potential bank robber or murderer?"

"You're way down on the list, baby, way down—even further down than me. We all have the potential. It's just a matter of degree. If the forces of nature converge at the right time, we all can become monsters."

"Jeez, I guess I should be grateful for that knowledge!"

"Listen, we should do something today—make the most of the day."

"Yes, good idea, but something where we're not freezing. It's below zero out there."

"How about a movie, and then we'll go out to a fancy restaurant? I'll even shine my shoes."

"I'll see what's playing," Josette said, putting her book down and picking up the Saturday paper.

Just then the phone rang. They both looked at each other.

"Don't you dare," Josette grinded out.

The phone rang three more times.

"It might be important," Eddie said, but he didn't dare make a move for it.

"I'm sure it is, but they can do without us for a day."

The ringing continued.

"Shit!" Josette said, and she went for it. "Hello ... Oh, hi ... Okay. Wow! ... Yep. I see ... Yes, absolutely ... Okay." Then she hung up. "That was Jack. He said the sketch of the guy is done, and there's a big break in the case."

"And?"

"He wanted to know if we could come and see him at police headquarters."

"What did you tell him?"

"I told him yes, absolutely."

"Okay, let's go."

———— «●» ————

Mr. Henry Jacobson from Cincinnati, Ohio, sat in his rented Ford Fairlane across the street from Eddie Wade's apartment on Saint-Urbain, his eyes glued to the front door of the building, smoking a cigarette. He didn't particularly like his new name, but he didn't think he'd have to use it much, mostly at the hotel. He expected to be back in Ottawa in three or four days with his mission completed, and that would be the end of Henry Jacobson. In the meantime, he'd just have to suffer through it.

He had gotten there early this morning, so he'd be sure not to miss his target. Today, and maybe for the next few days, he would be following Wade around, trying to get a sense of his schedule and scoping out appropriate sites for an accident. He had been here in Montreal several times before for extended stays and knew the downtown area fairly well, along with most of the east and west ends of the island. If he had to venture off the island to either the north or south shores, he'd probably have to ask for directions. He had passed through the south shore getting here, but it had been mostly a straight road, and he had simply followed the signs.

He leaned down to put his cigarette out in the ashtray, and when he looked up again, he saw his target coming through the door of the apartment building. He was with a woman. The file said nothing of a woman, and he wondered who she might be.

He watched them get into a car parked out front. The target made a U-turn and then drove straight down the street, going west. Mr. Henry Jacobson from Cincinnati followed behind at a safe distance. After several miles of driving on the same street, he thought that they might be going into town. The target then turned right onto Dorchester, drove for several more blocks, made another right turn and then a left turn a block away, and pulled up to a police station. Henry Jacobson drove past them but watched in the rearview mirror and saw them get out of the car and start toward the building. He continued for another block, made a U-turn, and came back, parking on the opposite side of the street and down away, so he had the front of the building in view.

His target was obviously conferring with the police. The woman with him could be another investigator on the case. Mr. Jacobson might have to act sooner than he had anticipated. He also might have to include the woman in the accident.

At the moment, the world abounded with possibilities.

———«●»———

Jack Macalister opened the bottom drawer of his desk and then looked over to Eddie and Josette sitting to the side of him. "A little morning nip, anyone?"

"My adorable husband here frowns on any of his apprentices partaking in alcoholic beverages before midafternoon. Says it not good for the concentration. I'm afraid I'll have to pass, but thanks anyway, Jack. Don't let me spoil your fun, though."

"As you know, Jack, I have only one apprentice, and she does whatever she damn well pleases. I'd like to think that I maintain a modicum of control over her, but I'd be kidding myself. Far be it for me to deprive her of a shot of whiskey. I'll take a rain check myself."

Macalister shrugged and then closed the drawer. He reached for a file and opened it. "Da Vinci said that because the photo was clear, he thought that he was pretty accurate with the face; however, he could only guess with the hair since the guy was wearing a wig. He decided to give him short hair for obvious reasons." He placed the file on the desk, facing Eddie and Josette. "This is what he came up with."

They both stared at it for a long minute; then they glanced at each other.

Before Macalister could say anything, Eddie beat him to the punch. "Okay, this'll be helpful. We'll see what we can do with it. You said you had something more—a break in the case."

Macalister leaned back in his chair, a wide grin spreading across his face. "Sometimes you have to chase down leads that go nowhere. You waste time and money and become frustrated. You start pulling at your hair and cussing everyone you come in contact with. You're about to fall over a precipice." He paused a moment. "And then there are times leads just fall in your lap like manna from heaven."

"Come on, Jack," Eddie said. "This is Saturday. The day will be over soon. This is playtime for Josette and me. We want to do something special today that doesn't concern business, like take in a movie and go eat out at a restaurant. Spit it out."

"If you want something special, I think I can give you two that right now. But I'm afraid it does concern the case."

"Spit it out," Eddie said again, "or we're leaving."

"Don't mind him, Jack," Josette said. "He's always peevish when he doesn't have enough coffee. He had only two cups this morning. He needs four more to reach anything that resembles a civilized state. Don't take it personally."

"You guys heard of the big fire at the Soviet embassy in Ottawa on New Year's Day?"

They both nodded.

"Apparently, it was caused by faulty wiring on the third floor. The embassy people wouldn't let the fire department into the building until after the fire had spread, and most of the building went up in flames. All the firemen could do was stand there in the freezing cold and watch the Russians carry out boxes, probably containing classified documents. At one point a fight broke out when several firemen tried to get into the building. Something like that."

Macalister went on to say that the press had arrived shortly after the fire began. A reporter from one of the Ottawa papers was watching near the front of the building, where the Russians were loading the boxes into cars. A file dropped out of one of the boxes. It went unnoticed, so he picked it up, folded it, and put it in his coat pocket. He thought he could get some kind of story out of it, besides the fire itself. Later that day at the office, he discovered what it was and called a friend who worked for the RCMP. It turned out to be something of massive importance. The file wasn't complete, but it contained a few names of Soviet KGB agents across Canada who were working as spies. The RCMP officer worked in the counterespionage department. "The Mountie sat on it until yesterday, deciding what to do about it. Last night he called me."

"Why did he call you?" Eddie asked.

"I'm getting to that. As I said, the file wasn't complete; after it was translated, only a handful of names were found to be in it. But there was a bio and picture of one particular Soviet agent named"—he picked up his notes and read from them—"Anastasia Alekseevna Nikandrova."

Macalister then told them the remarkable story he'd heard from the RCMP counterespionage officer. Before he died, Joseph Stalin had drawn up plans for Operation Duckpin. Only a handful of people knew about it, and even fewer were involved. Its mission had been to assassinate the president of the United States, Dwight D. Eisenhower. Stalin had handpicked Nikandrova to carry out the plan. She'd been planted in the United States in early 1953, three years ago. The assassination was to be carried out before the November elections this year. But then Stalin had suddenly died.

Last year Khrushchev had become aware of the plot and ordered it stopped. Nikandrova was recalled to Moscow, but she refused to go. She had received direct orders from Stalin himself, and she planned to carry them out. The KGB immediately began a search for her, but she had gone underground, and she changed her identity and location often. But they eventually found her. They assigned an agent in Montreal to draw her out. He and Nikandrova had done some training in Russia together, and she trusted him. He reassured her that all Moscow wanted to do was have her return so that they could reassign her. At that point, she was tired of being on the run. Without the resources and support she needed for the assassination, she relented. The agent then lured her to Montreal on the pretext of providing her with a safe extraction to Moscow. When she got to Montreal, he killed her on orders from the KGB. Apparently, she could no longer be trusted.

"It was all in the file in so many words," said Macalister. "The last name Nikandrova had used was Anne Lovingate. Ottawa contacted me because they knew we were working the murder. They don't know the name of the KGB agent who was assigned to kill her because the file wasn't complete, but his code name was Blackbird."

Eddie and Josette looked at each other in disbelief.

"Does the name Igor Gouzenko mean anything to you?" Macalister asked them.

"Wasn't he the Russian cipher clerk," Eddie asked, "who defected from the embassy about eight or nine years ago?"

"Correct. He sort of works with the counterespionage unit of the RCMP when they need him. They asked him if he thought the file was credible. Was the assassination plot even possible? He told them that it was not only possible but highly probable. At least, under Stalin it was. He said that

Khrushchev never would have followed through with a plot to assassinate the president of the United States."

"So we know who Lovingate was," Eddie said. "What about Blackbird?"

"No, we have no idea who he is, but most likely he's still somewhere in Montreal, working under some kind of cover. Montreal was his permanent assignment." Macalister paused briefly, then continued. "Regardless of who Lovingate was, she was murdered within the city limits of Montreal, and this is still my turf. You have a sketch now of what Blackbird might look like. I'm going to have copies made and give them out to my men with the orders not to be obvious about searching for him. We don't want to scare him off." He looked at both Eddie and Josette. "The guy is a KGB agent and dangerous. You still want to look for him? You won't have much time. I would expect the Mounties to be all over the city soon, screwing up the search."

"Need you ask?" Eddie said.

"If you find him, you'll get some good press. The city might even see fit to pay you for your time. They might even give Wade Detective Agency a shiny plaque to put on your wall. Catching a Soviet spy would be a big break for the department as well. The mayor would love it."

"Pay us for our time? I won't hold my breath."

"The Mounties won't like you working the case. They're very possessive about certain things. They could cause you some trouble."

"I had a run-in with them a few years back," Eddie said. "Those boys play rough, worse than the mob. Listen, how about a little shot before we leave?"

"Thought you'd never ask."

"Why in the hell would the Soviets name their operation Duckpin?"

"I posed that same question to the Mountie I talked with. He said that Eisenhower was given that nickname because he loved to play duckpin bowling, which has smaller pins and balls than those used in traditional bowling. Stalin must have thought it was a cute name."

"Wonderful," Eddie said.

They downed their shots of whiskey, and then Eddie and Josette left.

Outside, Eddie let the car idle to warm it up.

"Who would have thought that Anne Lovingate was a Soviet assassin, handpicked by Uncle Joe?" Josette asked. "I thought she was nothing more than just a woman who wanted to break up with her boyfriend."

"What did I tell you about women? They can be as ruthless as men."

Josette rubbed her hands together to warm them. "That sketch sure looks like someone we both know."

"I'm glad you didn't say anything to Jack when he showed it to us. The hair is different, but that face …"

"'Spit it out' is the phrase you're so fond of using lately, so spit it out!" said Josette. "It has Symeon Peters's name written all over it, doesn't it?"

"Yes, but don't get too excited, though. Sketches are simply sketches. They can look like hundreds of people. A lot of times, they look nothing like the criminals the police are trying to catch. Sketches have even put innocent people behind bars. I've seen it done. Like I said, a sketch is a sketch, something to help you along the way but not to be taken too seriously."

Josette twisted around and narrowed her eyes at him. The frown was undeniable. It said, *Who are you trying to convince? Me or you?*

"Okay, you got me, but listen. The guy's an asshole, but it doesn't necessarily make him a KGB agent."

But Eddie remembered what Gigi had said about Peters's sudden shift in behavior since the beginning of the year, the time frame in which Lovingate had been murdered. The sketch so resembled Peters that it was nearly photo-like, and it was hard to argue otherwise. Josette's eyes narrowed even more, and the frown continued to droop.

"Fine," Eddie said. "It seems bizarre, but we'll have to take a closer look at him."

———————»«●»«———————

Ottawa
The same day

Colonel Alexey Ivanovich Trifonov sat in his makeshift office with two of his agents at the temporary embassy that was primarily housing the Soviet commercial counselor on Blackburn Avenue. The former embassy had been a total write-off, costing the company that had insured it over 250,000 dollars.

The office was no more than a large broom closet, but somehow it had to function as the new communications room until the new embassy was built, which would be at least a year or more. The cipher machines sat along one wall, and the boxes of documents were piled high along the other walls. There was barely enough room to walk from the door to the small table at which they sat. How could the Kremlin expect Alexey to run the entire Canadian KGB operation out of this tiny room? Normally, he'd have six men monitoring the electronic equipment at any given time. Now, with three men in the room, it seemed impossible to squeeze in three more.

"I have an important assignment for you two," Alexey said. Then he reached for the bottle of vodka on the table and poured some into the glasses beside it.

They each picked up a glass and said together, "*За ваше здоровье!*" For your health!

The alcohol stung his mouth and throat as it went down, but Alexey did nothing to show his discomfort—not in front of his men. He was their leader, and leaders didn't flinch. Leaders remained stoic in the face of adversity. How could men look up to a leader who winced from a little vodka, who winced when ordering them into battle, who winced when ordering them to assassinate someone?

Alexey stared at Turgenev without expression for a full five seconds, which must have seemed like an eternity to the man. Then he did the same to Smirnov. The stares were important. They said, *I am your commander; I am your superior. You are my subordinate. I give you orders, and you follow them—unquestioningly. If you don't obey, you will pay for the disobedience with your life.* That was what the stares implied; that was how the stares were taken—always. Turgenev knew it; so did Smirnov.

"An important file went missing after the fire. What it contained does not concern you." He would not tell them that it was the Lovingate file because that would breach security. Besides, they didn't have to know; not even the Soviet ambassador was privy to that information. "I now know," he continued, "that it fell into the wrong hands. The code name of one of our Montreal agents was in there: Blackbird. My informant tells me that the RCMP and the Montreal police are actively searching for him. I sent Blackbird a message to return to Ottawa immediately." He paused a moment before continuing. "Unfortunately, I don't think he will comply. I believe Blackbird will either defect or go black."

He remembered hearing about Igor Gouzenko, a cipher clerk who had defected nine years before from the same embassy. He'd ruined their intelligence network by stealing top secret files and then passing them on to the RCMP. If

Blackbird defected, he could set Alexey's operation back five years with the information he had. Certainly, there was no evidence that Blackbird would do such a thing, but Alexey believed there was that possibility, and because he believed so, he could no longer trust him. Because he no longer trusted him, he had to act.

"I want both of you to drive to Montreal tonight and make Blackbird disappear. His cover name is Symeon Peters." He pushed an envelope across the table. "You'll find the pertinent information inside. Memorize it and then return it to me before you leave this building. Do you have any questions?" He had selected these two men because of their experience in making people disappear. They knew how to do it and had a vast array of methods at their fingertips. He knew that they wouldn't have questions, but he wanted to afford them the courtesy of asking.

Both men shook their heads.

Alexey poured more vodka into their glasses. "Then here's to your success," he said, raising his glass. As they drank, Alexey stared at them again over his glass. He was confident that his message was clear.

After the men left, Alexey poured himself another drink. He was a moderate drinker at the best of times, but for nearly the past two weeks, he had been hitting the bottle more than usual. Actually, the drinking had started before that, just after he received the order from the Kremlin. If only Anastasia had come in from the cold without hesitation, she would still be alive now, probably working in Moscow at KGB headquarters. But she had always been pigheaded, and because her file had gone missing, now Blackbird had to be eliminated at well.

Pigheaded was the right word. She had nearly been kicked out during the initial training phase of the KGB. She had wanted to do things her way. She definitely would have been thrown out of the program—75 percent of each class was rejected during the various training phases—had it not been for her immediate supervisor, who had seen some depth in her that he could exploit. But she had been headstrong and self-willed long before that.

Alexey remembered a time when they were but tender teenagers completely in love with each other. It was a beautiful winter day, and Anna—everyone called her Anna in those days —wanted to go tobogganing at their favorite spot in an isolated area near their town of Plyos. When the weather was good, hundreds of youngsters enjoyed themselves going down the gently sloping hills. But that day Anna felt more adventurous. There was a hill about a hundred meters away, but most of the kids stayed clear of it because it was full of trees all the way down to the bottom. Only the daring would venture onto that hill.

Anna was adamant; she wanted to try it out at least one time. Alexey tried to talk her out of it, telling her it was too dangerous. The hill was steep, and there were too many trees to dodge. Many kids had been badly hurt each winter. Anna wouldn't hear of it; she wouldn't listen. She even teased Alexey by calling him a little girl. Suddenly, Alexey's manhood was a stake, even though he was only sixteen. He relented.

Anna insisted she wanted to steer the toboggan, which would put her in the front, the most dangerous place should an accident happen. They argued again. If they were to do this, Alexey demanded to be in the front. And again, Anna won out.

The snow was slick, almost like a sheet of ice. The toboggan was gaining speed, and both of them felt exhilarated. Anna steered left, then right, expertly avoiding the thick trees. Again, she sheered left, missing a tree by mere inches, and then again she veered to the right, narrowly missing another. But when she did that, she suddenly saw a huge tree directly in front of them. They were going too fast at that point to turn. She had lost control. Before they knew it, the toboggan hit the tree, and Anna went over the front headfirst, directly into the tree. Alexey had seen it coming and grabbed her by the waist, but when he'd tipped himself over the side, hoping to take her with him, she had slipped out of his hands.

Alexey hurried himself up and went to Anna. She was lying there unconscious, her arms and legs thrown in awkward positions in the snow. Her chin was tucked down to her chest. Alexey's first thought was that her neck was broken. He knew from his first aid training that he shouldn't move her, but he had to get her to the medical clinic somehow. It would take him too long to leave her there and go for help. He had to place her on the toboggan without causing her further injury and then pull her back up the hill and onto the road and hope to find someone who could transport them to the clinic.

He got to the road just as a man in a horse-drawn cart was approaching them. The man stopped and helped Alexey lift the toboggan with Anna in it onto the cart. It was a short ride to the clinic. After a doctor examined her, which seemed to take hours, he told Alexey that Anna had a bad concussion, but she hadn't broken her neck. If Alexey hadn't brought her in when he had, she might have died. She'd be in the hospital for a least a month.

But the experience didn't deter Anna—before the winter was over, she returned to that same hill and tobogganed down it twice more successfully.

Anastasia was intelligent and brave and took risks. She became one of the best covert agents the KGB had, which was why Stalin came to know about her.

After receiving the directive from the Kremlin, and after he'd given the order to Blackbird to assassinate her, Alexey had gotten drunk in his apartment and stayed that way for the next day.

Now he picked up the bottle of vodka again and poured some more into his glass. Instead of drinking it, he placed his elbows on the table and buried his face in his hands. He whispered her name—"Anna"—but it came out more like a moan.

Everything had been going well since he had been posted to Ottawa as chief of the KGB operations in Canada years ago. Now it all seemed to be falling apart with this Lovingate ordeal. First, he'd had to send his best man to Montreal to eliminate an investigator who was getting too close to the truth. And now he had to send two more to take care of Blackbird. He knew that both missions were high-risk, but having his intelligence network in Canada exposed was an even higher risk.

He picked up the glass of vodka and gulped it down in one go. He was the most powerful man at the Soviet embassy, even more so than the ambassador himself. But he wondered just how long that would last.

The clock was ticking away on him too.

Chapter 17
A CHANGE IN DIRECTION

EARLY SUNDAY MORNING, JACK MACALISTER sat at his desk shuffling papers. That was all he seemed to do since his promotion in homicide. He could barely see the top of his desk; the paperwork formed mountains of various heights. He was a beat cop at heart and missed the action in the streets. Most of all, he missed the regular hours. Now all he did was make sure that the paperwork his men turned in to him was correct and direct murder investigations from his desk. He'd go on investigations himself on bigger cases, but for the most part, he spent his time at the helm in his office, making sure that the ship didn't sink. He worked late and on the weekends. His social life was nonexistent, and Molly was getting pissed at him because she rarely saw him anymore. But this was the life he had chosen to live, and he wasn't about to spend his time pissing and moaning about it.

He leaned back in his chair, put his hands behind his head and his feet on the desk, and wondered whether it was all worth it. He had joined the force after the war, following in his father's and grandfather's footsteps. Molly had been supportive and still was, but the job had evolved into something that was taking over his life. He didn't particularly care about himself, but it was unfair to impose this life on Molly. He knew it wasn't going to get any better. The further up the ladder he went, the more responsibilities he would have. Maybe if he could just walk a beat again, things would be different. But that was nonsense, and he knew it.

Just then, his door swung open, and a man wearing a heavy, dark-gray overcoat and a black felt hat with the brim pulled down to his eyebrows stepped in. He was tall, maybe six-three or six-four. He stood at the side of the desk and looked down at Macalister. He looked shady, menacing, like some of the jokers Macalister had arrested over the years. He could easily pass for an extortionist or a hitman.

Macalister stared at him. "Don't you knock before entering an office?" When the guy didn't answer right away, he sighed and then said, "Can I help you with something?"

"If you're Jack Macalister, you can. If not, you could tell me where he is."

Macalister still had his hands behind his head and his feet on the desk. Without changing positions, he said, "I'm Macalister. What do you need?"

"I'm Garrison Edward Meaghers, a federal agent from Ottawa. You talked to one of my men recently. I need to clarify a few points with you."

Macalister jerked himself into a more suitable position in the chair: shoes planted squarely on the floor, hands on the top of his desk. "Sit down. I assume you're referring to the Lovingate case. I thought my conversation with your guy was pretty clear."

Meaghers dragged a chair from the wall and sat down. "Not clear enough," he said. "He didn't know that we were taking the case over. This is a federal case involving foreign espionage. What he told you was classified information. He shouldn't have."

"What agency are you with exactly? There are so many of them, I can't keep them straight." He chuckled a bit and then picked up a pencil and bit into it.

Meaghers saw nothing funny to chuckle about. "I head the counterespionage unit of the RCMP." As an afterthought, Meaghers reached into his pocket for his wallet. He showed Macalister his badge and identification card and then replaced his wallet. "What you learned about the case, you're going to have to unlearn. I need to control the flow of information. You're not on the flow chart, so you can't divulge anything you know about it." He leaned in a bit. "Am I making myself clear?"

He was indeed making himself clear to Macalister. What was also becoming clear was that Meaghers was an asshole. The feds and the local police had never been bosom buddies, but they did tolerate one another and show a modicum of respect whenever they worked cases together. This guy seemed to be a jerk.

"I understand," Macalister said. "I assume you need something more from me, since you came all the way from Ottawa."

"You're a smart guy, Macalister—I mean like intelligent."

"Thanks for the clarification," Macalister said. It sounded like a wisecrack, but he couldn't be sure. "What do you need?"

Macalister decided that he was going to cooperate with the agent. He shouldn't have been investigating the case in the first place, but murder was murder, and it had occurred in his city. Now he could walk away from it with a clear conscience—one less murder case to investigate. He was glad that he had no choice in the matter. Let the feds have it. Maybe they could even find the Russian who'd killed Lovingate. Macalister hadn't been able to. He had a multitude of other cases that would keep him busy and his wife cranky at him.

"I need everything your investigation turned up, every little detail. Besides that, I need your personal input—your thoughts on the case, your speculations on where it might go. I'll be frank with you, Macalister. I hate to say this, but we have no idea who we're looking for. We know this guy is a KGB agent assigned here in Montreal and that his code name is Blackbird, but that's about all. We don't know what he looks like or what his cover is. We were hoping your investigation would provide some of that."

Macalister sensed a little humility trickling out of Meaghers and realized he was holding a better hand than he thought. Macalister would deal the cards from the top of the deck, but he decided to keep one hidden: Eddie Wade. How could he tell this federal agent that someone who wasn't on the police force, a mere civilian and a goddamn gumshoe at that, was a major player in the investigation?

For the next two hours, Macalister brought Meaghers up to speed with what they'd discovered. He turned over the complete Lovingate file, including the list of people who had called in when Macalister's team was trying to identify the woman. Additionally, he included the picture of the disguised Russian taken at the Windsor Hotel as well as the sketch of him without the disguise. All the while, Meaghers looked amazed by the work they had done.

"You boys have been busy," Meaghers said. "I'm impressed. Can't say that about many things. Your cooperation is greatly appreciated."

Macalister resisted the temptation to say that the man responsible for the majority of this information was a private dick.

"If we can catch this guy," Meaghers continued, "we may be able to cut some kind of deal with him if he exposes other KGB agents or if he has other good intelligence to share with us."

"You're saying he could go free? How about the murder he committed?"

"Oh, he won't be going free; I can guarantee you that. But we'll pull the hangman's noose off the table to get him to cooperate. You'd be surprised how fast people start talking like a chatty parrot. If it reaches that point, all he'll be concerned with is staying off death row."

Macalister was skeptical. He knew that the feds cut deals with murderers that set them free for the right kind of information. It didn't happen often, but it did happen. He decided to let it go, though. This was no longer his case.

After they shook hands and said their goodbyes, Macalister picked up the phone and called Eddie. "Meet me at the Lion's Den in thirty minutes," he said. "We need to talk."

———«❂»———

"You're off the case."

"Whaddya mean I'm off the case?"

"You're off the case, just like it sounds. I should say, we're off the case. The feds are taking it over."

"What feds?"

"The federal government—the Mounties. The guys with the funny hats. Can't say I'm sorry. They can probably catch the killer faster than we can. They have more resources."

Eddie scratched his forehead, pushing his hat further back on his head. He couldn't believe what Macalister had just told him.

Bruno walked down from the other end of the bar where he'd been cleaning. It was still early, and the Lion's Den wasn't officially open yet. "Are you guys going to order something, or are you just going to warm those stools you're sitting on? It may not look like it, but I'm a very busy man."

"I'm okay," Macalister said. "But because you're so busy, I'll leave you a tip."

"A tip from one of Montreal's finest? Your humor overwhelms me." He turned to Eddie, who simply stuck out his hand like a traffic cop.

"Okay," Bruno said. "I'm opening in an hour. If you want to leave before that, hunt me down, and I'll unlock the door. I'll be somewhere on the premises. Between a cop and a private detective, you should be able to find me. Put your heads together—you should be able to do it."

Eddie turned to Macalister. "Why didn't we just meet at my office?"

"I wouldn't put it past the feds to tail me, see if I lied to them. I did, as a matter of fact. I told the agent everything we know about the case and gave him the picture of the murderer at the Windsor and the sketch of him without the disguise. But I didn't mention your name. Meaghers—that's the guy who came to the office this morning; he wanted to sound official, so he used all three of his names—anyway, he would have a shit fit if he knew that you were the lead investigator on the case. He was sort of an asshole to begin with, and I didn't want to throw gas on the fire. Turned out he loosened up a little the longer he stayed."

"Was that what I was, a lead investigator?"

"Something like that. Come to think of it, I think I was, but you did all the legwork."

"So it's suddenly over?"

"I'm afraid so."

"And you gave him everything on the case that we had?"

"I had no choice. They're the feds, and it's their case. If he found out later that I withheld information, he'd raise holy hell, and I'd be up shit's creek without a paddle."

"What about me?"

"That's our little secret."

Eddie had an ace in the hole—his own little secret. He hadn't told Macalister that he thought he knew who the killer was. Hell, everyone in law enforcement withheld information at some point.

"Well, that's it then," Eddie said.

"Yeah, that's it then. The game's over."

Eddie nodded, as if in agreement. *It's not over yet*, he thought. *We're just going into extra innings.*

―――――――――――

After Macalister left, Eddie returned to his office next door. Josette was studying at her desk. He poured two cups of coffee, grabbed a pipe off the rack on his desk and filled it, and then explained what Macalister had told him.

"So it looks like we have two options," he said. "One, we could go to the feds and tell them that we believe Symeon Peters might be the Soviet agent who killed Lovingate."

"Nikandrova," she said, correcting him. "Her name was Anastasia Alekseevna Nikandrova."

"You remembered that?"

"I remember everything, so you better watch your step. What's the second option?"

"Amazing," he said, and then puffed a few times on his pipe. "Anyway, option two is that we continue with the case and look further into Peters ourselves."

"Option one would be the right thing to do. I see nothing wrong with that. It would be the morally correct thing to do. We might even be legally required to hand over the information about Peters, but I'm not certain about that. There's just one problem with option one."

"I think I know what you're going to say, but go ahead."

"If Symeon Peters is our guy, then he covered his tracks well. We know that for a fact. That's his cover name, of course. I'm dying to know what his real name is. Something unpronounceable, I figure. He must have had language training in Moscow, because that English accent of his is spot-on. His cover is obviously solid. If the feds arrest him, indict him, and then put him on trial, his lawyer could introduce exculpatory evidence that could set him free. That's a distinct possibility. We just don't have enough hard evidence yet for a conviction."

"Jeez, you really have been studying that manual. You sound like a prosecuting attorney. Go on."

"So do you agree with me about all that could happen if we go with option one?"

"Yep."

"Then the only option left is the second one. We find enough direct evidence to link him to Nikandrova and convict the bastard of murder."

"*Bastard*? You're starting to sound like a gumshoe now."

Josette indeed had a good mind, and she was learning the business with amazing speed. But she was only an apprentice and therefore inexperienced. Eddie needed to remind her of a few finer points in investigations.

"We're assuming that Symeon Peters is a KGB agent. He very well might be, and if he is, that means he's a spy and a professional killer. Things do seem to point in that direction. If we're right about that, he knows all the tricks of the trade, and he's used to cleaning up after himself. Look at the crime scene at the Windsor. He didn't leave behind a single thing to identify himself. Besides, he's already killed at least one person, and we can assume that wasn't the first time. If we're right about him, then he's a dangerous man."

"Yeah, Eddie, I've considered all that. That's why the decision should be yours to make. You're the one who's going to be doing all the work. I'm just an unlicensed apprentice."

"But you're my wife, and we're partners. We make decisions together. What I do affects you. You have a say in this too."

Josette got up and paced the room. Eddie sat back and poured a couple of shots and smoked his pipe. He had already known what he wanted to do before he and Macalister had ended their conversation. But his agency was no longer a one-man show. He had a wife and partner to consider; he had to involve her. It had to be *their* decision.

Going after evidence to convict Peters of the murder wasn't going to be easy. But even the most skillful, brilliant criminal didn't operate flawlessly. There was always at least one piece of evidence somewhere that would nail him. Getting to that evidence could sometimes be arduous, time-consuming, and dangerous. That was the reason so many murders went unsolved. Eddie realized that he could be spinning his wheels, and what was worse, he wasn't getting paid for his time. Nevertheless, this was a once-in-a-lifetime case for him. He'd helped put criminals behind bars before—plenty of them—but never a Soviet agent and assassin. Hell, he'd even pay to work this case.

Josette stopped pacing and sat down. They each picked up a shot glass, hoisted it in the air, made a silent toast, and downed it.

"Okay, baby doll," Eddie said. "What say you?"

"I say full steam ahead."

"I'll drink to that ... again."

———«◉»———

Even with the engine running and the heater turned up, Mr. Henry Jacobson from Cincinnati, Ohio, was cold. He could do with a strong cup of hot coffee right now. Better yet, he could do with a couple of shots of vodka. That would warm him up. Doing surveillance in the wintertime in a cold climate was never fun, even while sitting in a warm car. It never seemed to be warm enough.

There was a lull, so he mentally reviewed what he'd seen. He had a good memory, but he wished he could write some things down once in a while just for the convenience. He had been parked down the street from Eddie Wade's apartment when he saw him exit the building and walk to the Lion's Den. Wade had knocked on the door, so the bar must not have been open. Jacobson had then moved the car up to the church for a better view. Minutes later, another man had driven up to the bar, parked outside, and gone to the door. Like Wade, he knocked and was let in.

Wade must have been meeting this guy there. The guy looked as if he could have been a plainclothes cop. It made sense. So did the meeting place if Wade wanted to avoid his office or apartment. After approximately forty-five minutes, the guy left the bar and drove away in his car. Five minutes later, Wade left the bar and went to his office next door. Mr. Henry Jacobson could only speculate as to their conversation, but if he were a betting man, and he was, he'd put his money on the Lovingate case.

He had considered the possibility of shortening this mission by a few days and killing the target sooner rather than later. Jacobson didn't know what was being said between Wade and the police, and Wade was meeting with them frequently. The meeting today had looked secret, and that wasn't good.

Yes, he would kill the target tomorrow. That would put an end to all his meetings with the police. If it were Jacobson's choice, he would just shoot him and be done with it. He already had plenty of opportunities to do so. But it wasn't his choice. His boss had said to make it look like an accident, so an accident it would be. It would take a little more time, but he had the perfect accident planned.

And tomorrow night he'd be back in Ottawa when it happened.

Chapter 18
THE DROP

GARRISON EDWARD MEAGHERS HAD THREE names and made use of them to the best of his abilities.

Even before starting his career in law enforcement, as a third-year student at the University of Toronto, he had begun experimenting with his name. He had tried various ways of writing it, even going so far as to leave out his middle name completely. He had settled on G. Edward Meaghers, and for a time, he'd been satisfied with the truncated first name. He had gotten the idea from his American hero, the G-man J. Edgar Hoover. However, it was short-lived for two reasons. First, his fellow students thought he was being high and mighty and even resorted to mocking him. They started calling him J. Alfred Prufrock after reading the poem one day in English class. It became a big issue on campus. He couldn't have that.

And then there was Hoover himself. Meaghers had understood why—or at least he had made an educated guess as to why—Hoover used the initial rather than spelling out his first name. His first name was John. Besides sounding too biblical in the general sense of the word, he shared the name with John the Baptist and John Dillinger. Things hadn't gone well for those fellows at all, so he was right to chop off three of the letters. He was, after all, the head of the FBI. The name John would have made him seem weak.

When Meaghers went back to the drawing board, he realized that "Garrison," however, didn't have that issue. Furthermore, Meaghers liked the initial sound the name made: the hard consonant *G* followed by a vowel. He had done some research at the library and discovered that the sound was called the voiced velar plosive and was pronounced with the back part of the tongue against the soft palate. The sound it produced was strong and commanding. As an added benefit, the name itself conjured up the image of military troops stationed in a fortress, ready to defend, protect, and secure. It was close enough to what he was after and suitable for the Royal Canadian Mounted Police, to which he aspired. His fellow students approved. From then on, he had decided to use all three of his names.

Meaghers sat at a round table in his room at the Laurentian Hotel, his temporary command center, with four of his field agents: Jones, Williams, Walker, and Davies. After giving them an extensive briefing on their mission, he assigned them in pairs to follow up on the interviews initially done by the Montreal police. He told them they were looking for a dangerous Soviet KGB agent who had already killed. It was worth the time and trouble to interview these people again. They might have some information that they didn't know they had. He wanted the Russki, and he wanted him alive.

When they left and he was alone, he took out the bottle of whiskey he'd brought with him from Ottawa and poured some into one of the hotel glasses. He knocked it back and then poured another. He wanted to get this Russian agent, but he had to have him alive. He couldn't very well interrogate a dead KGB agent. No doubt he was part of a network. Meaghers knew that if he could capture the spy, he could turn him. He'd done it before; he could do it again. He knew exactly what to say and what goodies to dangle in front of his face. He'd offer the Russian the stars and the moon if he'd reveal his network. Forget the murder Blackbird had committed. Lovingate/Nikandrova wasn't Canadian. She had been just another Soviet agent—one less to worry about. The more they killed each other off, the better, as long as Meaghers had a live one for himself. Even if Blackbird was stuck up to his neck in Soviet ideology, Meaghers knew that once he started dangling the Canadian way of living, the big cars and big apartments, even a house of his own, things that only the top echelon of the Communist Party could afford back in Russia, Blackbird wouldn't be able to resist the temptation. In Canada, he would have freedom for the first time in his life; back home in the Soviet Union, he would continue to be in the grip of the party. Meaghers knew that if Blackbird returned home, all he would have were a few rubles in his pocket, an apartment the size of a Canadian clothes closet, a car that wouldn't start in the winter, and a chest full of glorious Soviet medals.

Not that Blackbird would ever see the likes of his motherland again anyway if Meaghers caught him. He would make it simple for the Russian: talk and live the good life on Canadian soil, or remain silent and drop six feet from the gallows with a noose around his neck. Meaghers felt those were reasonable options. He didn't feel the least guilty about lying to Macalister. If Blackbird cooperated and provided solid Soviet intelligence to the RCMP, Meaghers would forget about Lovingate's murder. That was the way things worked.

Besides all the Russian intelligence Meaghers would acquire if he captured Blackbird, it would also be a boost to his career. His position as chief of counterespionage was beneficial in its own right, but Meaghers had long ago set his eyes on something higher. He didn't want sideway promotions—what good were they? They were essentially all the same with the same pay, regardless of the department. He wanted vertical promotions. At the very top was the position of commissioner. Breaking up a Soviet network of spies would be a big step closer to that.

He tipped the glass back and began to doze on the bed. Capturing Blackbird and maybe a half dozen or a dozen other Soviet spies would put his name on the front pages of every paper in the country—and probably in the Western world—and keep it there for some time. Everyone would know the name Garrison Edward Meaghers.

———«o»———

The night was brutal.

At midnight, the temperature had dropped to minus twenty degrees Fahrenheit. Blackbird had parked his car at the corner of Avenue Papineau at Ontario East and was walking toward the southeast edge of La Fontaine Park. He had only a block to walk, but it seemed to be taking an eternity. He was wearing the parka that he had bought at an army surplus store when he first arrived in Montreal. It had a three-quarter-length sage-green silk and nylon outer shell and was padded with a wool blanket type of material. He had zipped the hood up, leaving only a small opening from which to see out. In spite of that, the wind ripped and cut into him like a homicidal maniac slashing into his victim with a knife, leaving him feeling maimed, wasted, and weak. Everything was ripe for him to find a suitable place to lie down, shut his eyes, and slip deep into the abyss of unconsciousness, if he so willed it. It would be a resolution for all of his problems. At least that option would be available to him for the next fifteen or twenty minutes.

He stopped at the edge of the park and looked around, trying to get his bearings. The tip of his nose was numb. The drop site wasn't far away, that much he knew, but the area looked different in the winter. There wasn't a single soul around, which was good, just as he'd planned it, but he suddenly felt alone and isolated, not only physically but emotionally. He was on shaky ground with Gigi and wondered where the relationship might go. Being alone in the world and not being able to tell another human his innermost thoughts was a terrible thing. Not that he had ever confided much in Gigi. All he'd told her were lies, mostly. More accurately, all he had told her was the cover story developed by the KGB for Symeon Peters. At times, he had been indifferent and unsympathetic toward her—even dispassionate. Now he could use some of the warmth and passion she often bestowed on him.

He turned right and continued on, the snow cracking under his boots. He was making a slow go of it. His body was moving as if it were freezing as he walked. His toes and his gloved fingers were ready to break off. He was risking severe frostbite, but there was nothing he could do. There was a message at the drop site that he had to get. He should have gotten it days before, but the time hadn't been right. There were many trees on either side of him, and they all looked the same to him: gelid, raw, rime-covered, and naked, a formation of winter corpses. No matter—he was looking for only one of them.

He slowly plodded on until he saw in the glow of an overhead park light an X marked in chalk at the base of a tree, just above the snow. He stopped before it and looked around him. Again, he saw no one. Who would be crazy enough to be out in this weather besides him? He stepped off the path and its padded-down snow and sank down five or six inches. With his gloved hand, he began clearing the snow away from the base of the tree directly under the X. Soon, he came upon an envelope wrapped in a cellophane bag. He picked it out of the snow and placed it in one of the pockets of his parka. He was eager to read it then and there but feared what it might say.

It would have to wait. He kicked the snow around the base of the tree with his boot and then walked around the immediate area, to leave the impression that some kids had been playing there, before returning to the path.

Back at his car, he started the engine and sat for a minute, to let the car warm up a bit before he began driving. The windows fogged up immediately, so he took a rag out of the glove compartment that he kept for that purpose and tried to use it to clear them. Useless. The fog had frozen immediately, and he didn't have a scraper. He could, however, see slightly out the windshield. It would have to do. In five or ten minutes, the defroster would kick in, and he would be able to see better.

He drove up Papineau and took a left turn onto Sherbrooke going west. After a mile or so, the car was warming up, and he felt a little better, but he was still cold down to his bones. He turned left again at Atwood, drove another block, made a U-turn at the intersection of Lincoln, and pulled up to his apartment building.

Once inside, he sat down on the couch. He pulled his hood off but kept his parka on. He was still shivering. You'd think that a Russian would be used to the cold, especially one who had trained in the army in cold-weather combat tactics, but not Blackbird; he hated the cold.

He had served in an airborne infantry unit during the war. Immediately after the war, he had joined the security services. He had undergone extensive English language training for five years and learned the British dialect to perfection, along with cultural training. In 1951, he had been posted to Canada as a British immigrant, using documents prepared by the KGB. He'd gotten a job right away in Montreal as an accountant with the firm of Fitchburg, Sterling, and Rycroft. His mission was to sit tight, blend in, and wait for an assignment. But no assignments came, and he felt that all his talent in espionage was being wasted. Had they forgotten about him? If he had wanted to become an accountant, he could have done so in Moscow as a civilian. Then, when he finally had gotten an assignment, it had been to kill a fellow KGB officer. That had left him with a profound sense of disappointment, because he had known the woman and had gone through some of his training with her. Nevertheless, he had obeyed the order down to every last detail.

He reached into the pocket of his parka and pulled out the cellophane bag containing the message. He set it on the table in front of him and then picked up a bottle of vodka and poured some into a glass. He knocked it back and felt the burning sensation as the vodka went down. It felt good; he felt warm inside.

He removed the message from the bag, tore the envelope open, unfolded the single sheet of paper, and read:

> O blackbird! sing me something well:
> While all the neighbours shoot thee round,
> I keep smooth plats of fruitful ground,
> Where thou may'st warble, eat and dwell.
> Alfred, Lord Tennyson

The message was in code and from his handler, Colonel Trifonov, code-named Tennyson. The message had been prearranged years before and would be used only if something happened that would necessitate Blackbird going to Ottawa and finding safety within the Soviet embassy compound. The embassy was, in fact, Soviet territory, immune from Canadian laws. The Canadian authorities would not be able to arrest him for any reason once he was safely inside.

Blackbird was confused. He read the message again. Why were they telling him to go to Ottawa? He wasn't in trouble, and his cover hadn't been broken. Why then? Could it have to do with his recent assassination of Nikandrova? It had gone off perfectly. He had left nothing in the hotel room that would identify him. Then it dawned on him—the file that had gone missing after the embassy fire. His name must have been in it after all.

Now the message was clear beyond doubt. They wanted him in Ottawa not to protect him, but to kill him.

He was done—finished. An exposed operative was a liability, not to mention an embarrassment. If the Canadian government captured him, he could trade Soviet intelligence for his freedom. Colonel Trifonov would never allow that to happen. Blackbird remembered Igor Gouzenko, who had defected the previous decade in Ottawa. He had caused a scandal and done irreparable harm to the Soviet mission in North America. Blackbird had always considered himself a loyal member of the Communist Party. He was a Russian, a Soviet, through and through. The thought of being a traitor and defecting was abhorrent to him. How could Trifonov ever think he would do such a thing?

But here he was. Trifonov must have concluded that there was a chance that Blackbird would defect, and he was not going to take any chances on someone who was exposed. Blackbird had never thought he'd be in this position, so expendable, so he had never thought about what he would do. *Those rotten bastards*, he thought, *both Trifonov and the Kremlin.* He had given his life to his country, and what did he get in return? A death sentence! *Damn it!* What was he going to do?

He picked up the bottle of vodka again, his hand shaking, and poured more into his glass. He drank half of it and set the glass down. He read the message again. It was no use. He came to the same conclusion as before: he was marked. He was a dead man. One thing he was certain of: he wouldn't be going to Ottawa voluntarily. He was late in getting the message, by a couple of days. They would be expecting him soon, maybe today, maybe tomorrow. They would not wait long before sending men to get him. His time was running out. He had to do something, but he didn't know what. He had to remain calm and think this through. He finished the vodka in his glass and poured another one.

He had to escape. Crossing the border into the United States would be the easiest and safest way. He could get through with just his Canadian driver's license. Whatever he decided to do, he needed to do it quickly, but he had to appear as if nothing was wrong. He'd have to stick to his routine as closely as possible in case they were keeping an eye on him now. How much time did he have? He didn't know—maybe a day or two at the most. When he didn't show up in Ottawa, they'd send a team to get him. Maybe he should send Trifonov a telegram telling him that he'd be delayed. That would give him some extra time to make his escape. No, that wouldn't work. Trifonov would know something was up and come after him faster.

Yes, he should go to the States. He would be safe there, at least safer than he would be in Canada. It was a big country, and the cities were jammed with people. Maybe he'd go to New York and then, after a time, to South America. They'd never find him there. Right now, he had to stay calm and not do anything rash.

He got up and went to the closet in his bedroom. He opened the door and pushed aside his hanging clothes and some large boxes on the floor. He reached down for a metal box about the size and shape of a fishing tackle box. He opened the lid and pulled out a revolver and a box of rounds. In the five years he'd been here, never once had he needed a gun. He had gotten it when he first arrived in Montreal as protection against street criminals in the city or in case his cover was blown and he got in a tight situation with the authorities that he couldn't get out of by other means. It was the means of last resort. Over time, he had almost forgotten he had it. Now he needed it as protection from his own people.

His hands were shaking as he put six cartridges into the chambers. He closed the cylinder and put the box of ammo into the pocket of his parka. He then went back to the couch and sat down with the revolver in his hand on his lap. He had to come up with a solid plan of escape.

How was he going to leave Montreal without arousing anyone's suspicion? He'd have to assume he was being watched.

And when?

Chapter 19
WHEN THINGS GO WRONG

ON MONDAY MORNING, BOTH EDDIE AND
Josette had gotten up early, fed the cats, had a light breakfast,
and decided to have their coffee at the office to discuss
strategy.

"As the situation stands," Eddie said, puffing away on
his pipe, "we have no direct evidence linking Peters to the
murder. That's a big problem—a major one, even."

"What about the cab driver, Leo Lemaire? Couldn't he
testify that he picked up Peters and Lovingate at the airport
and drove them to the Windsor Hotel the day before the
murder? And then there's your friend Angelo Mancini, who
saw a man running out the Windsor at the loading dock and
taking off a disguise around the time she was murdered. That
would link Peters to the photograph of him in disguise with
Lovingate when she checked into the hotel."

"I'm afraid that wouldn't hold up in court. It's all
circumstantial evidence. There's no proof that it was Peters
whom Angelo saw. And the cab driver might be able to identify
Peters as the person accompanying Lovingate, but that doesn't
prove he killed her. With the lack of forensic evidence from

the hotel room, there's no way the police could get a warrant for his arrest."

"So what we need is solid direct evidence—"

"That proves beyond reasonable doubt that Peters committed the murder."

"How are we going to get that?"

"When I find out, baby," he said with a wink and a nod, "you'll be the first to know."

"What are you planning to do today?"

"I'm planning on sitting here at my desk, smoking my pipe, drinking coffee, then switching to whiskey at the appropriate time, and thinking about how we're going to avoid having a judge dismiss the case against Peters for lack of evidence. Didn't I tell you that private investigators spend half of their waking hours just sitting and thinking? I'm sure I did."

"Aren't you getting ahead of yourself? Last I heard, there is no case against Peters."

"There will be, and when there is, we don't want a judge to throw it out, which means we've got to have irrefutable evidence—"

"I know, I know—beyond reasonable doubt. While you're doing that, I'm meeting up with Gigi for coffee in an hour, so I'll need the car. But I need to do a few errands first." She walked over to the coatrack and started to put on her coat.

"Listen, I think you should tell her to stay clear of Peters," Eddie said.

"She'll want to know why. What do I tell her?"

"You'll think of something. Tell her he's got a bad case of leprosy. Tell her it's infectious."

"Leprosy it is then. Should I tell her anything else?"

"No. Absolutely not."

Her eyes caught the shoulder of Eddie's overcoat hanging beside her on the rack. "What happened here?" she said, fingering his coat.

Eddie craned his neck to see what she was talking about. She was looking at the spot where a bullet had ripped through the shoulder of his coat that night in St. Paul, narrowly missing him. He had forgotten to get it fixed when he got back and hadn't wanted to mention the incident to Josette. He still didn't.

"Must have caught it on a nail or something. Oh, I forgot," he said, changing the subject. "Can you take a cab today? I may need the car in case Jack calls and wants us back on the case—officially, that is. We can write the cab off on our taxes as a business expense."

"But it's personal, not business."

He looked at her for a long moment. "And your point is ..."

⸻

Thirty minutes later, Josette was racing across town to Atwater in a taxi. The driver was an old fart and knew the city like the back of his hand. He'd taken some shortcuts, so he pulled up to Josette's destination in no time flat. She paid him, gave him a tip, and got out.

She looked around and saw a phone booth on the corner. She pulled the collar up on her coat and walked the quarter of a block to the phone. It was freezing cold. Inside the booth, she dropped a dime in the slot and dialed Symeon Peters's number. She let it ring ten times and then hung up. Good. He must be at work.

She walked back to the Atwater apartment building and went inside. She found Peters's second-floor apartment, then took out her pick and wrench from her purse and went to work on the lock. If Eddie knew what she was about to do, he'd have a coronary.

A few months earlier, Eddie had surprised her with flowers and a gift. There was no particular occasion, but

Eddie had decided that if she was going to be an investigator, she needed to know how to overcome possible obstacles, like locks. He had presented her with her own set of picks. He also had given her instructions and then let her practice on their own apartment lock as well as the lock on their office door. After practicing for a week or so, she'd had it down to thirty seconds. It was all in the fingertips and ears.

She opened the door slowly a few inches and then listened for a full minute. After deciding it was clear, she walked in and closed the door behind her. Eddie had told her during one of his training sessions to always lock the door behind her in case someone came back while she was inside. If the door was left unlocked, it would alert the person that something wasn't right. She locked the door behind her.

She stood with her back to the door and looked around the apartment. She felt strange doing this. She had never done anything like this before. She felt out of place and nervous. What if Peters came home and caught her there? What could she possibly tell him that would justify her breaking into his apartment? She had no answer for that. She should have thought about that earlier, before she decided to do something as foolish as this. She could still pull out—leave before something disastrous happened. No, she was here, Symeon Peters was at work, and this might be her only opportunity to find something that would link him to the murder. She didn't know what that might be, but she was certain she'd know it if she found it.

The apartment was tidy, which surprised her. She had been expecting a mess; Peters was, after all, a bachelor. She decided to start looking in the living room. She walked carefully to the couch, making sure not to make any noise. If there was evidence of his crime, he might have hidden it somewhere. She removed the cushions and ran her hand along the inside edges of the couch. Nothing. She replaced the cushions and then looked underneath. Again, nothing.

She noticed a door near the entrance. She went over and opened it. Inside the closet were winter boots and a parka. She went through the pockets, on both the outside and inside. Nothing. There was nothing else in the closet.

She went to the small dining room table and looked underneath the top. Then she went to a desk in the corner and sat down. There was only a cup containing pencils and pens and a pair of scissors on the desktop. There were three drawers along the right side, and she opened the top one first. It was empty, not even a scrap of paper. So were the second and third drawers. She thought that highly unusual. The apartment was so clean and contained so few things that it almost appeared as if no one was actually living here.

She decided to leave the kitchen for last and went into the bedroom. This was different. The bed was unmade, clothes were hanging off a chair, and socks and underwear were balled up in a corner. At least it looked like Peters was actually living here. She looked at her watch; she'd been in the apartment for twelve minutes. Eddie had told her always to keep track of time and limit herself, no matter what. He'd also told her that the first thing she should do when breaking into a strange place was check for another exit, another way out. She had forgotten that until now. Oh well, it was too late for that. She decided to give herself another ten minutes and then leave, whether she found anything or not.

It was strange, she thought, for Eddie to have taught her these things, given that he was so against her breaking into any place. By teaching her all this, had he been giving her his tacit approval? She didn't know, but she was well aware that he wouldn't be pleased with her now.

She looked under the bed and then pulled out the drawers in the nightstand. There were two of them, and they were both stuffed with books and magazines. She looked around the room for a closet and found it to her left. She walked over to it and opened the door. It was messy. The clothes hanging up were tightly packed, and there were shoes and boxes on the floor. There were too many things for such a small closet. She didn't have time to go through each pocket of every shirt and pants, so she shoved them aside and moved the boxes out of the way. This exposed a metal box on the floor, which she reached down and picked up by the handle. It looked like a tackle box, and she wondered whether Peters fished. She brought it out into the light and opened the lid. She immediately saw an American passport. She picked it up and beneath it found a fake mustache, glasses, and a wig at the bottom of the box. She opened the passport and stared into the face of Anne Lovingate. There were some things sticking out between the pages. One was Lovingate's Minnesota driver's license, and another was a folded piece of paper. She unfolded the paper and was about to read it when she heard the front door open. She froze in place. Her breathing stopped. There was dead silence.

Symeon Peters was back.

Later that day, Garrison Edward Meagher and his four agents gathered around the table in his makeshift command post as if the table were a cauldron bubbling up with anticipation. It had been a long day. Each man had been out in the freezing weather following up on the interviews that the police had already conducted. They were tired, they hadn't eaten all day, and all they wanted to do was go to bed.

"Let's make this quick, gentlemen," Meaghers said. "What do you have here?"

Jones was first to say something. "Nothing. Absolutely nothing. Most of the people I interviewed were crackpots. They should all be in a fuckin' loony bin. What's with these people in Quebec?"

Meaghers looked at the others; they all nodded in agreement.

"The same with me," Meaghers said. "Not a goddamn lead in the bunch. Several of them mentioned the name Eddie Wade. Said they already gave their statements to him. Was anyone else told the same?"

Walker and Davies answered in the affirmative.

"Okay then," Meaghers said. "I think it'll save us some time if I have a talk with Wade myself. Maybe he has something we can use. I'll find out tomorrow from Macalister where I can find him. In the meantime, I ordered some chow from room service. It should have been here by now. I don't want you skipping meals and getting sick. It looks like we're going to be here for a while. That Russki spy is somewhere in this city, and we're not returning to Ottawa empty-handed."

There was a knock on the door.

"Here's room service. I want you to eat up and then get a good night's sleep. You're going to need it. We're going to have a hell of a time tracking down that bastard."

"If he's still in Montreal," Williams said, "we'll get the son of a bitch."

"Yeah," Davies added, "right between the eyes!"

And they laughed.

But Meaghers didn't. "I want this guy alive, gentlemen, so enough with the bullshit."

———«•»———

Eddie looked at his watch for the umpteenth time that night. It was a little after eleven o'clock, and Josette still wasn't back from her morning visit with Gigi, and she hadn't called. She should have been back hours ago. Eddie was not the kind of person who easily panicked, but he had reached that point some time ago. He had phoned Gigi around five that afternoon and called her back every hour on the hour since, even though she had said she'd call him if Josette showed up. She also told him that she hadn't known anything about meeting with Josette for coffee. She had been at work all day and had gotten home around four. What was going on?

He picked up the phone at the office and called Gigi again. Maybe Josette was there, and Gigi had forgotten to call. It was stupid, but he dialed the number anyway. He was desperate.

"It's me again," he said into the receiver. "No sign of her? … Okay … Yes, I'll call when she come in. Thanks." He hung up and dialed his own number at his apartment. He let it ring for two minutes and then put the receiver down.

Josette had never done this before. When she was gone for an extended time, she always called him to check in. She'd been gone for over twelve hours now. He had no idea where she could possibly be. If she had decided instead to see her parents, she would have phoned him. He thought about phoning them but decided against it. He didn't want them to worry. Besides, there was nothing they could do.

Where could she be? Where would he even begin looking for her? He didn't know, but he had to do something. He put on his hat and overcoat. He wrapped a scarf around his neck and slipped on his gloves. He couldn't just sit in his office and wait. He locked up and went to his car just outside. Last night, he had thought about putting it in the underground parking garage because of the weather but had forgotten to.

He got inside and immediately caught a whiff of gasoline. That was strange. The car had been sitting there all last night and all of today. Was there a leak somewhere? The car had recently been at the garage for a routine checkup, and everything had been fine. His thoughts suddenly flashed to St. Paul and the gunman at Irving Park. The man had tried to kill him. Maybe he hadn't stopped trying. Maybe he had followed Eddie to Montreal. Maybe he had tampered with the car. If Eddie started the car, would it blow up? He wasn't about to find out. He got out of the car and returned to the office, wondering all the time whether this was somehow related to Josette being missing.

Damn it, he thought. *Damn it all to hell.*

————«•»————

They were halfway into their two-hour drive to Montreal before either man said anything. It was after two in the morning: the constant drone of the tires, the headlights shining on the two-lane highway enveloped by pitch darkness, the monotony of same thing. Turgenev was driving. He could barely keep his eyes open. He hadn't slept in thirty-six hours. Smirnov was slumped in the seat beside him, riding shotgun, fading in and out of consciousness.

"Talk to me," Turgenev said. "Tell me a story to keep me awake. You're good at that. Your stories are always amusing. Amuse me, Smirnov."

"Hmm? What did you say?"

"I said if I fall asleep, I'll crash the car in this godforsaken wilderness, and that will be that."

Smirnov sat upright. "For Christ's sake, keep your eyes on the road." He looked at his watch. "We've got only another hour before we're in Montreal. Don't lose it now. You want me to drive?"

"For someone who drove tanks for a living in the army, you're the worst driver I know. No, I'll drive. I want to get there alive, even if you might not."

There was silence again for the next five miles.

204 ⟪●⟫ John Charles Gifford

"He must have done something really bad," Turgenev said.

"Who?"

"Blackbird. He must have done something really terrible to piss off Colonel Trifonov."

"Trifonov doesn't need a reason to have someone killed," Smirnov said. "All he has to do is lift a finger, and poof, that person is gone. He's got us to make it happen."

"I suppose you're right. Loyalty is fragile; it's never a guarantee of survival."

Silence once again fell over them, and once again Turgenev broke it, attempting to stay awake. "Look what happened to Trifonov's own father. He was a loyal member of the party, a hero even, and they tied him to a pole in front of an execution squad."

"Ah, but he was rehabilitated! Let's not forget that."

"Ten years after they murdered him. A lot of good that did him."

"Hmm, that could happen to us, you know?"

"Anything is possible, I suppose."

"If we fail to make Blackbird disappear, I'm sure we'll find out."

"Fail?" Turgenev said. "Don't be a glupyy chelovek. Listen, we know where he works. We know where he lives. He won't be expecting us. This is a routine assignment. We'll be back in Ottawa before we know it."

"Yes, back in Ottawa with the mission completed, or in front of a firing squad if not."

"Smirnov, you can be such an idiot at times."

"Shut up and keep your eyes on the road."

Chapter 20
A TIME FOR CONFESSIONS

HOMICIDE DETECTIVE JACK MACALISTER WAS IN good spirits on Tuesday morning, which was uncharacteristic of him on most any day of the week. Overworked, underpaid, and trying to run a department on half the sleep he should be getting was standard operating procedure for him, but not today. He was still overworked and underpaid, but last night he'd gotten enough sleep and then some.

Yesterday, he had surprised his wife Molly by arriving home while it was still light outside. He'd taken her out for a fancy Parisian dinner at the Café de L'Est on Rue Notre Dame and then topped it off with a romantic evening at home with music and wine, which had inevitably led to them retiring upstairs to their bedroom. After about an hour, they were both sound asleep at ten o'clock, cuddled in each other's arms. He had made up for at least some of the nights he had arrived home after midnight.

So this morning, he was whistling a tune and as happy as any husband could ever be, still feeling the passion of the previous night. He had made his coffee and was now tidying up his office, transferring stacks of files from his desk to a small table in the corner where he was reorganizing them.

Nothing could happen today that would possibly change his mood.

But then the door swung open.

He turned around. He was still grinning from his thoughts about last night. "Garrison Edward Meaghers—what brings you here on this fine Tuesday morning?" he asked.

"I need to speak to one of your constables who conducted some of the interviews on the Lovingate case."

"Which one?"

"Eddie Wade."

Shit, Macalister thought. The grin left his face. He put his cup to his lips and took a sip. "Eh, he's not exactly a constable." He tried to smile, but his face wasn't working.

"What is he … exactly? A detective?"

"Well, no. He's not exactly that either."

Meaghers cocked his head, confused. "What the hell is he then? One of the janitors?"

"Actually, he's a private investigator. I don't have enough resources for the number of active cases, so I asked him to help out with the Lovingate case."

Meaghers stepped closer to Macalister, not precisely menacingly, but near enough that no one would dispute it. "Let me get this straight, Macalister. You had a lousy gumshoe working on a federal case that involved national security? Is that what you're telling me?"

"I didn't know it was a federal case when I brought him on board. As far as I was concerned at the time, this was a local homicide case." He took another sip of coffee and then put the cup on his desk.

"So this guy knows all there is to know about the case? For Christ's sake, Macalister, what kind of law enforcement officer are you, letting a goddamn civilian have access to confidential information?"

Macalister's mood did change, in fact, and quickly. He didn't appreciate Meaghers's tone. "Listen, buster. I don't care who you are. You don't barge into my office and accuse me of mishandling my job." He took a few steps forward, narrowing the distance between them. "I work for the city of Montreal, not you, so don't come in here and question what I do. If you want something from me, you ask in a reasonable tone of voice, or you can take your ass out of here."

Meaghers stood in front of him with his eyes narrowed, as if scrutinizing him. Macalister stared back at him with his hands on his waist, not backing down. It was a showdown. Macalister didn't know how long it would last and didn't care. He was good for the long haul. After a minute, however, Meaghers tipped his hat back with an index finger as J. Edgar Hoover might have done.

"Okay, Detective, I'll play your little game. If you would be so kind to tell me where I can contact this Eddie Wade, I would greatly appreciate it. As a matter of fact, I don't think it would be too outrageous of me to say that the whole goddamn Royal Canadian Mounted Police would appreciate it as well." He paused briefly. "Am I being *reasonable* enough for you? I could have another go at it, if you want."

Macalister turned away and walked around his desk. "I'll call Wade and have him come down."

"At the risk of being out of line, I'd like to go to him. I wouldn't want to disrupt your day any more than I have already."

Macalister looked up at him, about to say something, then decided not to. He wrote down Eddie's address and phone number on a paper and gave it to him. "Do you need directions?"

"I'm quite familiar with your fair city, Detective Macalister, having been assigned here at one point in my career, but thank you for the offer. That was very kind of you. Now, if you don't mind, I'll leave and let you get back to your duties, which I'm sure all of the taxpayers of this great city would find pleasing." With that, he made for the door.

Shithead, Macalister thought. *Don't let the door hit you in the ass.*

⸺»«●»«⸺

Turgenev and Smirnov pulled up to Symeon Peters's Atwater apartment building.

"This is the address, right?" Turgenev asked. They had been told not to write anything down, that they had to memorize everything.

"I think so. It looks right," Smirnov said.

They were parked across the street from the building. They both looked out the window on the driver's side.

"He might be at work," Turgenev said, "but let's go inside anyway in case he's there. Maybe he called in sick."

"Maybe," Smirnov said. "And maybe he's committed suicide. Then all we'd have to do is get rid of the body."

"That would be fine with me. We'd be back in Ottawa sooner that way."

Just then, they watched the front door of the building open and a woman come out. She turned right and walked up the street. They both followed her with their eyes.

Turning around, Turgenev said, "Wonder who she is."

"Someone who lives in the building. She's probably going to work."

"Maybe she's a prostitute. Maybe Blackbird was having a little fun before going to work."

"Let's go see if he's up there."

They got out of the car, crossed the street, entered the building, and made their way to the second floor. Smirnov knocked on the door, and both men kept their hands on their guns at their waists. When no one answered, Smirnov knocked again. They waited for five minutes, listening with their ears to the door. No movement inside. Turgenev got his pick from his pocket, squatted down, and picked the lock. Both men drew their guns while Smirnov twisted the doorknob and slowly pushed the door in. They followed their guns in and then shifted to the left and right, respectively. Turgenev motioned with his hand for Smirnov to check out the left side of the apartment while he took the right. The apartment was small, so after a few minutes, they met in the living room.

"He must be at work," Turgenev said. "What do you want to do?"

"Right now, I need a drink to warm up." Smirnov saw a bottle of vodka on the kitchen counter and walked over to it. "It's not open." He looked around for an open bottle but didn't find one. "What do we do?"

"Open the damn thing. I could use one myself."

For the next half hour, they sat in the living room and drank.

"His things are still here," Turgenev said, "so he hasn't skipped out."

"I don't think he would have taken anything if he did leave. If he had an idea that someone was coming, he'd leave everything here and make a run for it. That way they would think he's still in the city. What do you want to do?"

"Let's go and check out his work to make sure he's there. He doesn't know our faces. We could tail him back here and then take him."

"One more drink first?"

"Of course."

———《●》———

Eddie was pacing the office, going out of his mind with worry. Josette still had not called, and he had absolutely no idea where to look for her. Besides that, the garage had towed his car so they could check it out. He decided to wait until noon for her to either return or call, and then he'd call Jack Macalister.

He hadn't slept at all and had spent the night drinking coffee. The pot was empty, so he decided to make some more. Just then, the door opened, and in walked Josette.

He ran over to her and wrapped his arms around her. "Jesus, I've been going crazy wondering where you've been. Are you all right?"

"I'm fine. Sorry. Let me take my coat off. I need something warm to drink. I'm freezing."

"I'll put a pot of coffee on." He went into the backroom, filled the pot with water, added the coffee, and then put it on the burner. He returned to the office. "Okay, where have you been? Couldn't you get to a phone?"

She stared at him for a moment without saying anything. Then she sat down in one of the chairs in front of their desks. "You're not going to like what I have to say," she said.

"Listen, baby, you're here and in one piece. Nothing you can say will make me upset."

"Okay then. I'll hold you to that."

Eddie sat on the edge of his desk and smiled, relieved to have his wife back.

"Don't interrupt me while I'm talking, okay? Just let me talk, and you can ask questions after."

"Jeez, Josette. What did you do?"

"I broke into Symeon Peters's apartment."

"You what?" he said, standing up.

"You said you weren't going to interrupt me. Now sit back down and shut up. This is hard enough as it is."

He leaned his backside on the desk this time and folded his arms across his chest. He wasn't happy.

"Okay then, no more interruptions until I'm finished. I broke into his apartment to find some evidence that would directly link him to the murder. You said that the evidence had to be solid enough to hold up in court. Well, I found it. There was a large metal box in his bedroom closet, and in it was Anne Lovingate's passport and driver's license. I also found the disguise he used: the mustache, wig, and glasses, the same as in the photo. About the time I discovered them, he came back. I've been stuck in the back of the closet, hiding behind clothes, ever since then. I could only leave after he went to work this morning. And don't come too close to me right now, because I peed in my pants." She looked at Eddie as if she expected him to say something, but he didn't.

"I was so scared that he was going to open the closet door and find me that when he finally left this morning, I was so relieved and frightened that I forgot to take the evidence with me. But it's there for the police to find. I knew you would be worried, and I'm sorry for that, but I had no way to contact you and no way out until he left. Okay, now you can talk."

For a long moment, Eddie didn't say anything, and he had no expression on his face for her to read.

"Say something," she said, prodding him.

"I'm extremely happy that you're back. I'm also giddy that I won't be going around the city trying to find your body parts. I'm sure I mentioned this, but just in case I didn't, Symeon Peters is a KGB agent and extremely dangerous. Had he found you, he would have known a dozen different ways to kill you, and no one ever would have found your body. Nod if you understand that."

She nodded.

"Good. I'm glad that's cleared up. And let me remind you, if you had taken the evidence, it couldn't have been used in court because you illegally broke into his apartment to get it. The judge might think that you planted it. And in order for the police to enter his apartment and get the evidence, they would need a search warrant, which they wouldn't be able to get because they have no—let me repeat—they have no probable cause."

Josette thought for a minute. Her eyes flittered about the office before squarely landing on Eddie again. "Then let's say, just as a hypothetical, that Peters took the evidence and dropped it inadvertently somewhere outside his apartment, in the front or back of the building—it doesn't matter—and either you or I saw him drop it. Could it be used then?"

"I don't like what I'm hearing, but I'll answer anyway. Yes, but that's unlikely to happen."

"Oh, I almost forgot." She reached in her pocket for a slip of paper and handed it to Eddie. "I found this folded in the passport; I thought it might be important. I was reading it when he came back, and I put it in my pocket without realizing it until I left. It's a poem, but it does have the word 'Blackbird' in it."

Eddie read it. "I don't understand it. It must be some kind of coded message from his people. But on the positive side of all this, you did establish that Peters is in fact Blackbird and that he did kill Lovingate. Unfortunately, we can't prove it because we can't legally get the evidence. It's just the way it is. I think at this point, we need to bow out and let the RCMP do their thing. The case is getting too complicated and too dangerous."

She got up and walked over to him, resting her forearms on top of his shoulders, which could be either a good or a bad thing, depending on what she wanted.

"Eddie, sweetheart, let's sleep on it before you make a decision. It would be difficult, but I think we can get this guy. We're so close as it is."

He sniffed the air around him.

"I wasn't lying when I said that I peed in my pants."

Just then the phone rang.

"Saved by the bell," Eddie said, and he walked over to his desk to answer the phone. "Wade Detective Agency ... Yes ... Okay, shoot." He listened for the next few minutes, then said, "Hang on to the device, will you? ... Okay, I'll pick the car up sometime this afternoon. Thanks a million. I owe you." Then he hung up.

"What's wrong with the car?" Josette asked.

Eddie sat on the edge of his desk again and folded his arms across his chest. "Okay, it looks like this is confession day for both of us." He told her about the gunman in St. Paul and how he'd nearly gotten killed by making the stupid decision to meet an unnamed man at one o'clock in the morning somewhere partially remote within the city. He explained that he hadn't told her about the incident because he hadn't wanted her to worry. But she took it well now; she said she understood.

"If we're going to be partners in this agency," she continued calmly, "you can't spend your time trying to protect me. We've got to be equal partners. We can look out for each other, but you can't be obsessed with trying to protect me all the time."

"Something else happened that I think is related to St. Paul. It's about the car."

He told her that he'd smelled gas when he got into the car yesterday, so he'd called the garage early this morning, and they'd towed it in. The mechanic had called back just now and told him that the brake lines had been sliced slightly. They would have been okay braking at slow speeds, but wouldn't have held at anything over 25 to 30 mph. The gas line also had been tampered with. If he had driven the car and had run into something at a normal speed because he couldn't stop, there most likely would have been an explosion. The mechanic had discovered something like an ignition device near the gas line, set to go off at impact. He had never seen anything like it before but had read about the devices in magazines.

"Someone placed it under the car because he wanted to kill me. That's the second time. All the more reason to drop the case. Besides, we're officially off the case anyway."

"Let's give ourselves just a few more days before making a decision. We've got too much invested in this to just quit."

"Okay," Eddie said. "Three more days, but we're going to have to be careful. We're not going to put ourselves in any more danger. Someone wants to kill me. They think it'll stop the investigation, but it won't, because the RCMP is on it now."

Just then, the door swung open. Three men walked in, wearing long overcoats and felt hats with the brims down to their eyebrows. Two of them fell in behind the tallest one, who reached into his pocket for his wallet. He opened it and held it out at arm's length.

"I'm Agent Garrison Edward Meaghers. This is Agent Walker, and this is Agent Davies. We're with the Royal Mounties. May I ask your names please?"

Eddie's first thought was to ask whether they had the option of saying no. But he remembered his one and only prior encounter with the RCMP a few years back in this very office. He had been handcuffed to a chair, interrogated, and threatened with prison time by a couple of guys who looked just like the ones who were here now. Playing it straight might be the better option.

"I'm Eddie Wade, and this is my wife, Josette. Whaddya need, fellas? Always willing to help the Mounties."

Meaghers put his wallet back. "Detective Macalister tells me you've been working the Lovingate case. While we appreciate your input, I want you to remember that this is a federal case involving espionage and that your assistance is no longer needed."

"Yeah, Macalister mentioned something about that."

"Good. I'm here to remind you that anything you learned about the case is classified information, and it's a federal crime to reveal said information to anyone. It carries a minimum of five years in prison and a maximum of ten years."

Nothing like a bit of intimidation to keep people in place.

"Thanks for the reminder, fellas. Is there anything else?"

There was a long, uncomfortable moment of silence. Agent Meaghers's face was like a sheet of steel.

"As a matter of fact, there is something else. Detective Macalister gave me the file on the Lovingate case. We thought that perhaps there was something else you *forgot* to tell him. Something that might have slipped your mind. Withholding evidence on a case is also a federal crime punishable by a prison term—"

"I know, not exceeding ten years," Eddie said.

Meaghers stared at Eddie. "That's correct—not exceeding ten years. Now's the time to avoid that."

"Everything we know is in the file. Now if you fellas don't have any more questions, I have an errand to do."

Another uncomfortable moment of silence followed, along with another ice-cold stare from all three of the Mounties.

Meaghers gave Eddie his card. "If you remember something, anything, I can be reached at my hotel. I wrote the number on the back."

After they left, Josette was first to speak. "Okay, let's see. If we get the maximum sentence, we'll be out of prison—which will most likely be Bordeaux; no, scratch that, that's a provincial prison; we'll be sent to one of the federal prisons—in 1966. I guess if we take everything into consideration, that won't be too bad. Our hair will be a little gray, but I think we can handle that."

"He gave me his card, which means he left the door open. Listen, I don't like this at all. I'm giving us three days to decide what we're going to do about Peters. Then I'm going to

Macalister with the truth about him. Jack can tell the Mounties that he got the lead from an anonymous source; that way our names are kept out of it."

"Jeez, that's more than reasonable," Josette said, a happy lilt in her voice. "I thought for a moment you were going to run after him and spill the beans."

"We have three days," Eddie said as a reminder. "Listen, before I forget, would you please call Gigi and tell her you're fine? She's been worried sick about you." He went over to the coatrack to grab his overcoat and hat. "I'm going to the garage to pick up the car."

"Tell the guys I said hi."

"I'll do that."

"What about the coffee?"

"The whole pot is yours, baby. Oh yeah, you might want to consider going to the apartment to take a shower. You're starting to hum."

———«●»———

Agents Meaghers, Walker, and Davies left the Wade Detective Agency and went next door to the Lion's Den. They sat at the bar and ordered beer.

"He seemed cooperative," Walker said.

Davies nodded with a bottle to his lips.

"Too cooperative, if you ask me," Meaghers said. "I think he's hiding something. Everyone hides something during an investigation, even us. That's the nature of the game. Private detectives are better at it than most, the sneaky bastards."

"Are we going to do something about it, boss?" Davies asked.

"You bet we are. I want you two to put a surveillance on him. Get Jones and Williams on it with you. Four shifts, around the clock. The bastard knows something he's not telling. I could feel it in my bones. He was a bit smug, don't you think?"

Walker and Davies, sitting on either side of Meaghers, both nodded in agreement.

"Well, I'll cure him of that. We'll find out what he's not telling us, and then I'll lock his ass up for withholding information and interfering with an investigation. Maybe his wife too, but they won't be sharing the same cell."

"Sounds good to me," Walker said.

"Me too," Davies threw in.

Chapter 21
CHANGE OF PLANS

ON WEDNESDAY AT PRECISELY FOUR FORTY- five in the morning, Turgenev and Smirnov sat in their car across the street from Blackbird's Atwater apartment building, trying to keep awake. They'd been there since a little before two. Turgenev had driven again, because he didn't trust Smirnov behind the wheel, and he valued his life. Smirnov had wanted to drive; he claimed that if he could drive a T-34 tank—which he had done for two years in the Soviet Army before transferring to the security forces—he could certainly handle a car, but Turgenev threatened to walk if he persisted.

"The heater in this car is worse than anything we have at home," Turgenev said.

Smirnov grunted something unintelligible and then adjusted the blanket he had brought with him. They sat in silence for a while, listening to the wind blowing the snow around outside the car.

"Did you bring a flask?" Turgenev asked.

Smirnov changed his position, sitting more upright now than slumped in the seat. He twisted his head toward

Turgenev. "Does Nikita Khrushchev still have a forty-six-inch waist?" he asked.

"Don't be disrespectful," Turgenev said. "A simple yes or no would do."

Smirnov reached inside his overcoat for the flask, extended it toward Turgenev, and said, "Don't drink it all. It's got to last until we get back to the hotel room."

Turgenev unscrewed the top, drank some, and then gave it back. Smirnov, too, had a nip and then put it back.

At five o'clock, the light in Blackbird's apartment went on.

"That's his apartment, right?" Turgenev asked, looking up.

"That's it," Smirnov said, looking around Turgenev through the driver's window. "I doubled-checked the last time we were here. It's his all right."

"Then he's here; he hasn't skipped town since we saw him at work yesterday. That probably means that he has no idea someone has been sent. If he did know, he would most likely be gone. Should we take him now? It's the perfect time." Turgenev continued to stare at the apartment window. "We'll have the element of surprise. He won't be expecting anyone. He'll be only half awake. We'll have the edge. I don't feel like a big confrontation; it's too early for that."

Smirnov was silent for a long moment before he spoke. "Don't take this the wrong way, but you know, we could be him someday. Through no fault of our own, we could be hunted down because we made some mistake."

"It sounds like you're about to suggest something," Turgenev said. "Out with it then."

"I'm only suggesting that we take pity on the guy. Let him have another day of life. If he's lucky, he might get laid tonight. We know where he lives and works. We can get him tomorrow. We'll come back in the afternoon this time and wait for him to return from work. That'll be soon enough."

"You know," Turgenev said, "that might not be a bad idea. If we took him now, we'd have to return to Ottawa right away. If we take him tomorrow, we could go to one of the strip clubs tonight. The French know how to live! As we are acutely aware, there are no strip clubs in Ottawa. This might be our only chance to have a little fun here. Good thinking, Smirnov!" He then reached over and slapped him on the shoulder.

"It's settled then?" Smirnov asked.

"Yes, it's settled," Turgenev said. "Hand over the flask again."

————«◉»————

Symeon Peters sat in his small office at Fitchburg, Sterling, and Rycroft listening to his boss, Sterling, explain the new account he was assigning to Peters. Actually, he was only half-listening to him; he was preoccupied with more important matters at the moment.

"This company is looking to expand," Sterling said, referring to the new client, "and needs an accurate valuation from us."

Sterling was one of several owners of the firm. He was a bit stuffy but generally a pleasant guy to work for. He was in his sixties and always wore a white shirt with his collar unbuttoned and his tie hanging down. Outside of occasional social functions, Peters had never seen him with his suitcoat on in the five years he'd worked for the firm.

"They'll be seeking a bank loan or funding from private investors—they haven't decided yet, maybe both—so we need to look at their previous years' revenues and growth patterns to determine a reasonable value of their company to give to the bank and potential investors. You'll also need to work up pro forma financial statements and projections along with the company's financial history to calculate the data. They'll be needed for the expansion."

"When will you need this?" Peters asked.

"Well, let's say a week from now, but actually as soon as possible. We don't want to lose this client. It could mean some big money for us down the line—and of course, a nice bonus for you."

"I'll start today then."

"Good man. I'll leave you to it."

Good man, he thought after his boss left. How many times had he heard that before? In fact, Peters was one of the best men at the firm. He had to be; it was his cover, and he couldn't afford to screw up. His real boss at the KGB wouldn't be pleased.

But it didn't matter now. He had no intention of finishing the job. In fact, he might not even start it at all. At the moment, he had other concerns. He had to devise a way to escape Montreal. Maybe *disappear* was a better word. He would disappear, and no one would have the foggiest idea where he was. That was his priority now. Above all, he knew that until that happened, he would have to act normal, as if today were just another workday. He assumed that he was being watched by someone. He didn't think that Ottawa would have sent someone this soon, but he wasn't sure about that, and because he wasn't sure, he had to make it appear that this was just a typical day for him.

He hadn't worked out a plan yet, but he still was considering using his car to cross the border into New York State. It would be safer than flying. They'd probably have men at the airport watching out for him. The same would be true for the train station. Yes, driving across the border was his best option. He wouldn't take luggage with him, of course. Someone might see him loading up the car. Besides, there was nothing in the apartment that he couldn't live without. He could easily buy new clothes and personal items somewhere in New York. All he'd need were his phony British passport, his driver's license, and cash.

But what about Gigi? Could he leave without saying goodbye? It would certainly be safer to do so. If he saw her, he'd have to think up a story to break the engagement. Maybe he could tell her that he'd found a better job in Vancouver. She had often said that she couldn't live in English-speaking Canada. Maybe she'd break up with him, and that would be that. This was becoming complicated. He wasn't sure he could just leave her high and dry without some explanation, yet he didn't look forward to having that discussion with her.

Just then, something else occurred to him. As far as he knew, Ottawa didn't know about his involvement with Gigi. If he went to her apartment tonight to break the engagement and tell her that he was leaving the city, and if he was, in fact, being surveilled, then they'd learn about her. God only knew what they would do to her to get her to talk after he disappeared. She wouldn't have any information concerning his whereabouts, but of course, that wouldn't matter. They'd torture her just the same, thinking she must know where he'd gone. The stakes were too high for them not to. So now the decision became easier for him to make: he'd leave without seeing her; that would be best for both of them.

He looked at his watch. It was too early to leave work for the day, so he decided to start his new account for no other reason than to keep busy, with his mind occupied by something else. Someone else would have to finish it when they discovered the next day that Symeon Peters hadn't shown up for work and never would show up again.

He worked diligently until five without taking a lunch break and then left. In case he was being followed, he stopped at a grocery store to buy a few things and make it seem like a normal evening, and then he made one more stop at a gas station to fill up the tank for the drive to New York. Forty minutes later, he parked his car in front of his apartment building, and with his bag of groceries he entered the building and walked up to the second floor. When he unlocked his door and stepped inside, he was momentarily stunned to find someone waiting for him.

"Gigi!" he said. "What a surprise. Have you been waiting long?" He had forgotten that she had a key to his apartment. He had given her one last year, but she rarely used it. She was sitting in the armchair with her coat still on.

"We need to talk," she said.

"Certainly," he said. "Just let me put the groceries down in the kitchen. Would you like a drink?"

She stared at him for a moment and then shook her head.

He went to the kitchen, rehearsing in his head what he would say to her, put the bag down on the counter, and then reached for the bottle of vodka. Something was wrong—very wrong. This bottle had been new. He had bought it a few days before and hadn't opened it, yet half of it was gone. Someone had been here in his apartment. Someone had been waiting for him and helped himself. It had to have been yesterday or maybe even today. Ottawa must have sent a man for him. *Shit*, he thought. This confirmed it. Now he'd have to be looking over his shoulder constantly. He poured himself a drink, thought twice about it, and then set the glass down. Someone could have helped himself to the vodka, then poisoned the rest. He couldn't take the chance. He returned to the living room.

"You sound as if something is wrong, Gigi. What is it?"

She remained seated. "We have to talk about our relationship and future, if there's going to be one for us."

Symeon sat down on the couch opposite her. "Well, as a matter of fact, I was going to come over to you tonight and have a talk," he said, lying to her. What was another lie after two years of constant deceit? "I've come to a decision that I wanted to discuss with you."

"A decision?" she said. "Well, I suppose that's some progress." She didn't look sad or angry—just serious.

"Yes, a decision. You see, I was offered a better position in Toronto with a British firm." He had meant to say Vancouver, but he couldn't take it back now. Anyway, Toronto was far enough from Montreal. "More money and benefits. I've decided to take it."

She showed little surprise. "You've decided to take it without telling me first? You know how I feel about living anywhere besides Montreal."

Symeon felt heartless, but this was his only opportunity to end it, here and now. Leaving without telling her was no longer an option. "Well, that's the thing, Gigi. I feel that you'd be better off without me. I've realized in the last six months that marriage wouldn't be the right thing for me. I've lived alone for such a long time that I've become too used to it. You deserve better. Besides, I've always had a problem with commitments. It's nothing personal."

There—he'd said it. It was out in the open.

That last sentence must have been too much for her. *It's nothing personal.* It obviously was the clincher. How could she not take it personally? She threw the key at him and stormed out without saying another word.

Well, that went down better than I expected, he thought.

He didn't really give it another thought after that. His mind was diverted to something more pressing: the half-empty bottle of vodka sitting on his kitchen counter.

———«●»———

Eddie Wade sat in his car outside the Atwater apartment building and watched Peters get out of his car with a bag of groceries. He walked up to the entrance and went inside. Eddie had really never liked the guy, but he hadn't been able to pinpoint exactly why. Now he knew. Peters was a communist bastard. The Russians had been Eddie's necessary ally during the war because they'd had a common enemy: the Nazis. But after the war, they hadn't wasted any time enslaving half of Germany and spreading their vile propaganda to Eastern Europe. Since then, the Soviets would have liked nothing better than to enslave Western Europe and North America. Symeon Peters, or whatever his real name was, was a small part of the whole scheme but a deadly part nonetheless. Eddie hadn't fought the Nazi regime just to have the communists take up where the Nazis had left off, but that was what had happened. Now Eddie would have to be content in playing a small part against them. He'd start with Symeon Peters.

Just then, he noticed the front door of the apartment building open and saw Gigi come out. He slumped in his seat so she wouldn't see him. She turned right and walked up the street. She looked distraught. He wondered what had gone on inside.

———«◉»———

That night, Garrison Edward Meaghers, chief of counterespionage, sat at the table in his hotel room, his makeshift command post, with three of the four members of his team: agents Williams, Walker, and Davies.

"I assume Jones is on surveillance," he said.

"Right, boss," Walker said. "He just relieved me."

"Anything to report?"

"Not much," Walker continued. "Wade was at his office all day, except on Davies's shift."

All eyes turned to Davies.

"I followed Wade to an apartment building over on Atwater Avenue," Davies said. "Three sixty-one to be precise. He sat in his car for three hours and twenty-two minutes and then left. I then followed him back to his office."

"That's it?" Meaghers asked. "Any activity there?"

"A few people came and went, but nothing more. He just sat there as if he were on a surveillance himself."

"Who in the hell lives on Atwater that he'd be interested in?"

"Maybe he was working one of his cases."

"Yeah, maybe," Meaghers said, reflecting on that. "And maybe he's still running with the Lovingate case." He slapped his hand on the table. "Damn it, that son of a bitch knows something he's not telling us." He thought for a moment. "Okay, I'm taking over the surveillance on him myself. Let's meet here after breakfast tomorrow morning, and I'll give you your new assignments. Walker, drive over to Jones tonight and tell him to stay put until his shift is over. Tell him to meet us here at 0600. I'm going to get that smug gumshoe if it's the last thing I do. He knows something, and I'm going to find out what."

"When you do, boss," Davies said, "let me put the cuffs on him. I want to see his face light up."

"So do I," Meaghers said. "So do I."

Chapter 22

PACK UP ALL MY CARES AND WOES, HERE I GO, SINGING LOW, BYE-BYE, BLACKBIRD

EDDIE HAD GOTTEN UP BEFORE DAWN ON Thursday morning. Josette had still been warmly snugged under the blankets in bed when he arose, and he'd envied her and wished he were still making spoons with her. He'd made a pot of coffee, filled his thermos, and driven across town to Atwater Avenue. Now on his second cup, he sat and watched the front door to Symeon Peters's apartment building.

Jack Macalister had told him that he was off the Lovingate case. Garrison Edward Meaghers had done the same, in so many words, having gone so far as to explain to him that interference in a federal case carried a heavy prison term. These were reasonable men, even though Eddie thought that Meaghers was a little heavy-handed. Yet here he was, sitting in front of Peters's apartment, waiting for him to come out so he could tail him. What was wrong with him? Did he need his head examined by a team of psychiatrists? Did he have some sort of mental disorder he was unaware of?

In spite of Meaghers's implied threats to put Eddie behind bars if he was withholding information about the case, in spite of the fact that he wasn't being paid for his time on the case, and in spite of the fact that he didn't have any legally obtained evidence to go to the police with that would warrant an arrest, he had agreed to spend three more days on the case. And for what? To appease Josette because she'd said they were close to getting Peters? Close, he reminded himself, counted only in the game of horseshoes. Close to an arrest wasn't an actual arrest and maybe never would be.

And on top of all that, he had absolutely no idea why he was sitting outside Peters's apartment, waiting for him to come out to tail him. Tail him where? To his work? So what if he went to work? What would Eddie do once Peters got there? Wait for hours for him to come out and tail him home again? What would that accomplish? Eddie had always been a risk taker, and so was Josette. That was one of many qualities he admired about her. But this was ridiculous. He had to come up with another plan.

He finished his coffee and screwed the top down on the thermos. He knew what to do. He would tail Peters for the day and then go back to the office and explain to Josette why they were finished with the case. Two more days were unnecessary. They weren't about to get the evidence needed for a conviction. The RCMP had far more resources than they had to get the job done, if it was even possible. He would tell Jack to call Meaghers and report that an anonymous source had told him about Peters, the Lovingate passport, the license, and the disguise in his apartment. Let the feds take care of it. Wade Detective Agency would wash its hands of it. If Eddie wanted to capture a communist, he'd have to do it another time.

Just then, the front door of the apartment house opened, and Symeon Peters walked out. As he got into his car and pulled away from the curb, Eddie made a U-turn and followed him from a distance. Peters continued up Atwater and then made a right turn onto Dorchester. The morning traffic was starting to gear up, and Eddie let two cars squeeze between them. Peters drove by University and then Union with Eddie behind him at a safe enough distance. There were now three cars between them when Eddie caught a red light. The cars in front of him crossed the intersection, which left him at the crosswalk. When the light changed to green, Eddie shot ahead, but by then there were so many cars in front of him from the cross street that he couldn't see Peters's car. He continued on a couple of blocks before accepting that he had lost him.

When he had made the right turn from Atwater onto Dorchester about ten minutes before, he had noticed in his rearview mirror a black car behind him. It was still there. Was someone following *him*? He decided to find out. He made a quick left turn onto Bleury, drove a block, and made a right turn onto Sainte-Catherine. He drove for another block and looked into the rearview mirror again. The black car was still behind him. He had no idea who might be following him, but he didn't like it. He made a left turn onto Saint-Urbain, heading for his office.

In twenty minutes, he was parked in front of his office. He stayed in the car and watched as the car following him rolled by. He tried to see who was inside but couldn't make out the driver. The only person he could think of who might want to tail him was Meaghers—another reason to end the investigation. He wasn't taking a prison term lightly. Then a thought occurred to him: it might have been the guy who had tried to sabotage his car and failed. That was yet another reason to end this insanity.

He got out of the car and walked to the office door. It was locked, which meant Josette wasn't there. He hoped that she was still at home and not off doing something stupid. He unlocked the door and went inside. He went to the bathroom and then to his desk. He picked up the phone and called his answering service. No messages. He then called home and let it ring ten times. Josette didn't answer. He decided to drive over to Peters's apartment again, so that he later could tell Josette that he had been there all day and not have to lie about it. Then he'd break the news that they were dropping the case. He meant it this time. He really did.

He left a note for Josette on her desk, saying that he'd be back at suppertime, and then he filled his pipe and made sure he had enough tobacco in his pouch. He grabbed his paperback off his desk and went outside. After locking up, he scanned the area to his left and right. No sign of the black car. He waited for a moment longer and then got into his car and left for the Atwater apartment.

⚫

The taxi dropped her off at the corner of Atwater and Rue Saint-Jacques. Josette would walk the rest of the way to Peters's apartment building. It was windy and cold, so she put her coat collar up and pulled her hat further down on her head. As she'd done before, she went into the phone booth, dialed Peters's number, and let it ring a dozen times. No answer. Good, he was at work. She left the phone booth and walked toward the apartment building. She was certain that her plan would work. This time she would get the evidence that would convict Peters of cold-blooded murder. She would tell Eddie that she'd found the passport, license, and disguise wrapped in a bag in the garbage can in the back of the building. She'd tell him that she saw Peters throw them there. She would be a sworn witness to that in court. Peters, of course, would deny it, but his fingerprints would probably be on the passport and license. It wasn't the best plan—she'd have to lie under oath and to Eddie, which was worse—but no one else had come up with a better one. They couldn't let a Soviet spy and murderer get away scot-free when they nearly had him in the palm of their hands.

She walked in the front door and went up the stairs to the second floor. At the apartment door, she got out her pick and wrench and worked the lock. In thirty seconds, she was inside the apartment. She locked the door and went to the closet in the bedroom. She found the metal box and opened it. The evidence was still there. Good. She took out the items, closed the box, and returned to the living room. She needed something to put it all in, a bag or something. Just then, she heard a key in the lock. A second later, the door swung open.

"Josette," Symeon Peters said as he closed the door behind him. He seemed to be a little surprised, but only a little. Otherwise, he was calm.

Josette stared at him, unable to utter a sound. There was a long moment of silence, broken only by the wind outside, coming from the window casements and crevices.

"Thank you for getting them out for me," he said, glancing at what she was holding. "When I left a while ago, I forgot them, so I returned. You saved me a trip to the bedroom."

"You won't get away with this, Symeon." She was frightened, but she had to say something else—something, anything. She hadn't thought this would happen, not a second time, and therefore hadn't planned for it. "The police know I'm here, and they're on the way."

"What? To arrest you? You did break into my apartment, after all."

She stared at him defiantly and saw a sad smile on his face, as if he pitied her, as if he were as regretful about catching her as she was about being caught.

"I doubt that they're coming, Josette, but on the off chance you're not lying, I think I should be leaving." He took out his revolver and pointed it at her. "And I'd like you to accompany me, if you wouldn't mind terribly. Quietly and calmly, we'll go out together. Don't make any more foolish mistakes. My car is just outside, and I won't have to warm it up. It's already nice and cozy."

⸺«◉»⸺

Eddie had taken a different route this time, going west on Notre Dame. He turned right onto Atwater and had three blocks to go. As long as he was on his own time and wasn't being paid for his services, he'd sit in his car for the rest of the day, smoke his pipe, and try to finish his Mickey Spillane novel. He'd wait for Peters to return from work, and then he'd leave and drive home for supper. He'd tell Josette about his boring stakeout, she'd be content with his effort, and then he'd drop the news in her lap: he was ending their involvement in the case.

When he was less than a block away, he saw a man and woman exit the apartment building and walk to a car. He slammed the brake pedal down, and the car slid to a stop in the middle of the street. Jesus, it was Peters's car, and he recognized Josette's coat and hat. He watched them go around to the driver's side. Peters opened the door, pushed Josette in, and then got inside himself. It took Eddie a few seconds to register what was happening. Peters had *pushed* her into the car. He floored the accelerator, but his tires spun on the icy road. He eased up a bit until the tires got traction, but by then Peters was a block and a half away.

⸺«◉»⸺

About an hour later, Smirnov was spread out on Blackbird's couch while Turgenev was slumped in the armchair, his legs extended and his feet crossed one over the other. Smirnov himself was longer than the couch, so he rested his ankles on the armrest.

"If he comes straight here after work," Smirnov said, raising his head up slightly in Turgenev's direction, "he should arrive around five thirty."

"I hope he doesn't return earlier," Turgenev said. "After last night, I could use some more rest."

"Ha, after last night, I could use a permanent transfer to Montreal. I don't know about you, but I'm going to find it difficult to return to Ottawa. By comparison with Montreal, Ottawa is so ... what's the word? Bland, that's it. Ottawa has suddenly become tasteless to me, like the watered-down vodka our grandparents used to drink."

"I read somewhere that the Montreal mayor is trying to make his city more like Ottawa. He's cracking down on the strip joints and gambling. He wants to put them out of business. Doesn't the numbskull know that's why people flock to his city and spend money?"

"That's a depressing thought," Smirnov said. "Now that we've discovered Montreal, he wants to take it away from us. If he succeeds, where will we go to have a little fun?"

"That's a problem to solve another time," Turgenev said. "Right now, we have to resist falling asleep. Blackbird might come home early. We have to be ready for him."

"If I fall asleep, kick me in the ribs, but don't break anything."

"I'll be sure to do that."

Chapter 23
AN HONEST CONVERSATION

SYMEON PETERS CONTINUED DRIVING, crossing the Jacques Cartier Bridge and eventually finding his way onto Route 9 on the south shore, heading toward the US border. He had exchanged no words with Josette, preferring instead to concentrate on his driving. He was only somewhat familiar with the southern shore of the St. Lawrence River, but now that he was on the road out of Quebec, he had gotten his bearings and felt more relaxed. He felt no sense of dread, no sense of trepidation. That worried him, because he thought he should. He couldn't say with absolute certainty, but it was reasonable for him to believe that Ottawa had sent someone, maybe even a team of men, to find him. After all, there was the opened bottle of vodka in his apartment. If they found him, they would not take him back; they would make him *disappear* as if he had never existed. His fellow Russians were experts at that. That in itself should have instilled fear in him. Because of the missing file, he most likely had been exposed, or would be with enough time. The Soviet mission in Ottawa probably believed he was likely to defect, to exchange highly classified Russian intelligence with the Canadian government for his freedom, like others had done. The KGB would never allow that happen, if it had the power to stop it. He knew that because he was one of them.

And yet he felt amazingly calm. This probably had to do with the fact that he was in his car and on his way to relative freedom. He could be experiencing a false sense of security, a possibility he had entertained, but he rejected that on the grounds of reason. Once in the US, he would have many more options available to him. He'd still have to be wary of his environment and those around him—he wasn't a fool—but he would no longer feel the crushing weight of Montreal on his shoulders. The conscious anticipation of that left him feeling nearly tranquil.

He still had one necessary task in front of him before he crossed the border. He glanced to his right, out of the corner of his eye, at that task. Josette sat still, her hands on her lap and her eyes looking straight ahead at the road. She looked serious but not afraid. Was she covering up her fear? That was a distinct possibility.

He cleared his throat. "How did you know about me?" It was a simple question, and Peters asked it in a sincere tone, truly wanting to know where he had gone wrong. When she didn't respond, he said, "You don't have to fear me, you know."

"Don't flatter yourself, Symeon. I don't fear you. If anything, I pity you."

He hadn't been expecting that response. It caught him off guard, but he recovered immediately, as would any good Russian spy who was worth his weight in gold.

"Pity, is it? That suggests you have some concern for me, for my suffering and misfortunes. I suppose I should thank you for that, for not being indifferent. We all suffer in life if we live long enough, even you."

"Did you have pity for Anne Lovingate when you murdered her?"

That stunned him for a moment. *Murdered* was such a harsh word. Her tone suggested that she wasn't asking a question, but rather was accusing him of something, of cruelty. He suddenly felt defensive, as if he had to justify himself to her. He admired her fortitude, however misplaced.

"Actually, I did," he said, "but you got her name wrong. It was Anastasia Alekseevna Nikandrova, and I did have a great deal of pity for her. But you see, I had an assignment to do, so I did it. I guarantee you she felt no pain whatsoever. She was unconscious at the time. Isn't that what pity is all about, really—the absence of pain?" He took another quick glance at her and then stared at the road again, suppressing a snicker. "Why all the concern? You didn't know the woman. She was a Russian, a committed Soviet soldier of the people, an avowed enemy of the West, a righteous workhorse for Stalin. She would have just as soon killed you as looked at you if the situation necessitated it, and the conditions were right. She was nothing to you."

Josette pursed her lips and continued to stare at the road in front of them.

He was annoyed by her lack of response, annoyed that she wouldn't engage him in discourse, annoyed that she wouldn't challenge his assumptions. He knew the facts; he had the upper hand. And he wanted to show her he did.

"So let me ask you again," he said. "How did you know about me?"

"Does it matter?"

"Yes, of course, it matters a great deal to me. It means that I did something wrong. I'd like to know what."

"So you can do it again to someone else without being discovered?"

His annoyance became simmering anger. His need to explain returned. Why, exactly, he didn't know, but he felt the urge to justify his actions to her, now, in this car on his way to relative safety. For some strange reason, he felt he could be honest with her far more than he had ever been honest with Gigi or even himself.

"You know, I had never killed anyone else before, except in the war, and never up close like that. It didn't feel good, if you want to know the truth. I nearly got sick afterward." The words came out angry and bitter. "I had been trained as a spy, to get secret information from your government, not as an assassin. Your Nikandrova whom you feel so warmly about was the assassin. She was the one who was going to kill the US president. And you're telling me that you feel sorry for her because I killed her? Had she lived, she might have tried and succeeded, and then there would have been another world war." He paused a moment because he felt himself losing control. "What do you have to say about that?"

Josette said nothing but continued to stare ahead.

"I am an accountant. I sat at my desk for five years, waiting for an assignment to spy against the Canadian government. You can judge me if you want, but your people spy on us as well. When I finally got an assignment, it was to kill a fellow Russian.—yes, to kill Nikandrova—or I myself would have been killed for disobeying an order. How do you think I felt about that? Please tell me—explain *that* to me."

Peters was at the point of losing it. He had always prided himself on his self-control, but now he was nearly becoming undone. He had fallen into the trap of having to defend himself. But from whom? A person he barely knew, a person who wasn't even Russian and who looked at him as simply a murderer. *She knows nothing about me!* he thought. It didn't make sense to him, yet he had this overwhelming urge to explicate himself, to her, to anyone who would listen. The reasons behind a grievous act should always be considered before a judgment was rendered. Damn her sense of superiority!

He continued on Route 9. The road was relatively straight, with some slight bends in it here and there. He would stay on it until a few miles to the border. Then he'd make a right turn into a heavily wooded area and drive for another mile or so. He'd stop the car, take her into the forest, and shoot her. Then he'd get back on Route 9 and cross the border into relative freedom.

"I think you probably felt some compassion for her," Josette said.

That surprised him. This time he hadn't been expecting a response.

He didn't answer her. He stared straight ahead at the long road ahead of them and listened to the wind whipping over the car, the drone of the engine, and the sound of the tires on the pavement.

⸺⊙⸺

Eddie followed Peters's car across the Cartier Bridge and onto Route 9 going south. The traffic was moderate, so he allowed two cars in between them. He still had visual contact; he could see occasionally the back of Josette's head and hat. Peters must be going to the border; that made sense. Why else would he be driving in this direction? However, he wouldn't risk crossing the border with Josette in the car. Eddie knew her well enough to know—and Peters likely suspected—that she would do or say something to alert the border guards. Maybe he'd let her out just before getting there. Maybe he had other plans for her.

"Damn it," Eddie said aloud, pounding the steering wheel with his palm.

What had Josette been doing at Peters's apartment? The first time she'd gone there, she'd nearly gotten caught. Why would she return a second time, knowing how dangerous

Peters was? Suddenly, Eddie felt a warm flush of guilt spread across his face.

This was all his fault. He hadn't taught her enough about the inherent dangers of going after someone capable of murder. She wasn't supposed to go after anyone! He'd thought he'd made that clear enough. She didn't have a license. Even if she had one, he never would have knowingly put her in danger. So why had she gone to Peters's apartment a second time?

Eddie still felt she'd make a great investigator, but her level of risk-taking did not match her level of experience. She had too much enthusiasm and not enough knowledge. Eddie knew that and should have been more forceful with her. He should have placed more restrictions on her and insisted she comply with them. Would he have done so had she not been his wife, but instead another guy? He might have fired a male apprentice after learning about his breaking into Peters's apartment the first time.

Yes, this was all his fault.

———— «●» ————

"What about Gigi?"

"What about her?" Peters asked.

"Is she all right?" She asked the question softly, almost tenderly, with a great deal of concern.

"You really think I'm some kind of monster, don't you?"

"I really don't know much about you," Josette said. "I know what you did, but I don't know what you're capable of. I don't know your limits."

Peters turned his head toward her briefly and scowled. "Good God, you really do think I'm a monster. I didn't *murder* her, if that's what you're asking. Of course, she's all right. I wouldn't harm a hair on her head."

Josette turned her face toward him. "Except if you were ordered to."

She was pushing him, but why? For what purpose? Peters sighed deeply and tightened his grip on the steering wheel. She didn't warrant a response.

"Does she know about you?"

This time, he couldn't help himself. "No," he said sharply. "I've kept my other life a secret from her."

"She knows something is wrong between you, though. She came to me asking what she should do."

"She came to you? What did you tell her?"

"I didn't know about your secret life then," she said, almost sarcastically, "so I told her you two had to have some heart-to-heart talks. She thought you were seeing another woman. Apparently, you've had some strange behaviors."

"That's all?"

"That's it. You've hurt her, you know, emotionally. When she finds out the truth, she'll be crushed."

"She'll get over it. She'll forget about me in a week."

"I doubt that. I doubt she'll ever forget you. She really does love you, terribly."

Just then, Peters slowed down and made a right turn off Route 9 onto a snow-covered dirt road. About a mile or so further down Route 9 was Saint-Bernard-de-Lacolle, and five miles beyond that was the US border. He'd double back when he was finished.

"Where are you going?" Josette asked, a note of concern in her voice.

"Down the road a bit to let you out."

"Let me out here? I'll freeze. I don't see any cars or houses around."

Indeed, there were no cars or houses in the area. That was why he'd chosen the location. There was just a thick forest with thousands of trees, most of them evergreens, some deciduous. The trees grew so close together that in most spots, you could barely see a few yards beyond them. He would have liked to tell her the truth, but she'd probably try to fight him off. He couldn't have that. It wasn't in his plan.

"I'll make an anonymous call to the police and tell them where to find you. You'll be fine until they arrive."

"Where are you going? The border's just down Route 9. You're going to cross over to New York, aren't you?"

"That would be obvious, wouldn't it? Why would you think I'd tell you where I was going? But if you must know, I'm going back to Montreal, and then I'm going to simply disappear. Feel free to tell the police everything you know. By then, I won't be around."

━━━«◉»━━━

Eddie watched Peters's car make a right turn off of Route 9. He slowed down nearly to a stop and then slowly made the same turn. He pulled to the side of the road and stopped. Where was Peters going? The border was further down Route 9. He grabbed his binoculars from the glove compartment and watched Peters's car continue down the road. Where was he taking Josette? All Eddie was concerned with now was her safety. He no longer gave a damn about Symeon Peters.

He accelerated the car slowly, with one hand on the steering wheel and the other holding the binoculars to his eyes. He drove that way for about three-quarters of a mile, until he saw Peters's car gradually come to a stop. Eddie crept forward a little way and stopped as well. He had a clear view of the car, but he was far enough back where he wouldn't be seen. His binoculars were focused on the car.

The door on the driver's side opened, and Peters stepped out. Eddie watched him walk around the car and open the passenger door. He reached in and pulled Josette out of the car by the sleeve of her coat. Once outside, she broke free of him and then kicked him between the legs. Peters bent over, holding himself, presumably in pain. Josette then ran into the wooded area parallel to the road. She moved awkwardly since the snow was nearly to her knees. Peters straightened up, swung around, and reached inside his coat.

A white-tailed deer leaped across the road. A northern goshawk with its slate-gray cap and long single white eyebrow sat on a frosted branch of an evergreen and fluttered its wings. A secluded snowy owl nearby twisted its head, eyeing the scene suspiciously. A light breeze moved around some powdered snow.

Eddie got out of his car, still holding the binoculars to his eyes, and saw that Peters was aiming a gun at Josette.

Chapter 24
DO SOMETHING OR I WILL!

SYMEON PETERS HAD BEEN COMPLETELY unprepared for the kick he received from Josette, and it had been a good one at that—no doubt about it. While experiencing indescribable agony, while the pain radiated throughout his body like electrical currents, while his world suddenly turned black on him, all he could think of was how embarrassed he would have felt had it happened in front of his fellow KGB officers. That a mere 110-pound female had gotten the better of him was shameful, yet that was what had happened.

But only momentarily.

It had taken him a few seconds, and he had not come close to recovering yet, but he was able to fight through the pain and act. He forced himself upright and swung around in Josette's direction, at the same time pulling his revolver out of his coat. He extended his arm and aimed directly at Josette's back as she was trying to run away from him. She made a beautiful target.

He was about to squeeze the trigger when he heard two nearly simultaneous gunshots and felt the bullets whiz by his head.

He immediately squatted and then dived for the front of his car. He swung his head to the left but could no longer see Josette. Who could be firing at him? He couldn't see beyond the car and didn't dare expose his head for a quick look. The only conclusion he could come to was that someone, somehow, had followed him out here.

———«●»———

After Eddie fired off two rounds, he ran to the side of the road to a clump of evergreens, which provided him adequate cover but would do little to protect him should Peters decide to fire into the trees. He had seen Josette run off into the woods but could no longer spot her because the trees were too thick. He decided to fire off two more rounds in the direction of Peters's car. Peters returned fire immediately, but as far as Eddie could determine, Peters hadn't come close to hitting him. It appeared to be a standoff.

It suddenly became quiet. He looked for Josette among the trees, but she was nowhere in sight. There were so many trees and thick naked bushes in the area that he hoped she had found a place to hide. His own position afforded him such a view that if Peters decided to move in that direction, Eddie would easily see him. If Peters moved in the opposite direction and circled around, however, Eddie would be vulnerable. For the time being, at least, he thought Josette was safe as long as she was hunkering down somewhere. Her coat was brown, so she would blend into the trees and dense branches of the bushes.

Then suddenly, he heard crunching snow behind him. He swung around, crouching low, with his semiautomatic ready to fire. Garrison Edward Meaghers was plodding through the snow. Meaghers stuck up a hand and waved him off. Eddie lowered his gun and motioned with his hand for Meaghers to get down. About a minute later, the two men were face-to-face.

"Your man is hiding in front of his car," Eddie said, pointing in that direction. "He's got a gun, and he kidnapped my wife. She got away from him and is somewhere out there." He pointed into the forest. "She ran in that direction, but I lost her."

Meaghers looked at him, shook his head, and grimaced. "Aren't you curious to know how I knew you were here?" he asked.

"You tailed me," Eddie said. "I saw you. You've been doing it for at least a few days."

"And just who is *my man*?"

"Your Russian guy, Blackbird—the one who killed Lovingate, or whatever her name was. The one you came all the way from Ottawa to get. I only know him slightly; he was engaged to a friend of my wife. He's been going by the name Symeon Peters. He works as an accountant downtown. That's probably his cover. He had Lovingate's passport and driver's license in his possession, along with the disguise he used. I'm guessing they're probably in his car."

"Goddamn it, Wade, I knew you were withholding something. I could have your ass for that."

Eddie was only half-listening. He was looking toward the forest for his wife.

"Look at me when I'm talking! If you would have told me about Blackbird before now, this wouldn't be happening."

"We have to get Josette back. She's out there somewhere." He continued to look off into the forest.

"I'm taking over now," Meaghers said, determined. "But if something happens to your wife, hotshot, this will all be on you."

"It's happening right now to her. Do something, Meaghers, or I will!"

—————«◉»—————

It was quiet now, and Symeon Peters took the time to think through his options. He certainly had as much KGB training as others had, but would it do him any good now? He remained calm; he was always good at that. But he was disappointed in himself for the way he had handled Josette. He should have anticipated that she'd do something like what she had. It was an embarrassment for him, for sure. He had acted like an amateur when he pulled her out of the car. Unforgivable.

He glanced around the front of the car again. Josette was nowhere in sight. In assessing the situation, he determined that it was no longer possible to kill her. Someone had followed him here, someone with a gun. Who could it be? A fellow Russian who had been sent to kill him? That was a distinct possibility. Some law enforcement officer? Also a possibility, but less likely.

Just then, he heard voices behind his car, off in the distance. He risked exposing himself and looked in that direction, for just a second or two. He saw two men. Now he was convinced they had been sent from Ottawa to kill him. They obviously had been tailing him.

He hunkered down again. He had to formulate an escape plan, and it wasn't going to be easy. He had been taught during his training how to escape from various situations, but that had been so long ago. All he knew at the moment was that he had to do something now, or he'd never get out of this alive.

He reloaded his revolver. He exposed himself once again, pointed the gun in the direction of the two men, and then let loose.

Chapter 25
ONE STEP AT A TIME

A HAIL OF BULLETS SUDDENLY CAME IN THEIR direction.

Eddie and Meaghers lowered themselves further toward the snow-covered ground, their guns in the ready position, momentarily losing sight of Peters's car. Eddie was more concerned about Josette than he was about anything else. Peters appeared to be shooting wildly, which didn't make him any less dangerous. Then the firing stopped as suddenly as it had begun. Whenever that happened, whenever Eddie had been in a firefight during the war and the firing suddenly stopped, there had always been an eerie, undefinable silence that left him wondering whether he was still alive in this world or dead in the next. This was no different.

Eddie looked over at Meaghers. "Okay, Meaghers, you said you were taking this over. Do something now, or I will."

"You said that already. Don't you think you've done enough already, hotshot?"

"Call me hotshot again," Eddie said, grinding out the words but making sure to keep his voice down, "and I'll shove the barrel of this .45 down your throat."

"Do that and see how fast you'll end up in prison for assaulting a federal agent."

Eddie backed off. He raised his body up slightly and looked toward Peters's car. He couldn't see him, but he knew that was where the fireworks had come from.

Then Meaghers took over. "It's over, Peters!" he shouted. "My name is Agent Meaghers. I'm with the Royal Canadian Mounted Police. Surrender and you won't die."

No response, nothing. Silence.

"We know you're a Soviet spy," he continued, "and that you killed Nikandrova. We can work something out. You could trade Russian intelligence for your freedom. We could give you a new identity. That's better than dying, isn't it?"

Again, no response.

"You gotta be shitting me," Eddie said just above a whisper.

"Rest assured I'm not, Wade. We do this all the time. You'd be surprised how many former Russian spies are now upstanding Canadian citizens." He looked toward Peters's car again. "You can't escape, Peters. There's no way out for you. If you try for the car, you won't make it two feet. Let me help you. You'll stay alive. Your Russian buddies won't find you. We can protect you."

Nothing.

Out of the corner of his eye, to his right, Eddie caught sight of movement. In a second, he realized it was Josette. She was wading through the snow, coming in his direction. Eddie jumped up and started toward her.

Meaghers saw what was happening. "Wade, no! Get back here!"

But it was too late. Eddie was gone.

Meaghers stayed put with his gun pointed in the direction of Peters's car. He fired off seven or eight rounds, laying down suppressive fire to keep Peters in place, hoping not to hit him. In less than a minute, Eddie and Josette were back in position with Meaghers. Meaghers stopped firing and looked behind him, over his shoulder.

Silence again.

"She's all right," Eddie said to Meaghers.

"He confessed to being a spy," Josette told them, out of breath. "He also confessed to killing Lovingate, I mean Nikandrova. I can be a witness to that in court."

"He's not going to make it that far," Eddie said, anger building in his face.

"I want this guy alive, Wade," Meaghers said to Eddie. "If you so much as graze him with a bullet, I'll have your hide."

Josette looked at both men and seemed to realize that there was some tension between them. "The evidence is still in the car," she said. "The disguise and Lovingate's passport and license."

"Shh." Meaghers gazed toward Peters's car.

They stopped talking and listened, first for a minute and then for another. They heard nothing except the breeze turning into a gust of wind, sweeping the snow across the road.

"I don't think he's there," Meaghers said. "Wade, cover me. I'm going up to the car." He stood up, crouching, and cautiously moved forward, pointing his gun ahead of him. He would make a good target should Peters decide to fire. He stopped momentarily. Over his shoulder, he said to Eddie, "Don't you goddamn shoot him if he doesn't have a gun pointing at me. You understand me, Wade?"

Eddie and Josette watched the show play out. Eddie was pointing his gun at the front of the car where he thought Peters was, but his eyes were darting to the left and right, looking for any movement. He didn't much care for Meaghers, but the guy did have guts. He could say that much for him.

As Meaghers approached the car from the right side, he kept both hands on his semiautomatic, moving it slightly back and forth in a steady rhythm. As he got to the car, he looked into the passenger window and saw no one. Carefully, he followed his gun around to the back of the car and then to the left side, knowing Eddie was covering him from behind. He glanced toward Eddie and nodded, as if to say, *Okay, this is it*, and then proceeded to move toward the front of the car.

Eddie's finger was on the trigger of his own gun, ready to shoot if he saw Peters jump up with his gun.

Meaghers eased himself ahead, slowly following his gun to the front of the car. At the car's front, he relaxed slightly but then swung around to his left. He looked across the road at the thick forest, his gun steadily moving across the trees, in front of him and then to the left and right. After a minute, he lowered his arms. "He's gone, damn it."

Eddie and Josette made their way over to him.

"He can't get far," Eddie said.

"These guys are trained in winter conditions," Meaghers said. "They know this kind of terrain better than Canadians. He'd fare far better than either you or me."

"Then he's on the run."

"He'll get help from the Soviet embassy or from his Russian buddies in Montreal and be out of the country before my boss can say Anastasia Alekseevna Nikandrova. We'll never find him. In twenty-four hours, maybe forty-eight, he'll be in Moscow at some dingy bar, listening to music, gulping down vodka, and entertaining the old-timers with the story of his close call back in Quebec."

All three of them exchanged looks; there was nothing left to say.

———— ««•»» ————

Symeon Peters stood with his back to a clump of young hemlock trees. He pressed into one of them, its spindly branches laden with heavy snow, hoping to conceal himself but knowing he couldn't—at least not to the degree he needed—if they ran after him. He was breathing heavily from having sprinted across the road and into the forest. The snow was high, so he had had to lift his knees up nearly waist-high in order to trudge through it. He reloaded his revolver and then waited. Suddenly, he heard one of them firing his gun. He couldn't be seen from the road, so he stayed where he was. The firing stopped, and his breathing slowed down.

There were two of them, and they were dressed as he was, in suits and dress overcoats. He doubted that they would come after him, but he couldn't say for sure. If he'd had on his winter clothes from the army, things would be different. As it was, he'd wait a while longer, and then he'd move forward. But where would he go? Crossing the border now was out of the question. He expected one of the men would take his car; he'd left the keys in the ignition. He was maybe thirty or forty minutes from Montreal by car. God only knew how long it would take him to get there by foot. He would be a frostbitten corpse before he made it halfway. An icy blast of wind hit him. His nose was freezing cold, as were his ears. He had to decide on something and soon.

He looked in front of him. Before him was a carpet of glistening snow and then more coniferous trees. Green and white were all he saw, plus shades of brown and yellow. For a second, he thought he saw the pine trees dancing and heard some sort of funeral dirge. Was he starting to hallucinate already? He knew what the freezing cold could do to a man. If he could get to a farmhouse or a country home, he could warm up, eat whatever was in their refrigerator or cupboards, and then take their car. It might work, if Lady Luck was on his side. If he could only get back to his apartment for just a short time—maybe for an hour or two—he could recuperate and think this through. That was what he needed now: time to think. Maybe then he could have another go at the border—this time going straight there with no detours. That was it! That was what he'd do. It was risky, but no more so than staying where he was and freezing to death.

He put his revolver in his coat pocket, rubbed his nose with one gloved hand, and then placed both gloves over his ears. The icicles on the trees sparkled; the white sunshine glared off the snow; a snowy owl screeched in a distant pine. He lifted one leg out of the snow and then moved it forward, sinking it into more snow. One step at a time was all he needed.

Chapter 26
A CANDLE GOES OUT

"I DON'T THINK HE'S COMING BACK."

"You're a pessimist, Smirnov, a cynic, a miserable prerevolutionary naysayer." Turgenev gulped down some of Blackbird's vodka. "I would recommend that you go into that closet over there and shoot yourself in the head, but our orders were to leave the apartment clean, and I don't feel like cleaning up after you. It would take too much time. If you could just shoot yourself and then clean up after yourself, that would be a different story, something I could live with."

"You have Chekov's humor but not his subtlety." Smirnov paused to pour some vodka for himself before Turgenev drank it all. "It's nearly two in the morning, and we're sitting in the dark like fools, waiting for Blackbird, who most likely took to the skies and is winging it to somewhere unknown. Let's at least be reasonable about this."

"Don't worry; his wings have been clipped. He'll be returning to his nest."

"I'm not worried, but I can tell you truthfully that I'm bored. Thank goodness for this vodka. If we didn't have it, I might be forced to take you up on your recommendation."

It was 1:58 a.m. They stopped talking, each man deep in his own thoughts.

"Do you remember when we were in training and too tired to sleep?" Turgenev asked. "We lay in the dark in our bunk beds, you above me, and talked for hours until sleep finally came."

"How could I forget? About the time we fell asleep, the lights would come on, and the bastards would shout at us to get up."

"That's right. In our youth, we could go for days at a time with only a few hours of sleep."

"You have to admit," Smirnov said, "that we had many interesting conversations while everyone else was snoring away. They were far better than our lectures."

"I will admit to that, yes. We solved many of the world's problems, didn't we?"

"We did indeed. If my memory serves me, I believe on one occasion we concluded that if every country saw the world through the lenses of Marx and Lenin, they would all be good Bolsheviks, and things would be fine." Smirnov chuckled. "Ah, we were idealists back then."

"Are we not idealists now?" Turgenev asked.

Blackbird's apartment went dead silent for a long moment, and then both men burst into uproarious laughter.

"I'm afraid that we're too old for that bullshit now," Smirnov said, still giggling somewhat to himself in the dark. "There's nothing like a dose of reality to set you straight. I only wish it would have happened in our youth. How much wiser we would have been."

"Wiser but not much better off," Turgenev said.

"Now who's the cynic?"

Turgenev stood up to stretch and bumped his shin on a table. "Ouch! Goddamn it!" He leaned over to rub his leg.

"A wound!" Smirnov said. "Blood spilled for the motherland! You'll surely get a medal from the Kremlin for that one. Bump yourself again, and you'll get two!"

Turgenev sat down again and mumbled something.

At 2:23 a.m., silence had returned.

Turgenev could barely see his partner sitting in front of him. Only a little of the street light spilled into the apartment, enough to create shadows that created other shadows that created a sense of loneliness, a hollowed feeling of despair and longingness that sliced into his core and left him bleeding inside. He missed Kursk, the place of his birth and where he had spent his youth before entering the army and then the security force. He had been back there only two or three times since then, and now that he was middle-aged, he had begun to long for it again.

"Smirnov?" he said.

"Hm? I'm not sleeping, if that was what you were wondering."

"What will you do when you retire?"

"Retire?" Smirnov asked in a tone that suggested it was a ridiculous idea. "That's another ten, twelve years from now. I could be dead before that. What's the sense in wondering about something that may never happen?"

"And maybe you'll be alive too. There's a good chance of that. Now is the time to start thinking about retirement, not when you're on its doorstep. You see, you should be planning right now like me."

"I'll go back to Moscow and sell chestnuts on a street corner. I'll make more money doing that than living off a state pension."

"I'm serious," Turgenev said. "Me? I'm going to go back to Kursk and open up a bar."

"Good luck with that," Smirnov said, snickering.

"But before that, I'm going to put in for a transfer to somewhere warm. Maybe Miami or Los Angeles. The Americans call it the City of Angels. Either city would be a nice place to end a career. Warm weather suits me."

"I'll stick with my chestnuts."

Another period of silence followed.

At 2:41 a.m., Smirnov said, "Maybe Blackbird is at one of the strip clubs, having the time of his life."

"Isn't that why we gave him an extra day to live?"

"Yes, but he's greedy. He should have been here long before now. I still think he's gone. If he is, what are we going to tell Colonel Trifonov?"

"We'll tell him a half-truth—we looked for him, but he was nowhere to be found."

"Ha, we'll leave out the part where we found him, and instead of making him disappear when we had him, we gave him another day to get laid, and now he's escaped."

"You're beginning to understand how to deal with our superiors."

"I'm beginning to understand that Blackbird cheated death."

"But only we will know that—and of course, Blackbird."

"Don't kid yourself," said Smirnov.

Turgenev looked out the window behind Smirnov and saw snowflakes glistening under the streetlight as they fell. "Remember when we pulled guard duty during training," he asked, "and you told stories to keep both of us awake? You were always good at that. How about one now? If we don't do something soon, we'll both be snoring."

"Maybe I'll remember one; it's been a long time. One will come to me. Let's see." A minute later, Smirnov snapped his fingers. "I've got one, and I think it's just right for the occasion."

"It better be interesting enough to keep me awake," Turgenev said.

"I've never let you down in the past. But if I hear you snoring, I'll throw a copy of *War and Peace* at you ... or I would if I had one."

"Fine, get on with it."

"Okay, here's the story. Pay attention. In a small village called Dzhambichi not far from the Laba River—"

"Which district? I've never heard of the village."

"It doesn't matter. You want a story? Then shut up and listen."

"Don't be so touchy. Take another swig of vodka; it'll calm your nerves."

Smirnov sighed and gave him a cold stare in the darkness before continuing. "In a small village called Dzhambichi not far from the Laba River, there was a poor blacksmith by the name of Igor who could barely feed his ten children."

"Ten children? My God—so many mouths to feed!"

Smirnov pursed his lips and squinted his eyes. "Let me explain something to you that you obviously forgot," Smirnov said. "In storytelling, there is a certain flow and rhythm. If the storyteller is constantly interrupted, he loses that flow, and the story becomes flat. So save the commentary. Yes, *goddamn it*, he had ten children. When the eleventh one was born—" He stopped, pointed a finger at Turgenev, and squinted his eyes again.

Turgenev could barely see him, but the message came through nevertheless.

"When the eleventh one was born, Igor ran out to the main road of the village, determined to find someone to stand in as godfather to the child. Surely, someone would be willing to help support the eleventh child. The first one to pass by was God, but the poor blacksmith rejected him. 'God gives to the rich and takes from the poor. I'll wait for another to come.'

"Igor grew worried. Would anyone else come by? Before he could complete the thought, the Devil appeared, but he rejected him as well. 'He lies and cheats and leads good men astray.' He would wait for another to pass by who was more trustworthy for his son, whom he called Olezka.

"He didn't have to wait long before Death showed up. Igor reflected carefully. 'Death treats all men alike, whether rich or poor. He certainly would be trustworthy enough.' So he decided to ask him."

"Igor is crazy," Turgenev chimed in again. "Bad choice."

"If you'd keep your mouth shut and let me finish the story, you'd see. Am I asking too much of you? Is that beyond your capabilities?" When Turgenev didn't reply, Smirnov continued. "Death was confused by the question because he had never been asked that before, but he readily agreed. 'Your child will not lack for anything,' he said, 'for I am a great friend.'

"The years went by, and Death kept his word. Olezka lacked for nothing. When the boy came of age, Death appeared to him and whispered in his ear. 'It's time for you to go out in the world. You will become a great physician. Take this magical herb, the cure for all maladies. Look for me when you're treating a patient in bed. Now listen carefully. If you see me at the head of the bed, then give the patient a tincture of the herb, and your patient will be healed. But if you see me at the foot of the bed, you will know it is the patient's time to die. You will always be right, and because of that, you will be famous, not only in Dzhambichi but in all of Russia.'

"Death was true to his word. Olezka became the most famous doctor in all of Russia, and his fame spread all the way to the ears of a rich man in Moscow."

"What was the rich man's name?" Turgenev asked.

Smirnov ignored him. Turgenev was hopeless.

"The rich man summoned Olezka to his luxurious bedchamber. Olezka looked down at the rich man in bed. He was gravely ill; Death stood at the foot of his bed, ready to take him into the fold. As it turned out, the rich man was kind and generous and beloved by all. Olezka greatly wanted to cure him. Always the clever fellow, Olezka instructed the man's attendants to turn the bed the opposite way to fool Death. After all, Olezka was always right. He then proceeded to restore the man to health with a tincture of the magical herb. However, Death was not pleased by this deception. He shook his long, bony finger at Olezka and said, 'You must never cheat me again. If you do, it will not go down well for you.'

"Olezka understood the warning and vowed never to deceive Death again. But several months later, the rich man's daughter fell ill, and Olezka was summoned back. She was the rich man's only daughter, and he became desperate that she not die. 'Save her life, and I will give you her hand in marriage,' he told Olezka.

"Olezka went into the daughter's bedchamber. She was the most beautiful woman Olezka had ever seen. To be married to her for the rest of his life would be a reward beyond belief. But Death was waiting when he arrived, and he stood at the foot of the bed instead of at the head of it. It was clear to Olezka that Death was ready to take her away with him. 'Don't deceive me again,' Death warned.

"Olezka looked down at the daughter; he had already fallen in love with her. She was within his grasp, the most beautiful woman in all of Russia, and she was to be his bride. He couldn't resist the temptation. He ordered the attendants to turn her bed around, just as he had done with her father. He gave her a tincture of the herb, and she was immediately healed as Death had promised. But Death had also promised something else to Olezka, and he was a man of his word.

"He grabbed Olezka's arm tightly and said, 'You will go with me instead of her.' He took the young doctor into a cave, its walls covered with millions of flaming candles. 'Here,' he said, 'are candles burning for every life in Russia. Each time a candle grows low and goes out, a life has ended. This one,' he said, pointing, 'is yours.' It had burned down to a pool of wax, the flame barely visible.

"'Please,' Olezka begged, 'for many years, I was your faithful servant. Please, won't you light a new candle for me?'

"Death gazed at him without remorse. Olezka's candle sputtered and then flickered out. Poof! All that was left was a stream of rising smoke, and soon that too disappeared."

"That's a fine story, Smirnov. I sense it was a parable and that Olezka was really Blackbird."

"Your level of intelligence never ceases to amaze me."

"Okay, I see. Blackbird cheated death, but in the end, he won't be able to escape it. Okay, fine. But don't we all get it in the end, regardless of what kind of life we lead?"

"We do, Leonid, yes," Smirnov said patiently, as if this were a life-and-death situation that Turgenev should understand. "But that's not the point. The point is that Olezka's life ended in the prime of his life when he was looking forward to being with the most beautiful woman in Russia for decades to come. And why? Because he deceived Death by cheating him. He paid a heavy price. So will Blackbird. He cheated us, and when we catch him, his candle will flicker out in the prime of his life. Now you tell a story, and it better be good."

"I'm not a storyteller—you're much better than me—but I'll try my best," Turgenev said. "The story takes place in a tiny village east of Dzhambichi. It was approximately twenty-five kilometers from—which river did you mention? Saba? Something like that. The district, as you say, doesn't matter."

Smirnov suddenly interrupted him, holding up a hand. "Shh!"

Turgenev stopped talking, and both men listened. They heard footsteps in the hallway coming toward the door of the apartment. And then nothing.

3:34 a.m.

3:35 a.m.

3:36 a.m.

3:37 a.m.

A key slid into the lock and slowly turned. The door inched open, and then a moment later, it closed again. There was no movement in the complete silence; not even a breath could be heard.

3:38 a.m.

3:39 a.m.

And then a hand reached for the light switch by the side of the door. *Click!*

Smirnov was crouched behind the couch with both hands resting on the back. Turgenev was on one knee behind the armchair with his forearms braced on the back. Both men were pointing guns with long tubes screwed into the barrels. Blackbird had returned.

He stood there disheveled. His hat was smashed down on his head, and his pant legs from the knees down were stiff, covered with frozen snow. He was shivering, whether from the cold outside or from the fear inside, no one but he would know.

"Hello, comrade," Turgenev said. "You're late getting home. We were worried about you." He paused a moment, then said, "If you would excuse me for saying so, you look like shit."

And then Blackbird's candle went out.

Chapter 27
AMONG THE EVERGREENS AND CEDARS

Plyos, Russia
Two weeks later

COLONEL ALEXEY IVANOVICH TRIFONOV HAD borrowed a new government GAZ M 23 from a Muscovite friend in the KGB and made the trip to Plyos in less than seven hours. His hometown sat northeast of Moscow on the banks of the Volga River with a hilly pine forest at its back. In many ways, the area was idyllic, but few people these days were happy in the Soviet Union, and no one idealized their habitats. The car had a V8 engine and was fitted with an automatic transmission specially made for the KGB, so he made good time in spite of the icy roads. He'd made one stop at the town's only shop and bought some fresh bread, frozen fish, cigarettes, and vodka. The shopkeeper had discounted everything because Alexey was in uniform. What more could a fellow Russian ask for or expect? Alexey couldn't go empty-handed.

At his destination, he turned off the engine and stared at the izba, the small century-old log house. It hadn't changed since the last time he'd seen it, twenty or so years before—more weatherworn for sure, but otherwise just the same. In the spring, the kitchen garden in the back would be revived, and the hay shed would be cleaned out. Alexey himself had spent hours doing both tasks. He had been a frequent guest in the house in his youth and had been treated like a family member. He hoped that the long-ago occupants were still there, that they hadn't died, as his parents had. They'd be old now, perhaps in their seventies, with twenty more winters having challenged their weary bodies, twenty more winters in which they'd scratched out a living on the fringes of civilization. If a person could survive that, then old age was a blessing when it came—or maybe a curse. The amounts of alcohol and devout religious faith one had usually determined which one.

Alexey got out of the car and walked slowly to the house, clearing a path for himself in the snow. He knocked on the door and waited, looking down at his boots, holding a cloth bag in one arm. He was sure that the old couple didn't receive many visitors and were probably talking about who was at the door—maybe some young government official looking to collect something from them. He hoped they'd remember him. He was about to knock again when the door was slowly pulled back. A man wearing a heavy winter coat, a thick scarf around his neck, and a ragged fur hat stood before him but said nothing. Alexey hoped that his uniform didn't intimidate him. That was what a Russian would see first—first the uniform and then the face. In spite of the long hair under the old man's hat and the white beard—he had always been clean-shaven in the old days—Alexey recognized him.

"Nikolai," Alexey said, "it's me, Alexey Ivanovich!"

"Alexey?" the old man asked. "Can it be you? Yes, it is you. Come in, come in. What a surprise!"

Alexey stepped in and stomped the snow from his boots, then shook the old man's hand while holding his shoulder tightly with the other hand.

"Marina, come! It's Alexey Ivanovich!"

Marina got up from the chair she was sitting in and greeted her visitor with a hug. She stood only a little over five feet and had to reach up to him. "It's been too many years," she said to Alexey. "Let me look at you." She held him by his arms as she leaned back, her sad eyes sweeping across his generous frame. "You've become a fine-looking man, Alexey, a fine Russian man."

The living space and the kitchen were really one large room. Alexey placed the cloth bag on the small wooden kitchen table. "A little something for you," he told them.

Then the old couple led him to the other side of the room, and they sat down.

Before another word was spoken, Nikolai reached for a large clear bottle and poured some samogon into three glasses. Alexey had never been fond of homemade brews, but he accepted it with gratitude.

"To Russia," Nikolai said, raising his glass, and all three drank. The samogon, stronger than vodka, was fermented from various ingredients, and it left a sickly aftertaste in Alexey's mouth. But he was grateful for it, grateful to be here, and grateful that Nikolai and Marina were still alive. What he wasn't grateful for was what he had to tell them.

For the next two hours, they caught up on the last twenty years. They laughed, drank more samogon, smoked Belomorkanal cigarettes, and told stories about the past. Marina had some funny stories to tell about Alexey when he was growing up. Alexey enjoyed himself and enjoyed their company; however, there was one subject that everyone seemed to be avoiding. When he sensed that the old couple was starting to tire, and there were longer pauses in the conversation, Alexey dared to bring it up.

"I'm afraid I have some bad news for you," he said.

"No," Nikolai said, "don't say it. We already know. Speaking the words aloud would be like driving a knife into our hearts."

Alexey was surprised. He looked at Nikolai and then at Marina, confused.

"When the new year came," Nikolai said, "Marina had a dream, a terrible dream. That was when we knew that Anna wasn't coming back."

No one said anything for a long moment. They sat still, as if in mourning, and looked at the floor.

Alexey then reached into his coat and pulled out a leather case. He opened it and showed it to Anna's parents. "Anna was awarded this medal by the government, posthumously. It now belongs to you." With that, he gave it to Nikolai, explaining to both of them that it was a Gold Star medal for a "Hero of the Soviet Union." He also explained that as survivors, they were entitled to special privileges, including a pension, that would make their lives a little easier.

Just then, Alexey felt an overwhelming sense of inexorable shame and guilt. The Kremlin, the same Kremlin that had issued the medal, had given the order to kill their daughter, Anastasia Alekseevna Nikandrova, but he had been the conduit. It was he, Alexey, who had given the final directive that set it into motion. He had neither the fortitude nor the willingness to tell Anna's parents that. He was glad that he was guilt-ridden, because when that feeling diminished, and it would over time, he knew that all that would be left would be emptiness. He would rather feel guilty than experience the hopelessness of being empty inside. How could he carry on in life with the inevitability of that great burden?

They talked for another ten or fifteen minutes in somber tones, and then it was time for Alexey to leave. They hugged one another, and Nikolai and Marina told Alexey to come again soon for another visit. They emphasized *soon*; they didn't have too many more winters left.

Alexey started the car and drove through town. It looked deserted and run-down, but it had always looked like that in the winter, for as long as he could remember. Nevertheless, he had spent his joyous youth there. But now it looked aged, like Anna's parents, preparing for its final stage in life. He continued to the back of the town and up some hills that were used for skiing and tobogganing. There was no one there; today was a workday for the adults, and the children would be in school. He continued to drive further up the hills until he got to one in particular. There he pulled over and parked the car between two pine trees and got out.

He stood at the edge of the steep hill and looked down at the many trees below, evergreens and cedars mostly. It hadn't changed at all. It was the same hill that he and Anna had gone down more than a couple of decades before, when they were in their teens and very much in love.

He could see them now, Anna and himself. The snow was well packed and as slick as a sheet of ice. *Alexey, Alexey! Hold on tight!* And down they went, Anna steering the toboggan, zigzagging around the trees—Alexey behind her, holding on to the sides for dear life. They gained speed; it was exhilarating. The snow cracked under them, the wind at their faces. Then fear set in. It happened so fast. *Watch out for that tree, Anna! Watch out! Anna! Anna!* But it was too late. Alexey grabbed her on either side of her waist and then leaned to the side to throw them both into the snow, but she slipped out of his hands and went headfirst into the tree. He ran to her, but she was unconscious, with her neck at an inconceivable angle.

He didn't panic but instead placed her back into the toboggan and trudged back up the hill. *Anna, Anna, don't die. Please don't die.* On the main road, he found a man with a horse and cart who took them to the medical clinic. After the doctor examined Anna, he told Alexey that she had a terrible concussion, but she hadn't broken her neck. Alexey had saved her life with his quick action because if he hadn't gotten her to the clinic as fast as he had, the doctor said, she could have died from the concussion.

So long ago, but to Alexey, it seemed like yesterday.

Today was cold, and there was a light breeze, but otherwise it was a fine day. The sun was out, and the sky was clear; what more could a Russian ask for or expect? Alexey, however, could think of something.

He would ask for another chance at life. He would ask to be transported back to this hill when Anna got her concussion. He would save her again, save her from a certain death. He would tell her that she was the most precious thing on earth, tell her that he wanted to marry her, have children with her, grow old with her. He would forget about joining the security service and convince Anna to do the same. He would become a teacher, and she would raise their children. They'd move to Moscow, the big city, and they would enjoy a life their parents had never dreamed of.

He remembered the night before he left for his government service. "Anna," he'd said as he held her in his arms, "it won't be too bad. We're both joining up. We'll be apart for a while, but we'll be busy, so the time will go by fast. We'll see each other again soon, maybe in a few years, and by that time, I know the rules will have changed. They'll let members of the security services marry each other, and by that time, we'll have some rank. We'll get married and make a good life together."

"Do you really think so, Alexey?"

"Yes, I'm convinced the rules will change. They have to. Will you wait for me?"

"I'll wait an eternity. I'm so much in love with you."

"I will love you for an eternity as well, Anna, for more than an eternity."

Tenderly, but with youthful passion, they made love that night.

But the rules never changed.

There are no more chances, Alexey thought, looking down the hill. He'd had but one, and now it was gone. Anna was gone.

His only hope now was that if there was an afterlife, they would be reunited. He and Anna, together again.

He took off his gloves and let them fall to the snow. He unbuttoned his coat, grabbed the grip of his semiautomatic pistol, racked a round into the chamber, flipped the safety with his thumb, put the barrel to the side of his head, and pulled the trigger.

The sound echoed down the hill and into the forest.

——«•»——

Montreal
The same day

"Since this is only our second session, I'd like to remind you that what is said in this room is not shared with anyone else. Also, I'd like to take the time to ask you whether your goal is just the same as it was at our first session last week. If it has changed, that's perfectly fine, but I need to know so I can adjust the focus of our sessions to accommodate your needs. Is your goal still the same?"

Gigi Bonnet stared at her psychotherapist. He was a tall, thin man with wispy gray hair and a pencil mustache. He was perhaps shy of sixty. His diploma on the wall was from McGill.

She didn't know whether she liked him or not. She had never been in therapy before, except for that one time last week. She still really didn't know what to expect. He wasn't the warmest person she had ever known. Rather, his expression was always neutral, never showing shock or dismay when one would expect him to, and he was analytical in dealing with her, very analytical. He hadn't even cracked a smile during the first session. She couldn't figure him out. She had gone to him on a recommendation from a friend. He had helped her, her friend had told Gigi, so she had decided to give him a try, and here she was. It didn't matter whether she liked him or not, she concluded. That wasn't within the framework of her goal.

"Yes, it is," Gigi said softly.

"Good then. You wanted to know how you could have been so naive as to fall in love with a person who had hidden his real life from you so well as to be a completely different person from who you had thought he was. You wanted to know whether you had any flaws in your character that might account for that. Have you mulled that over the past week since our first session?"

"Yes."

"And?"

She changed position in her chair, placed her hands on her lap, and sighed. He was asking her a direct question, as he had during the first session, that required her to think about things that were painful. Maybe that was why she didn't like him—if, in fact, she didn't.

"There's something desperately wrong with my brain."

"Why do you think that?"

"Symeon wasn't even English. He was a Russian spy who had murdered a woman. We went out that night for dinner and dancing, on the day he killed her. Don't you think I should have sensed something?"

"Do you think you should have?"

That's right—throw it right back at me! "Yes, of course."

"What, then? What should you have known that would have shed some light on his background and made you aware that he'd just killed someone?"

"I don't know, but something."

"How long have you known Symeon?"

"Two years."

"Tell me about the first time you met him."

"We met at a social function his firm put on. He was an accountant, and I work at a bank that did business with them."

"Did he approach you, or did you approach him?"

"Neither. We were at the punch bowl together."

"Who spoke first?"

"Symeon did. I think he said something like wasn't it a nice party."

"How soon after that did you see each other next?"

"The following weekend. He called me at work and asked me out."

"How did that make you feel?"

"Happy. Yes, very happy."

"Did you think at the time that you could have romantic intentions toward him?"

"Oh yes. He was handsome and intelligent, and I loved the way he spoke with his English accent."

"Did he impress you because he was English?"

"Yes, very much so. Of course, I didn't know he wasn't English at the time."

"Why were you so impressed by him?"

"I'm not sure, but I think it had something to do with him being so mysterious, you know. He was from somewhere else, someplace very different from here. There's always mystery in that. There's something captivating about the unknown, something that draws a person in. It can be quite exciting—the unknown."

"And you were drawn in by him?"

"Very much so."

"Did he talk much about England, whether or not he had a family there?"

"A little, but always in vague terms, nothing specific."

"Did you probe him for more information about himself over the two years?"

"No, I didn't want to make him feel uncomfortable. If he didn't want to talk about his background, maybe he had a reason."

"Or maybe you were quite content that he remain a mystery to you. That way, you could keep the excitement going."

She hadn't looked at it like that before. "Maybe you're right."

"He was hiding his background from you, as you now know, and as long as you didn't probe him about it, as long as you didn't ask him personal questions about his life in England, then he must have felt safe with you. You became his perfect companion."

"Yes, I think you're right. I'm beginning to understand now."

"When did you notice a change in his attitude toward you?"

"After the beginning of the year. I know now that it was January 3, the day he killed the woman. Maybe a little before that."

"How had he changed?"

"He became aloof. He seemed to be avoiding me. And when we were together, it seemed as if he wanted to be somewhere else."

"How did that make you feel?"

"Dejected, as if he no longer wanted to be with me. I thought he was cheating on me. I went so far as to consider hiring a private investigator. Now I know the true reason. He must have been concerned about being exposed as a spy. His behavior makes sense now, but at the time, it didn't."

"You mentioned in our first session that he has never been caught by the authorities. What if he showed up at your apartment one day? What would you do? Do you still love him?"

Gigi was startled by the questions. How dare this man ask her that? What right did he have? Of course, she still loved him. You didn't just stop loving someone after two years. And what if he did show up one day? What would she do?

"I don't know," she answered.

"I would like you to think about that over the next week, Miss Bonnet, and we'll pick up on that again during our next session."

Gigi left the office and walked down the street to the corner to catch the tram. Her mind was still working through the question. *What would I do if he suddenly showed up and wanted to marry me and take me away to England or Russia or wherever?* She hadn't thought about that until now, but she knew exactly what she'd do. *Yes, of course, I'll marry you, my darling Symeon. I don't care where we go as long as we're together.*

The tram came, and the air brakes made a horrible screeching sound as the car came to a stop. It sounded like a terrible cry in the wilderness, echoing down a lonesome hill among a forest of evergreens and cedars.

EPILOGUE

UNSOLVED ISSUES

A week later

Eddie Wade sat behind his typewriter, pounding out a report on a recent case he had just brought to a conclusion. A woman had hired him because she thought her husband was cheating on her. She wanted enough evidence to proceed with a divorce. These cases were routine and the bread and butter of any private detective agency. Deceit and infidelity paid off, but more than half of the cases were based on unwarranted suspicions or misunderstandings. Lack of trust in a marriage from either party was a serious obstacle to peace and contentment. But in this case, as it turned out, the woman had been right. Eddie had followed the guy around town for three days and gotten some good photos of his extracurricular activities, which she could use to support her case when she brought it to court. As soon as he finished the report, he would take it along with the photos to the woman, and then he'd have five hundred more smackers in his bank account—their bank account, his and Josette's. He stopped typing, tamped the ash down in his pipe, and turned toward

Josette. She was sitting at her desk beside him, studying her manual on crime investigation. At this point, she was going over it for the third time.

"Now that the Lovingate case is over," Eddie said, "and the dust has had time to settle a bit, we should have a talk."

Josette looked up from the manual. "Do you have a particular topic in mind, or do we just share random thoughts? I'd like to know in case I need to prepare."

Just then, the phone on Eddie's desk rang.

"Wade Detective Agency, Eddie speaking ... Yep, no problem ... Okay, see you soon." He relit his pipe and blew some smoke across the desk. "That was Jake. I forgot to tell you that he's doing a feature article for the *Gazette* on the Lovingate case. He's on his way here for some more *substance*, as he calls it. That's his way of saying that he's going to poke and prod us for inside information." He relit his pipe again. "Now for that little chat."

"I think I know what it's about, but go ahead. I'm all ears."

"For weeks now, we both have been avoiding talking about your ... let's see, how am I going to word this?" He puffed on his pipe, looked up to the ceiling, and blew a mouthful of smoke in the air. Turning his head to Josette again, he said, "Your excursions into territories that *were*, and for the next five months *are*, off-limits to you."

She looked at him, waiting for him to say more. "Go on," she said. "I'm listening."

"I'm not one to give lectures. I hate being lectured to, and I'm not about to impose that on anyone else, especially my own wife. But there comes a time when a guy has to take the bull by the horns." He put his palm out in front of him, as if to halt an onslaught of words. "I know— that's fraught with danger. I could get gored. Blood could flow." He stopped to tamp his pipe. When he finished, he took a few more puffs.

"Look," Josette said, apparently fearing that her husband would take all day to make his point and fail in the end. "I'll make this easier for both of us. I'm not going to gore you, and I promise I won't spill any of your blood. I overstepped by boundaries. I broke the law by entering Peters's apartment. The reason was commendable, I must say myself, but nevertheless, I did break the law."

"Not once but—"

"Twice. Yes, I'm aware of that; I was the one there. Both times. But the evidence was just sitting there, waiting for us. No one else was going to do it."

"I'm not concerned as much about you breaking the law as I am about you placing yourself in the position, alone, of being in the apartment of a professional Soviet killer. You were lucky the first time and even luckier the second time. Had I not been there precisely when I was to see Peters shove you into his car, had I been a minute or so late getting there, we might not be having this conversation right now."

There was an uncomfortable moment of silence. Josette looked down at her hands and examined her nails. Eddie tamped his pipe.

"I'm not scolding you, sweetheart. I just want you to understand how dangerous that was. You could have been killed out there in that field had you two been alone. It was just plain luck that you weren't."

She looked up at him. "I know," she said just above a whisper. "It was really stupid of me."

"I don't want you to feel stupid. But I do want you to understand the danger of going after a killer, especially someone who is trained and knows all the tricks. You were no match for him. As experienced as I am, I might not have been a match for him."

"Point taken," she said.

Eddie stared at her. Had the point been taken? Did she really understand that there were sick and demented people in the world who killed others out of desperation, or for pleasure, or from some crazed ideology without remorse? Symeon Peters had been the first one she had encountered, but he most likely wouldn't be the last if she stayed in the business long enough. He hoped she understood that; she had to understand that if they were going to continue as a team.

"On the positive side," Eddie continued, "kicking him in the balls was a clever move. He never saw it coming."

"Thank you," she said, the corners of her mouth forming into a slight grin. "The opportunity presented itself, and I went for it."

Eddie put his pipe down and went over to her. She stood up, and he gave her a bear hug, holding her tighter than he ever had before. Tears welled up in his eyes.

"The only thing I could think of was that I had lost you," he said. "We had just gotten married six months before, and now you were gone. That's all I thought of. And it was all my fault."

"I'm so sorry, Eddie. I *was* being stupid. It wasn't your fault. You warned me. It won't happen again."

He stopped hugging her and held her by the shoulders in front of him, looking into her eyes. "It can't happen again—ever," he said, and then kissed her hard and long.

When they had recovered, they each sat down again at their desks.

"The thing is, Josette, you're going to make a terrific investigator. You're obviously intelligent, but more important than that, you've got all the right instincts. You can sense things that other people can't." He picked up his pipe and puffed a few times. "We're going to make a great team, you and me. We are already, but we'll be even better after you get your license."

"I think so too, Eddie," she said. She paused for a long moment before continuing. "As long as we're talking, I need to bring up something myself. I've been thinking about this for a while, and I've mentioned this before, but it's important enough to bring up again. I had more to say the first time we talked about it, but we got interrupted. I don't think it got through to you the first time."

"As you said, I think I know what this is about, but go ahead. I'm all ears."

"It's about St. Paul."

"Bingo! I was right."

He had been waiting for this. He hadn't known when and where she was going to bring this up again, but he'd known she would. For a time, he had tried to craft a solid defense for himself, tried to anticipate all the angles from which she'd come at him, but in the end, he'd thrown up his hands. She had a stronger case against him than he had a defense for himself. He had decided that when it did happen, he'd simply listen to her prosecution and try to understand.

"If we're going to make this work, you can't continue to protect me. I'm not a child who needs protection. Okay, I screwed up, and you just taught me a valuable lesson. But I'm your partner. If I had been a man, you wouldn't have hesitated to tell me that you had made a foolish mistake and met someone you didn't know in a park at one o'clock in the morning without any backup or safeguards and nearly got yourself killed. Let's face it. You didn't tell me that because I'm a woman and your wife, and you thought I was too fragile to handle the news, and you didn't want to cause me any unnecessary anguish. I understand that, I really do, and I love you for it. But what else will you protect me from tomorrow? Or next week? Or next year? Maybe at some point you won't give me a case because of those same reasons. And then what kind of partnership will we have?"

Eddie had been sitting back in his chair, puffing away on his pipe, and looking directly at her the whole time she talked. She knew that she was right, and Eddie knew she was right. It wasn't fair. If he continued to protect her from the harsh realities of the world, from perceived danger, it would stunt her growth as an investigator. The agency wouldn't last, and neither would their marriage. There was too much at stake for him not to change his attitude. In her diplomatic but lovable way, she had him against the wall and had issued an ultimatum. It was now or never for Eddie. He had to come to his senses.

"Point taken. I'm sorry. It won't happen again."

"I'm a full partner in this agency," she continued, undeterred. "We look after each other and share the risks equally."

"Yes, equally as full partners—you and me."

This time Josette got up and went to him. She leaned down, pulled the pipe out of his mouth, and kissed him hard on the lips, as he had done with her just a few minutes before, an added benefit of being married to a partner.

Just then, the door opened, and Jake Asher walked in.

"Excuse me if I'm catching you two lovebirds at the wrong time," he said, "but you did say I should come over now."

"Yes, I did indeed," Eddie said, looking over at him, still recovering from a moment of passion. "That was fast."

"Come in, Jake, and close the door," Josette said. "You don't need an invitation to come in. You're family."

"You're lucky it's me," Jake said, shutting the door behind him, "and not my Uncle Milty. You wouldn't be so hospitable."

He took off his rubber boots and placed them by the door. Then he put his hat and coat on the coatrack, while Eddie and Josette cleared off space on Eddie's desk for him.

"Listen," he said, "I won't keep you two long. I just want to verify a few things so I don't get them wrong. Before you know it, I'll be gone, and you can resume your romantic midday interlude."

Josette looked at Eddie confusedly. "Were we having a romantic interlude?"

"Well, it is midday, so we must have been."

"Okay, okay, enough already," Jake said. "I'm the one with the wisecracks. It doesn't suit you two." He sat down in front of Eddie's desk, spread some papers out, and took a pen from his pocket. "Okay, I want to make sure I got the name correct. I have it as Anastasia Alekseevna Nikandrova." And then he spelled the name out. "That's a mouthful!"

"Correct," Eddie said, "and yes, it's a mouthful."

"And she was a KGB spy and assassin who was supposed to assassinate Dwight Eisenhower, president of the US of A. She went by the name Anne Lovingate, a Soviet code name." He looked up. "Correct?"

"Correct, I think. We don't know for sure whether that was her original code name or an alias she used on the run when the KGB was looking for her, but it was the last name she used."

Jake appeared to think for a moment. He moved his cigar from one side of his mouth to the other and thought some more. Finally, he took the cigar out of his mouth and set it in Eddie's ashtray.

"This is going to be the story of the decade, folks—a Soviet assassination plot against the president of the United States with some primary source material from you as well as secondary sources. I might be able to get a book deal out of this. You guys can help me write it. I'll include your names on the cover as well as on the article, of course."

"Well ... there's just a few wrinkles we'd like ironed out first," Eddie said. "We don't want our names used, and we don't want you to write about the assassination plot."

Jake did a double take. He picked up his cigar again and puffed on it while considering what he'd just heard. A minute ticked away before he said anything.

"This does not make me pleased. You're going to have to tell me more. Why not the assassination plot? Why not your names? It'll be good publicity for you. Besides, it'll lend credibility to the article."

"That's what we don't want—the publicity," Josette chimed in. "We've had enough problems with this case and don't want anymore. And accusing the Soviets of planning an assassination brings it to a different level. An accusation like that could cause an international crisis. You never know what the Kremlin might do, or for that matter, the KGB. That's why we want our names left out. Just write that you came to this information about Lovingate being a KGB agent from anonymous sources."

"Besides," Eddie said, taking the handoff from Josette, "if you were to write about the assassination plot, the Mounties and the FBI would come knocking on our doors five minutes after the paper was out, demanding to know the leak. And those guys play rough. If you just identify Lovingate as a KGB agent shot and killed by another KGB agent, they won't have a problem with that. As a matter of fact, they most likely will be thrilled that you broke the story. Makes the Russians look like a bunch of idiots. And you can be certain that the feds are already on top of the plot behind the scenes, and they'll want to keep it behind the scenes. Putting it in the paper, as Josette said, would make it an international issue between two powerful countries, with us, all of us, right in the middle of it."

Jake didn't say anything right away. He just sat there, contorting his face, moving his cigar from one side of his mouth to the other. Eddie found him amusing; Josette was serious. Both were waiting for some kind of response from him.

"I'm still not pleased," he finally said. "I am a reporter. I report facts! I don't withhold them from the public. They have a right to know. We're living in a free society. However—" He stopped to relight his cigar. He drew on it several times and then blew clouds of smoke across the desk. Eddie and Josette fanned their hands in front of their faces.

"However," he continued, "not pleased as I am at the moment, you have given me food for thought. Okay, it's anonymous sources and no plot. Now let's move on. Lovingate's killer was one Symeon Peters." He looked up briefly from his notes. "Just what in the hell kind of name is *Symeon*?" He looked down again without waiting for an answer. "Anyway, he was also a KGB agent who worked as an accountant here in Montreal." He looked up from his notes yet again. "Correct or incorrect?"

"Correct," Eddie and Josette said at the same time.

"Do you know his Russian name? Yes or no."

"No," both of them said together again.

"I won't mention the firm he worked for," he said and flashed them a rude smile. "And this Peters escaped imminent capture at the hands of the RCMP. They won't like me writing that, but there's nothing they can do. It's a fact; they screwed up. Now, Eddie, the last time we talked, you mentioned how Lovingate got her name. Tell me again. That detail will be of interest to the readers, if you *allow* me to print that." Another rude smile.

"The KGB has their hands all over North America. That's a fact, ready for you to print. How she got her name is only speculation, but I think I'm right. I just can't prove it." Eddie went on to tell him that the name Anne Lovingate was unusual. The police couldn't find another one in Canada or the US. The only person with that name had been a little girl from St. Paul, Minnesota, who had died when she was a year old, over thirty years before. Her date of birth had been the same date that was on the Russian's passport and Minnesota driver's license. That was not a coincidence. But the records office in St. Paul had no record of the girl's death. Eddie thought that the Russians had had a contact person in the office destroy it so they could establish Nikandrova's identity as Anne Lovingate.

Jake had his head down, writing away. After a minute or so, he looked up. "That's good, that's good. Little details like this make for good copy. I'll put this in quotation marks as a statement from the anonymous source. Now let's go back to Symeon Peters for a moment. What was his code name again?"

"Blackbird," Josette said.

"Blackbird," Jake repeated. "Good. Code names always go down well in stories like this, you know—drama, suspense, espionage. I'll also relate your encounters with him and the evidence, but of course, I'll leave your names out of it. You also mentioned that Peters had a fiancée. What was her name?"

"No, Jake," Josette said. "You can't use her name. She's been traumatized by all this. She'd be ruined by all the publicity. The whole world would know that she had been engaged to a KGB agent. The circumstances wouldn't matter to them. She would be looked at as suspicious for the rest of her life. She might be fired from her job, and then who would hire her? She'd be ruined by it all, and then she might—"

"All right, already, then don't tell me her name. With all of your editing, maybe you guys should be paying me my salary instead of the *Gazette*. How's she doing?"

"She's a lot better now and recovering. She mentioned being in therapy. But she was devastated, and remember, Peters hasn't been captured. He's still out there somewhere; he might even be in Montreal. There's no telling what he might do."

"No," Eddie said, "he's probably sitting in some bar in Moscow, drinking vodka."

"Okay, okay," Jake said, "nix on her name, but her friends might put two and two together and figure it out. Eddie, you said she'd been engaged for a year. It would have been natural for her to tell some close friends and people at work about him."

"Nothing we can do about that," Eddie said.

"Maybe there is, Jake," Josette said. "Couldn't you just use the name Blackbird to identify Peters? It would have the same impact, and there would be no link to the fiancée. Her close friends would never know it was her."

"Fine," Jake said with an annoyed look. "Anything else I should include in the story? Maybe we should share the byline."

Eddie and Josette looked at each other and shrugged.

"Okay," Jake said. "My editor wants the story in two days. If you think of anything more, let me know before then."

"Will do," Eddie said.

Jake examined his notes and this time blew a cloud of smoke over his own head. "Now," he said, setting down his pen, "I believe I have a good title for the article. My editor might change it, but I'll give him hell if he does. Before I tell you, I want to give both of you the opportunity to have your say. I don't want you to jump all over me and go stark raving mad when the article comes out. A body can take just so much punishment from the pair of you, know what I mean?"

Josette nodded.

Eddie said, "I can live with that."

"Okay then. I'm going to title the article 'Lovingate.' It's plain and simple, and the whole thing started with her murder. Everything in the story follows from that. Maybe someone will write a book in fifty or sixty years, telling the complete truth." He chomped on his cigar, eyeing them over. "Yes, just 'Lovingate.' Whaddya think?"

Silence.

Thirty seconds went by. Then a minute.

"That works for me," Eddie said and then looked at Josette.

"Me too," she said.

Printed in the United States
by Baker & Taylor Publisher Services